A Mysterious Creature

Something fell out of the chandelier and landed *splat* on the floor. I jumped up, freaked out because it might be a bat. A very sick bat, a baby, maybe an albino, pinkish beige. It lay there quivering. I tiptoed over, trying not to make noise.

It wasn't a bat. I thought it might be a huge moth, because of the wings. They were open but limp-looking, as if whatever they belonged to had forgotten how to use them.

Then I noticed that the thing had a dress on, which seemed strange for a moth. So I figured it was a doll. A tiny wind-up doll with wings.

I crouched down for a closer look.

The little thing sat up, tears running down her cheeks, let out a scream that managed to be both tiny and quite ear-splitting. She squealed something that sounded like "Salty May!"

She wasn't a doll. She was a living lady, three inches tall. With wings.

OTHER BOOKS YOU MAY ENJOY

SMALL PERSONS with wings

ellen booraem

PUFFIN BOOKS
An Imprint of Penguin Group (USA) Inc.

PUFFIN BOOKS

Published by the Penguin Group

Penguin Young Readers Group, 345 Hudson Street, New York, New York 10014, U.S.A.

Penguin Group (Canada), 90 Eglinton Avenue East, Suite 700, Toronto, Ontario, Canada M4P 2Y3

(a division of Pearson Penguin Canada Inc.)

Penguin Books Ltd, 80 Strand, London WC2R 0RL, England

Penguin Ireland, 25 St Stephen's Green, Dublin 2, Ireland (a division of Penguin Books Ltd)

Penguin Group (Australia), 250 Camberwell Road, Camberwell, Victoria 3124, Australia

(a division of Pearson Australia Group Pty Ltd)

Penguin Books India Pvt Ltd, 11 Community Centre, Panchsheel Park, New Delhi - 110 017, India

Penguin Group (NZ), 67 Apollo Drive, Rosedale, Auckland 0632, New Zealand

(a division of Pearson New Zealand Ltd)

Penguin Books (South Africa) (Pty) Ltd, 24 Sturdee Avenue,

Rosebank, Johannesburg 2196, South Africa

Registered Offices: Penguin Books Ltd, 80 Strand, London WC2R 0RL, England

First published in the United States of America by Dial Books for Young Readers,
a division of Penguin Young Readers Group, 2011
Published by Puffin Books, a division of Penguin Young Readers Group, 2012

1 3 5 7 9 10 8 6 4 2

THE LIBRARY OF CONGRESS HAS CATALOGED THE DIAL EDITION AS FOLLOWS:

Booraem, Ellen.

Small persons with wings / Ellen Booraem.

p.   cm.

Summary: When Mellie Turpin's grandfather dies and leaves her family his run-down inn and
bar, she learns that for generations her family members have been fairy guardians, and now that
the fairies want an important ring returned, the Turpins become involved in a series of magical
adventures as they try to locate the missing ring.

ISBN: 978-0-8037-3471-5 (hc)

[1. Fairies—Fiction. 2. Magic—Fiction. 3. Grandfathers—Fiction.
4. Lost and found possessions—Fiction.]
I. Title
PZ7.B646145Sm 2011
[Fic]—dc22 2010008400

Puffin Books ISBN 978-0-14-242054-6

Designed by Nancy R. Leo-Kelly
Text set in Aldus

Printed in the United States of America

For Fletcher
and
Louise Booraem

Contents

Chapter One

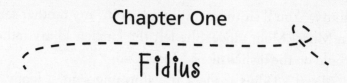

Fidius

LAST JUNE, MY PARENTS JUMPED OFF A ROOF because of a pinky ring.

Beware of jewelry, especially if it's more than a thousand years old. And definitely beware of your own brain. Imagination is part of life, but also it sucks.

I'm not actually allowed to say "sucks."

Fidius had imagination. Every bedtime until I was almost six, he curled up on my pillow in his tattered jacket and knee breeches, not too close because touching him could give a person frostbite. Three inches tall, barefoot, and scraggle-haired, he told me about his elegant youth: the beautiful clothes, how everyone insulted each other, what they ate, how popular he was. I dreamed of (a) cockroach fricassee, (b) minuets, (c) winged ladies dressed up like Cinderella.

If you organize your thoughts and assign numbers and/or letters to them, they stop being imagination and turn into scientific inquiry, which is safer.

Fidius lived with us in our Boston apartment, which was the size of a French king's closet. One day when I was five, I sat in the tiny kitchen with my Winnie-the-Pooh plate empty except for summer squash, all soft and slimy. "You'll sit there until you eat it," my mother said, in Model Mom mode. She left the kitchen so my father could do the dishes like a Model Dad.

"Pssst." Fidius made a transforming sign, a loopy *q*. The squash turned into candy corn, which I didn't love, but anything beats squash. I scooped it into my mouth, realizing too late that Fidius hadn't done a thing to (a) the taste or (b) the sliminess, only (c) the looks.

"Bleah," I said.

Fidius cracked up. "That's what you get for having a sense of taste," he whispered. He wasn't mean—there were just things he didn't understand about being big and warm and human. I gulped my milk and I didn't feel hurt at all. Not. At. All.

A week later, I scattered three sets of LEGOs over my bedroom floor, organized by shape and color because Fidius was going to make Versailles, the palace of the French kings. Mom said I had to put them all back in the right boxes so she could vacuum. "They're organized by shape and color," I told her. "We're going to make the palace of the French kings."

"It's too late to make the palace of the French kings to-day," Model Mom said. "You should know that, Fidius." She wasn't looking at him—she hardly ever did—so he went all beady-eyed and stuck out his tongue at her. "The two of you, pick up those LEGOs or no macaroni and cheese, just broccoli."

We ignored her, because it was my room and she wasn't

the one with a building plan. But then I smelled macaroni and cheese, which is my favorite, and broccoli, which isn't. Mom yelled, "I'm coming in there now. Those LEGOs better be picked up, dang it." She didn't actually say "dang it." She always uses a swear word that means exactly the same thing and yet I can't repeat it until I'm sixteen. This makes no sense but what can you do.

Anyway, Mom was coming and Versailles was all over the floor. Fidius flew around and moved his pointy fingers in a "go away" sign, like brushing a spider off your sleeve. One by one, the piles of LEGOs disappeared. "Whoa. It worked," Fidius said, so low I almost didn't hear. He sounded surprised.

"Where'd they go?" I panicked, because he didn't sound like he knew what he was doing.

"They're still there. Or somewhere."

"What happens when she vacuums? Will she suck them all up because she can't see them?" I felt around with my hand, but there was only carpet.

Fidius's iridescent wings turned mud color. "Am I a *magus?*" he snapped. That's what his people call a scientist, and talking about *magi* made him cranky. "I don't know where they went." But then his wings lightened; some faint purples and pinks appeared. His thin lips stretched in an almost-smile, the closest he ever got to an expression on his pale, pointy face. "Don't worry, Turpina. They're pretending to be gone. It's a trick of the eye."

Fidius almost always called me Turpina—my last

name with an *a* stuck on the end, which made it a girl's name in Latin, his first language. When I annoyed him he used my full name, Melissa Angelica Turpin, which he said was "of lineage," although he never explained what that meant.

He pronounced "Turpin" in French, his second language, with not much *r* and absolutely no *n*—"Tooghh-peh," kind of. Grand-père pronounced it that way too. Dad said "Turr-pinn," with as many *r*'s and *n*'s as he could shove in there.

Fidius tried to be helpful. One time he fixed a hole in my jeans before my mom saw it, but the hole opened again ten minutes later. He said he was too lonely and depressed to make a spell last. That's why he was all raggedy—he had some magic in him, but not enough.

He made My Little Pony come alive and gallop around the room for five whole minutes, which was cool except that she ate a hole in my Wild Things bedspread and pooped squishy blue plastic BBs, and when the magic died she didn't have any tail left. I started to cry and Fidius laughed.

"Bring back her tail," I sobbed. "You can do it. You're a fairy."

Fidius whirred at me, wings darkening, tiny, sharp fingers curled into claws. "Fairies!" he snarled. "Figments!" His frigid fingers were an inch from my eyes.

I cowered and that lightened him up, wings and all. "We are not fairies, Melissa Angelica Turpin," he said.

"We are Small Persons with Wings." He went out to the living room to watch the DVD player open and close, so I was the one who had to clean up all the blue plastic poop, and my pony never got her tail back.

I never saw anyone love appliances as much as Fidius did. "Electricity is the same as magic, Turpina," he said, "except it doesn't decay your body." I didn't know what he meant by that, and he wouldn't explain because he was too busy posing for himself in the mirror. He unfurled his wings in towering iridescent glory, the shimmery pearls and blues and golds catching the light and improving it.

He always expected you to gasp when he unfurled his wings. And I'm sure I always did, always.

Wings have to be groomed. Fidius pulled them through his sharp fingers, the way a bird pulls a feather through its beak. They flowed through his hands as if they were liquid, the colors rippling and swirling like oily puddles at a gas station when you stir them with a stick. Imagine having something so beautiful on your body, and you'd flap them and they'd carry you up into the air.

No, don't imagine any such thing. It doesn't happen. It's not real. Item A on the list of made-up stuff.

It was my fault that Fidius went away. One day he was sleeping on my pillow and disappearing the Cheerios off the floor, the next he was gone and I had a little china guy that looked like him except he had a chipped elbow and no wings. I talked to the china guy as if he were alive, even though I knew he wasn't. Not for one minute did I think that little guy was anything but china, with that stupid painted smile.

I remember every second of Fidius's last day, and I do think a lot of it really happened.

Nobody said not to talk about him. Nobody said, Talking about a little guy with iridescent wings won't get you invited to Janine Henry's birthday party, won't help you ride a bike, won't take away your excess vocabulary. You will still be not-skinny with not-blond curls and say "not necessarily" and "who's SpongeBag SquarePants?"

It was the stupid birthday party that set me off. Everybody in kindergarten was going except me and Marshy Talbot, who threw up every time she ate ice cream and insisted on eating it anyway. They were going to Janine's on the school bus Friday, and all the parents had to write notes saying that was okay. Except mine and Marshy's.

Marshy cried, but I didn't. Did. Not. When Inez Whatsername asked me right out loud if I was going—she knew I wasn't invited—I said I had something important to do.

"Oh yeah? What?"

Everybody kept doing their puzzles of the fifty states, but they all were listening. I didn't decide to say it, I heard the lie coming out of my mouth: "It's Fidius's birthday too. He is my priority."

"What does that mean, prioriddy?" Inez knew perfectly well that I couldn't define half the words I used. I couldn't define this one either, and I turned red.

"If something is a priority, that means it's important," the teacher's aide said, being nice.

"Fidius has wings," I said. "And he's teeny and he cleans up my Cheerios."

"So he's a *f-a-a-a-i-i-iry*," Inez said, and everybody hooted like a streetful of car alarms.

"A Small Person with Wings," I said.

"Fat Mellie has a fairy friend!" That was Inez again, chanting. "Fat Mellie, Fat Mellie has a fairy, fairy, fairy!"

"Fairy Fat," Janine screamed.

"Fairy Fat, Fairy Fat," they all chanted. It took a full five minutes for the teacher's aide to calm them down.

"Hey, hey, hey," she said. "We all have imaginary friends."

"He's real," I said. "He vanishes dirt and turns squash into candy corn."

"That must be why you're so fat," Janine said. "Too much candy corn."

"I'm not fat. I will grow into my grandeur." My mom told me that when I started school and found out my family was officially overweight. I was an alien from Round World stranded on The Skinny Planet.

I couldn't define "grandeur," but it sounded all right to me.

"What's grandeur?" Inez screamed. I returned to my puzzle and pretended I was deaf. Inez was inconsequential, which means she didn't matter.

At recess, Mina Cardoza and three other girls cornered me by the swings, but they didn't poke me in the belly like usual. "Do you really have a fairy at your house?" Mina asked.

"A Small Person with Wings," I said.

"What does he look like?" another girl asked.

I told them about Fidius's raggedy clothes and beautiful wings and the LEGOs and I don't remember what else. They sat with me at snack and story time, voted for me to put the sun-and-clouds sticker up on the weather report board. As we tidied up the classroom before the bus they grumbled at Janine because I wasn't coming to her party.

"She can come if she wants," Janine said, but I couldn't because I didn't have a note for the bus driver. When Marshy and I got off the bus at the Shady Acres Day Care stop, all the girls hugged me good-bye except Janine and Inez. Marshy was bawling, and nobody hugged her.

"Bring your fairy on Monday, okay?" Mina whispered. "You're my best friend."

I spent the whole time at day care trying to figure out what had just happened to me. Up to that year Mom and Dad had shared one teaching job, so I spent all my time with one or the other of them or with Fidius. When I got old enough for kindergarten, my parents each took a full-time job in the industrial arts department of Alton H. Blackington High School and cast me into the world.

I'd never had anything interesting to tell the other kids before. When it was my turn for show-and-tell, I brought in my mom's palm sander and found out that I had no idea what it did.

During nap time at the day care center that afternoon, it dawned on me that not everyone had fairies living with them. I imagined the whole class and the teachers spell-bound at show-and-tell, while Fidius groomed his wings and vanished the craft aprons. I imagined my next birth-day party, to which I would invite everyone except Janine and Inez. Mina would sit next to me because she was my best friend.

"Did you have a good day at school?" my mom asked driving home.

"Yeah," I said, with more feeling than she was used to.

"Really? That's great. What happened?"

There was no simple way to explain. "Nothing."

"But what was so good about it?"

"We had cupcakes for snack."

She frowned, and gave me the lecture about food not being recreation, even though we both knew when we got home we'd sit down with Dad and eat one chocolate chip cookie apiece. We'd break off pieces and pretend each one was a whole cookie.

"I know all about food not being recreation, Mom."

She snorted. "You're not supposed to achieve that tone of voice for another seven or eight years." She's always complaining about how rude teenagers are. But even at five I knew Mom liked a girl to stand up for herself. I hoped she never saw the way I was at school.

I couldn't wait to tell Fidius that Mina was my best friend, and that he was coming to school with me Monday.

The walls of my room were a jungle. Fidius waved his hand and the palm trees swayed in a breeze. I lifted my face to feel the breeze on it, but there wasn't one. It was all pretend.

"Look quick," Fidius said. "I can't keep this going for long."

I wandered around admiring my private jungle. Pretty soon it all faded into my dad's plain cheery yellow paint. I didn't care, because now I could tell Fidius about my day. I didn't tell about not being invited to Janine's party—I didn't want him to look down on me, since he'd told me he was so popular at home. I made it sound like everybody was talking about their pets and I happened to mention him.

I don't know why I thought it was a good idea to compare him to a pet.

He was curled up on my pillow. Before I finished talking he unfurled his wings with an angry *fwap!* and flitted around like a wasp, banging off of things. His wings were brown as mud, mud, mud.

"I didn't mean a *pet* pet." I ducked as he buzzed past my head. "I didn't mean to say anything about you at all. It just came out." *Zip! Zoom!* "But you have to come to school with me Monday, so I can show them—"

He hovered in front of my nose, wings beating. "I am not your servant. I am your secret."

"Why? Why are you my secret?"

He put his hand on the end of my nose, kept it there until it froze me so much it burned. He made a swoopy gesture with the other hand, stared into my right eye.

A memory burst into my head, but it wasn't mine. I was trapped in a jar, no room even to unfurl my wings. A boy's nose and eyes appeared, huge. A girl said, "What is it? Give it to me a sec." Hands fought for the jar, and I crashed from side to side. I pounded my fists against the glass.

The memory faded. "I'm sorry," I said.

"You take me for granted. You think everyone has a Small Person with Wings making magic for them. And now you betray me, as the large always betray the small."

"I don't take you for granted." But I kind of did, and we both knew it. I felt I'd broken something that couldn't be repaired, and I was scared of what might happen next. It never occurred to me that he might leave. I couldn't remember a life without him.

He slept on my pillow that night, wings all calm and colorful, and the next day he was gone, leaving the little china guy in his place.

I stayed in my room almost the whole weekend, waiting for Fidius to come back. My insides felt like sawdust. I couldn't believe he'd leave for good because I did one stupid thing. Sunday night I almost smashed the little china guy to wipe the smirk off his rosebud lips, but then I couldn't because he was a present from Fidius.

Mom and Dad came in not looking at each other, always a sign of trouble. They sat on my bed and waited for me to talk.

"He's gone," I said. "And it's because of something I did. He made a frostbite handprint on my nose. And he left me this china thing."

"Don't break it," Mom said. She reads minds. "You'll be glad to have it later."

"It always seems like it's your fault when they go," Dad said. "But it isn't. Fidius left in his own good time."

"This happened to you before?"

"It always happens. Life goes on and gets better."

"You'll have to eat squash on your own, that's all," Mom said.

"Or you could cook something that wasn't yucky," I said.

She smiled. "There's always that possibility."

On Monday morning I woke up with a knot in my stomach and tears behind my eyelids. I'd never cared before, but I'd been popular for half a day on Friday and I was hooked. In desperation, I took the china guy to school.

Normally everybody would have spent Monday talking about Janine's birthday party. But it turned out that the kids had spent Janine's entire party talking about my fairy, wondering what would happen Monday. They expected me to come in with some little creature on my shoulder.

I would have given anything to have had Fidius on my shoulder. I felt like throwing up.

The classroom went silent long before it was supposed to. Everybody was in their assigned seats, and every single person was looking at me, even the teacher and her aide. Their eyes tingled my neck as I rummaged in my backpack.

I pulled out the sad little china guy, made myself turn to face them. I discovered I had nothing to say. I stared at my toes.

"Is he here?" Mina said, nearly breathless. "Is that him in your hand?"

I made myself look up, and the first person I saw was Janine. Our eyes met, and in that instant we both knew everything. She knew I didn't have a fairy on me. I knew she'd never let anyone forget this moment.

"We had a fight," I whispered.

"Speak up, Mellie," the teacher said.

I didn't want to speak up. Speaking up was going to suck.

Chapter Two

Pigs in Slush

I SHOWED THEM THE CHINA GUY. I spoke up, but the furnace blower was on, so maybe no one would hear. "Fidius is gone, but he left me this. It looks like him."

They heard. The world stopped while the class gawked at the stupid china guy.

"That's him?" Janine hooted. "That's your fairy? That's not real. He doesn't even have wings."

I was not going to cry. Was. Not. "It's not really him. He *was* here, but now he—"

"I knew it," Inez said. "I knew she didn't have a fairy. Fairy Fat."

"I don't get it," Mina said, her face all scrunched up as if she might cry. "Why did she tell us she had a fairy if she didn't?"

"I did have one," I said. "I promise, really, I really did." Mina scowled at me. I could tell she'd lied about being my best friend.

"I have a dinosaur model," a kid yelled. I think his name was Anthony. "*Six* dinosaur models."

Everybody blinked at him, then realized what he was saying. "Oooo, Anthony," Inez screamed, approving. "That means you have six *real dinosaurs.*"

"I have a real live miniature elephant and Thor and Merlin," somebody else yelled. Everybody was standing up and whooping and hollering about what animals and supernatural beings they had living with them at home. Mina and her real friend Whatsis started poking me in the stomach so hard I almost did puke.

The teacher's aide made everybody sit down and zip their lips and keep their hands to themselves. Being rescued by a grown-up was the final humiliation. I returned the china guy to my backpack, wrapped in my recess sweater. I was not crying, although I stood there with my face in my cubby for a long time to make sure.

I promised myself I would never talk about Fidius ever again. But I didn't realize then what an enemy I'd made of Janine when I'd wrecked her birthday party. As long as Janine was around, nobody at Barbee O. Carleton Elementary and Middle School would ever forget about me pretending I had a fairy at home. Which meant I couldn't forget it either.

"How's the fake fairy?" Janine started asking when I got on the bus, every single day. "Has he grown wings yet?"

I tried to explain—*again*—that the china guy (a) wasn't Fidius and (b) was a present Fidius left behind. But before I got out a whole sentence, Janine and Inez would start chanting "Fairy Fat" and the whole bus would join them, even Mina.

By the time we started first grade, everybody called

me Fairy Fat, or sometimes FF or Effy. Mostly I ignored them, but when somebody confronted me about it I *had* to say Fidius was real. I mean, didn't I? I didn't want to let him down. It felt like our honor was at stake.

This began to annoy people, I guess. I guess when you're round and curly and not blond, you should learn to fade yourself into the background.

One gym day in second grade, I walked out of the girls' locker room to see Inez standing there running the water in the drinking fountain to make it extra cold. "You'll get a cold water headache," I said.

She grinned, never a good sign. "*I* won't. Go, Benny." Somebody grabbed me and he and Inez shoved my face into the icy water. It went up my nose and down my front—I could breathe through my mouth, but I almost forgot how because of the way my nose was freezing, inside and out. They held me there and held me there, and boy, did I get a cold water headache.

They did this every single gym class, three days a week. Mr. MacClaren looked at me funny because I was wet all down my front, but he never said anything and he never saw because the fountain was around the corner from where he stood and blew his whistle.

I was a Stoic, like these ancient Greeks I read about who believed emotion opens you up to misfortune. I learned to relax and shut my mind down when Benny grabbed me, easy-peasy, and pretty soon it was over for the day.

It was a relief when our classroom teacher, Mrs. Whipple, got sick of hearing about Fidius and brought in Ms. Appleby, the school counselor, to rid me of an Unhealthy Fixation. Ms. Appleby smiled like a horse, with all of her gums showing, and asked me did I mind missing a couple of gym classes a week. I did not mind. I wanted to keep her interested so I could keep missing gym class.

At first, she asked me about my family every single week, as if there was going to be something amazing and new. There was never much to say about my parents, who were shop teachers by day and artists the rest of the time. They wanted to be full-time artists. They split all the household chores. Sometimes my mom was the boss, sometimes Dad, but mostly Mom when you thought about it.

Ms. Appleby approved of all that.

One day, desperate for something to tell her, I added that my dad didn't drink any alcohol. Ms. Appleby asked why that was, and I said because of Grand-père, who owned the Agawam Inn and Bishop's Miter Pub in lovely, seaside Baker's Village, forty-five minutes northeast of Boston. Dad said Grand-père was a bad example to us all, but especially him.

"We went to visit him," I told Ms. Appleby. "We pulled up to the curb and he threw old whiskey bottles out of an upstairs window and they smashed all over the sidewalk. Mom said that's it, we're not going back there until the crazy old coot sobers up and apologizes."

Grand-père stories always scored big for my parents

at the Friday night potluck—their friends loved that he was in the French Foreign Legion and came home with a French wife and a bad temper. But Ms. Appleby pinched up her face and said I was being disrespectful to the elderly, which didn't seem fair because (a) she was the one who asked and (b) it actually happened.

After a month or so, Ms. Appleby decided it was time to bring in my parents. I kept insisting that Fidius was real—I mean, I did have that frostbite handprint on my nose and it tingled sometimes in the winter, and where else would it have come from?

Ms. Appleby refused to look at it close enough to see that it looked like a hand.

"Such an imagination," she said. When I left her office that day I went into the girls' bathroom and shredded a roll of toilet paper into the wastebasket until I calmed down.

My parents made an appointment for a Thursday, three fifteen, after the last bus. They would have to leave the high school fifteen minutes early to get there on time, but Dad said he'd do anything to get a look at Ms. Appleby. I'd told him about the horse smile.

Mom took a change of clothes to school, her usual drapey stuff in cool colors that make her look like a queen even though she's round with curly brown hair like an extra-large cherub. Dad's round and bald and wears the same wire rims as Mom because they got a deal. But he has a honker like Julius Caesar, which could be mistaken for grandeur in the right circumstances. He wore a tie that day, and there was hardly any paint on his pants.

I was sure they had told Ms. Appleby that they knew Fidius too. I was looking forward to the three of us telling Ms. Appleby to widen her horizons and smell the coffee.

"I wanted to talk to all three of you together," Ms. Appleby said when they arrived. "Can anyone tell me why?" Mom stiffened, because Ms. Appleby sounded as if all three of us were in the second grade instead of just me, and that is not the way you talk to Veronica Sanford Turpin.

Dad put his hand on Mom's knee and said, "Why don't you tell us, Ms. Appleby?"

"Mellie is a smart and imaginative girl," Ms. Appleby said. "But I do think enough is enough when it comes to the little man with the wings. I get the sense that Mellie really believes in him. This does her no good with her peer group, and may become Unhealthy."

"What do you want us to do about it?" Mom asked.

"It's clear Mellie respects your opinions. I need you to tell her that this little man exists only in her imagination, that she made him up to substitute for real human friends."

Mom stayed in her chair, but in spirit she rose up on her webbed feet and flapped her wings like a mother swan. "I do not choose to tell her any such thing. Mellie can make up her own mind about her imaginary friend."

"Kids grow out of them on their own," Dad said. "I've been teaching high school for fifteen years, and I have yet to encounter a teenager who still believes in an imaginary friend."

"Me neither," Mom said. "I think we should let nature take its course."

For a second, I was happy they were standing up to Ms. Appleby. But then I realized what they were saying. They were saying Fidius wasn't real. That he *was* my imagination.

I fingered the end of my nose. "I have a frostbite handprint."

Ms. Appleby blew air out of her mouth. "I keep hearing about this frostbite handprint. What is *that* all about?"

"I'll thank you to maintain a civil tone when talking about my daughter," Mom said. "Particularly when she's sitting right here."

"Mom, I have a frostbite handprint. It's real."

Dad patted my shoulder. "Of course it is, honey."

"No!" I stood up. "I don't want you to say stuff to make me feel better. You *knew* Fidius. He made squash into candy corn."

Dad looked miserable. "Honey—"

Something physical happened to me then, as if somebody ran an eraser across whole sentences in my brain and wrote in new ones. My parents and I always pretended we believed in Santa Claus even though we didn't. It flashed on me then that Fidius . . . that Fidius . . .

Wasn't real either.

My innards were gone. Fidius was gone. Part of my life—the good part—gone, gone.

I made him up. He's a china guy with a stupid smile. I deserved to have my head pushed into a fountain. I was nuts.

I forgot Ms. Appleby was there. All I had were Mom, Dad, and what used to be my friend Fidius. "Daddy, am I nuts?" I never called him Daddy.

Mom made a choking noise. Dad surged up, hugged me hard. "No, honey, no, no, no."

Mom grabbed my elbow, flapped it. "It's perfectly normal, Mellie. *Perfectly* normal."

My head was jammed against Dad's chest, facing Ms. Appleby. She smiled like a sympathetic yet self-satisfied member of the equine species. "That's enough for today," she said. "We'll meet at our regular time Monday, all right, Mellie?"

The next morning on the bus, when Janine asked if my fake fairy had wings yet, I did not explain for the gazillionth time about the china guy being a present from Fidius. I said, "You don't still believe in that fairy, do you?" I grabbed an empty seat and counted telephone poles all the way to school, fighting the feeling—*still*—that I was being a traitor to Fidius.

I had three enemies at that moment: Ms. Appleby, Janine, and Fidius, who still hadn't left my mind. I could see him. I could hear him talk. If I rubbed my nose, the frozen handprint burned. My imagination was fooling my entire, physical body.

Fidius wasn't my friend anymore. Fidius scared me.

As second grade became third, I figured out who the real enemy was, and it wasn't Ms. Appleby and it wasn't Fidius. It was my own brain, with my imagination rampaging around in there like King Kong in that old movie my dad watches.

I knew I had to control the beast. I had to stop daydreaming about Fidius, stop making up stories to put myself to sleep. I would read fake stories at school because I had to, but at no other time. My loves would be addition and subtraction, order and alphabets, geography. Nature studies. Lists.

I was still Fairy Fat. I was round and clumsy and vocabulary-enhanced, and I had my head in the drinking fountain every gym class until Mr. MacClaren caught on and started keeping an eye on Benny. But someday I would leave Barbee O. Carleton Elementary and Middle School, and I would start over. I would grow up to be an extremely successful . . . I don't know, scientist or tycoon or something. Janine and Inez would be cobblers or beggars or washerwomen.

That was something to look forward to.

From that time on, I was a new person. I spent recess organizing the classroom crayons by size and color. I became the best speller in my class. I absorbed grammar and punctuation. After a long day of refusing to enjoy

Roald Dahl, I taught myself to multiply and divide. I memorized biological classifications in Latin, down to genus and species.

You can't avoid imagining things entirely. One recess in fourth grade I alphabetized my class's Laura Ingalls Wilder books by title. (This caused a furor a week later when Mina found out she'd read the fifth book first.) One of the book jackets sent me jolting across the prairie in a covered wagon, and I found myself wondering if Fidius could have made my room into a sod cabin.

I developed a defense for these moments. If I caught myself wandering off, I'd mutter "Fairy Fat." That reminded me how everything imaginary—Fidius, SpongeBag Whatsisname, Laura and Mary in the Big Woods—can suck you into believing in them and ruin your life.

My parents didn't know what to think about my new personality. You can see why. There they were painting pictures and watching *King Kong,* and one day their daughter had alphabetized the spice rack and wouldn't read fairy tales and had a list of Real but Unbelievable Things, from artichokes through sumo wrestlers to the Venus flytrap.

"Sheesh, Mellie," Dad said, "you're going to make a great scientist. Or maybe an accountant." He was bewildered.

My parents fought back. They started Family Movie Night on Fridays, with pizza (vegetarian, no extra cheese). I sat through every Walt Disney movie ever made, plus

The Wizard of Oz and a gazillion others, each more imaginative than the last.

I fought back too, and as a result I can tell you that *The Wizard of Oz* uses the word "witch" sixty-two times, "heart" thirty times, "brain" twenty-five times, and "courage" nineteen times.

They fought harder. Dad gave me a huge book about Edgar Degas, this French painter from the late 1800s who believed people should be plump. The name's pronounced "Day-gah." There's a ballerina he did, she's having a great time dancing and yet there's this light coming up from the floor that hits her face in a way that makes your stomach jump. Which is a figure of speech—your stomach doesn't do that *physically*.

I became very, *very* interested in art, and Dad and Mom joyfully bought me every secondhand art book they could come up with. But then I started a scrapbook of selected post-Renaissance artists in chronological order, with subcategories for religious, mythological, and civic subject matter. Did you know that the *Mona Lisa* was stolen for two whole years? Well, she was. And Pablo Picasso (1881–1973) created more than 20,000 works of art.

When Dad saw my scrapbook he went silent for several minutes and said, "Sheesh."

Mom put me in Girl Scouts. I got eighty-four badges and went to Maine for Girl Scout camp two weeks every summer. I made friends at camp, where they celebrated nerds, but they all lived two hours away.

Marshy Talbot, who had thick glasses and the skimpiest hair you ever saw, tried to be friends for a while. But she was as stupid as everyone else and obsessed with Japanese cartoons.

I was better off alone. I was happy. I was fine.

As fourth grade became fifth, and sixth ran into seventh, the other kids in school got so they really hated me. I was the spelling and geography champ and aced Science Fair. The teachers gave up on making me read stories, and let me be some math/science/art history freak. I often recited interesting tidbits from the lives of Degas and Cézanne and van Gogh.

For example: Degas' relatives called themselves "de Gas" because having a "de" in front of your name makes you sound noble in France. I figured the whole class would laugh at that because of, you know, "gas." This turned out to be one of the times when everyone pretended I wasn't there.

They all wanted to be on my team in Science Brainiac, though. In seventh grade, when we won and were cheering, Benny gave me a one-armed hug, so quick that nobody noticed and afterward I wondered if it had happened. Benny was tall with blue eyes and freckles, and wasn't totally stupid. That night I kept waking up and feeling his arm around me and this electric zing.

The next morning I met him at the classroom door and looked him in the eye and smiled. He said, "What're you so happy about, Fairy Fat?" and muscled past me into the room.

Marshy's mom told her that boys were not to be trusted. I could see what she meant.

Seventh grade was the year Janine and Inez started wearing eye makeup and push-up bras, which could be considered a victory for them. They kissed boys and Janine had hot pink streaks in her straight blond hair. I wore an undershirt rather than a fake bra like Alice Whatsername, who was as flat as me. I kept my hair short and curly and brown, and wore T-shirts and a sweatshirt with a hood. My nose had turned into a Julius Caesar honker like Dad's, which Mom kept telling me I'd appreciate when I grew into my grandeur. But I wasn't growing into anything now, except maybe size fourteen.

Somehow everybody in my class knew I didn't have my period yet, which gave Inez the idea of sticking a tampon in my back pocket as I was getting up to do a math problem at the board.

I heard everybody giggling and it dawned on me that I had something in my pocket. So I reached around and pulled out the tampon and examined it, because at first I didn't know what it was. That brought the house down. I was about to rip open the wrapper when our teacher Mr. Higgins swooped down on me, grabbed the tampon, and threw it away.

"Grow up, you barbarians," he said. But he was trying not to laugh too.

By that time I'd figured out what the stupid thing was and was trying to pretend it was funny, but also I was Titian red. (Titian, who actually was named Tiziano Vecellio, lived in Italy in the 1500s and painted a lot of naked round ladies with red hair and got a color named after him.)

"You can sit down if you want, Mellie," Mr. Higgins said. But I was a Stoic. I turned my back on them all and worked on the math problem until I was winter-pale again. Got it right too.

At lunchtime an hour later, I was at the little kids' end of the school, sitting on a bench against a wall steaming with March sunshine. I was leafing through my Degas book, my refuge in times of stress and tampons. It had snowed overnight, and I could hear the other kids in my class having a slush-ball fight around the corner.

"Hey, Effy," Janine said, sitting down on my left. Inez sat down on my right. They had on too much competing perfume. I sneezed, managing to close my Degas book first so I didn't get any snot on *Musicians in the Orchestra*.

"Nice math problem," Janine said.

Inez snickered. "Yeah. Guess you never saw a Tampax before, huh?"

I didn't open my Degas book again because I didn't want to draw their attention to it. I had a bad feeling.

"So what's in that book, anyways?" Janine asked. "That's the de Gas man, right?"

I made sure my rubber boots were flat on the pavement, ready to run. "Don't even ask. You'd never understand, any of you."

Janine reached for the Degas book. Her mittens were soaked, filthy with slush-ball grunge. I jerked the book away from her and ran. But I was soft and clumsy, and they were basketball stars with eye shadow. They caught me at the jungle gym, shoved me into the monkey bars. The Degas book flew out of my hands and splashed into a puddle.

"Wooo," Benny yelled. "Lookit Fairy Fat." I clung to the monkey bars, watched the pages of my Degas book darken with the wet, the book jacket half off, floating.

"She said we were stupid," Janine crowed. "All of us."

A slush ball hit me in the back of the head, ran down my neck. I wasn't crying, was not going to cry. More slush hit the side of my head, but I would not wipe it off my face. I watched my Degas book, willing the moisture not to reach *Prima Ballerina*.

A slush ball hit the floating book jacket, submerged it. Slush balls exploded on the ground all around me and my book.

"Aw," Inez said. "Poor Fairy Fat." Another slush ball hit the dirt.

"Recess is almost over, leave her alone," somebody said, maybe Mina Cardoza.

"Hey!" somebody else yelled. Mr. Higgins. "Get off her, you little . . ." He used a word I'm not allowed to use until I'm eighteen because it's biological and not usually the best word for the occasion. It was the perfect word for this occasion.

The playground went quiet. I picked up my Degas book, tried to wipe it on my coat. The book jacket fell apart in my hands. Water ran out from between the pages.

"Maybe we can dry it off." That was Marshy, who still thought she could eat ice cream.

I couldn't look up because I might, after all, be crying a little. I stared at the toe of Janine's yellow boot.

Before my eyes, it turned into a cloven hoof, attached to a pink, hairy leg. This surprised me so much that I did look up.

Everyone, including Mr. Higgins, was a bright pink pig on its hind legs, all dressed except for having no shoes. The image lasted a second and then they were themselves again.

Inez looked sick. "Hey . . ." she said to Janine, "did you see something weird?"

"No," Janine said. "No, I did not. I didn't. No."

"I didn't either," Benny said, pale as popcorn.

Mr. Higgins sat down in the snow on the end of the slide and got his pants all wet.

Chapter Three

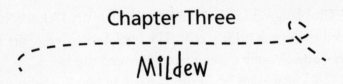

Mildew

I COULDN'T FIGURE OUT THE PIG THING. Losing control of my brain like that freaked me out. What had Janine and Inez and Benny seen? And Mr. Higgins?

I would never know, since nobody was going to talk about it. I read up about how our body chemicals react to stress and decided the answer was in there somewhere. I stored the mystery away for when I was a famous scientist.

And anyway, a month later I had something new and big to think about. We heard Grand-père had died, which was a dream come true. That sounds callous, but wait and see.

The phone rang a couple of hours after dinner. I answered it, and some lady who sounded like she was in a tunnel asked for "Rho-longh Tooghh-peh," which is the French version of Roland Turpin, which is my father.

It was bound to be a serious phone call at that hour, but Mom and I got no information from Dad's side of the conversation.

"Huh," he said at first, followed by "When?" Then "What was the . . . ?" And more *huh*s.

When he got off the phone, he stared at the wall for

three full minutes while Mom and I tried to be sensitive and unintrusive. Three minutes would be about our limit.

"So?" Mom said.

"He's dead," Dad said.

"Who's dead?"

"I don't believe it. I didn't think he was the type."

"What type? Who?"

"The heart attack type. He was so scrawny. And god knows he never held in his rage or anything. Plus, he drank red wine."

"Roly, if you don't tell me *this instant* . . ."

"My father," Dad said, annoyed as if she should have known. "He had a heart attack and died. That was his lawyer calling."

"Oh, Roly," Mom said. "I'm so sorry."

Dad jutted out his chin that way he has. "Why?"

Mom eyed him as if he'd handed her a stapler for a screwdriver. "It's gotta feel weird, Roly. He's your dad. I know you didn't get along, but you must have at some point."

"Nope. Not once."

"Never once?" I couldn't imagine not getting along with my dad.

"Zero," Dad said. "Zilch. Nada."

"But Dad—"

Mom frowned me down. "Anyway. What happens next? Is there a funeral?"

"Nope. The lawyer says he wanted to be cremated and no funeral. He didn't leave any instructions for what to do with the ashes."

"He sent your mother's back to France," Mom said.

"So maybe I'll do the same with him. Plant him next to her and good riddance."

"Roly." Mom gave me a nervous look. I could tell we were inching toward things she wanted to protect me from. So of course you know what came next. "Mellie, it's past your bedtime. Good night, sweetie."

"It's Sunday tomorrow."

"Right, so you want to get up early to enjoy the day." She has an answer for everything.

I went to my room and read about Leonardo da Vinci and how he gave some lady with an ermine a Mona Lisa smile before he even painted the *Mona Lisa*. So it wasn't until the next morning that I heard the really big news: Grand-père had left us the inn, and we were moving. We'd finish the school year, then my parents would quit their jobs and we would move lock, stock, and bad memories to scenic, seaside Baker's Village.

Good-bye, Fairy Fat. Sayonara, Janine. A whole new life, that's what this was. "Dad, are we going to run an inn?"

"No, no! We're going to fix it up! And then we'll sell it! And we'll invest the money wisely, and live on the proceeds while your mother and I become full-time artists! And we'll add a bunch to your college fund too!"

"We know what to do, Mellie," my mom said. "Don't worry."

They are brilliant about everything visual, so I wasn't worried about the fixing-up-the-inn-and-selling-it part. The investing wisely part was a laugh, but you can't have everything.

We moved in late June, and it was the first time we'd seen the inn since the bottle-throwing incident five years before. I was shocked when we pulled up to the same curb and saw what the inn had turned into. It probably hadn't been in great shape all along, but you didn't notice when it was painted and fixed up, with geraniums in the window boxes and everything. Now it was peeling all over the place, streaks of rust running down the stucco. A couple of window boxes were missing and a couple more were dangling by one nail apiece.

"He couldn't get up there anymore, I guess," Dad said, eyeing one window box that might fall on us like a whiskey bottle.

"Or down here," my mom said, looking at the rotting doorstep into the pub.

Getting up and down was an issue at the Agawam Inn. Still is. It's four stories, not counting the basement pub, which is five steps down from the sidewalk. The building is square, four windows on a side, wedged between two normal houses on Agawam Street near the Oak Street intersection.

When Mom opened the inn door—it's at the corner

of the building next to the pub entrance, and opens onto a flight of stairs—she reeled and said, "Gah!" She has a fine nose for mold and mildew and rot, and Grand-père had left us plenty of each.

"Bring the bleach bottle in first," she ordered my father. She pulled an herbal tea bag out of her shorts pocket, held it to her nose, gave me one, and grabbed my hand. We stepped over a pile of old mail and ran up the stairs before we could change our minds.

It was bad up there. When we got to the top of the stairs, a mouse abandoned a hollowed-out onion on the reception desk and booked it into the kitchen beyond. Nobody had cleaned out the refrigerator and Grand-père hadn't exactly spent his last days mopping and dusting. Every surface was sticky and brown and lumpy.

Mom ran around opening the windows that weren't stuck shut. She poked her head out a window in the breakfast lounge and yelled to my dad: "Bleach, dang it! And trash bags!"

It was hot up there, and my mom's hair was curling around her face in full cherub mode. Nevertheless, you do not ignore her when she says "dang it" or any swear of equal or greater value. My father was up the stairs in three minutes, his bald head shining with sweat, bleach bottle in one hand, trash bags in the other.

The next two or three hours went by in a stinky blur. We threw away terrible things, sniffed our tea bags, bleached important cooking surfaces and obvious patches of mold, stuck our heads out the windows to breathe. Mom and Dad carried a damp sofa down from the second-floor family quarters, plus a carpet and anything else that had cloth, and dumped it all in the backyard.

This was just the first two floors. We didn't venture upstairs to the guest rooms, even though a clock kept bonging up there with no regard for the actual time. "Don't drop or slam anything," Mom said when it finally shut up. "We don't want to set it off again."

My dad washed all the floors. My mom emptied the refrigerator except for some stuff in the freezer—cheese, fancy French coffee, even fancier Turkish coffee. She washed the shelves and bins. Then she went around the corner to the store to get something to cook for dinner.

Left temporarily to myself, I wandered down to look at the Bishop's Miter Pub, which I'd never been allowed to see. I stood out on the sidewalk for a minute, enjoying the fresh air. A freckled kid about my age came out of the regular two-story house next door and started walking over. *Oh great*, I thought. *Animal life.* He was pretty scrawny, but he looked to be my age. His light brown hair was longish and straightish and flipped out at the ends like a misshapen ski hat.

I was not prepared to meet a boy my age, especially not one from The Skinny Planet. I was tired and filthy and smelled like bleach and my nose was full of dust. This was no way to begin my new life.

Like I'd be so impressive if I was clean.

"The inn's closed," the kid said.

"Obviously," I said. *Ooo, clever comeback, Mellie.*

The kid stopped walking and peered at our car, which had its trunk open and a toilet brush sticking out of a box of stuff on the roof. "Are you cleaners?"

"Who wants to know?"

"I live here."

"You don't live here," I said. "You live there." I pointed at his house.

"Obviously."

"I have things to do," I said. "Good-bye." I fumbled like a dork with the pub doorknob, because it was round and my hands were sweaty. I felt myself go red and hoped the kid wasn't still watching. Finally I got the knob to turn and scuttled inside.

"Nice to meet you," he called. I slammed the door and stumbled down the steps to the pub floor, hoping he wouldn't knock or anything. He didn't.

Way to make new friends, Mellie.

But then, who needs 'em.

The pub was gruesome, which was good because I was in no mood to cheer up. The wooden floor was stained with fifty years' worth of who knew what. Behind the greasy mahogany bar, the liquor bottles were all grimy and spiderwebby. The ceiling tiles sagged like they were holding in somebody's guts. But it didn't smell all that horrible by comparison—just mildewy, which I could handle.

Mildew

I sat down on a filthy padded bench attached to one wall, behind a table. I stared at the cracked Formica on the tabletop, trying to imitate Degas' *Glass of Absinthe*, a painting of this sad woman sitting in a bar in 1876.

Pretending to be a painting is not imaginative. Not. At. All. You find out whether it actually is possible for a person to slump like that on a bar bench. That's science.

I had my hands just like the lady in the painting and was thinking how perfect I had her expression when I heard this funny noise. Several noises. A rustle. A tinkling, which made me look up to see this fancy but filthy chandelier shaking like my dad's belly at the beach.

There was a teeny-tiny hiccup, a despairing little cry. Something fell out of the chandelier and landed *splat* on the floor. I jumped up, freaked out because it might be a bat. A very sick bat, a baby, maybe an albino, pinkish beige. It lay there quivering. I tiptoed over, trying not to make noise.

It wasn't a bat. I thought it might be a huge moth, because of the wings. They were open but limp-looking, as if whatever they belonged to had forgotten how to use them.

Then I noticed that the thing had a dress on, which seemed strange for a moth. So I figured it was a doll. A tiny wind-up doll with wings.

I crouched down for a closer look.

The little thing sat up, tears running down her cheeks, let out a scream that managed to be both tiny and quite ear-splitting. She squealed something that sounded like "Salty May!"

She wasn't a doll. She was a living lady, three inches tall. With wings.

I couldn't breathe. I couldn't hear. The whole world disappeared except for that little lady. My brain, my muscles, my whole body froze into the silence, except for this one faint voice screaming, *No, no, no, not again not again notagainnotagainnotagain . . .*

I squeezed my eyes shut. *Fairy Fat, Fairy Fat, Fairy Fat.*

The little lady was gibbering in some foreign language, maybe French.

I'm dreaming, I fell asleep on that yucky bench over there. Deep breaths. Fairy Fat, Fairy Fat.

But I was smelling all that mildew. I've never had a dream with smells in it. I don't think you smell things in a dream. I had to admit, the mildew was real.

I opened my eyes. The little lady was still there, still gibbering.

Options: (a) Unfreeze, run out the door; (b) Count the bricks in the foundation; (c) Both of the preceding options; (d) Stomp on her, just in case.

There's never a school counselor around when you need one.

Chapter Four

Turpina

BLINKING DIDN'T HELP. Neither did deep breaths. This wasn't like the Pigs at the Playground Incident. This one didn't go away.

I've finally cracked.

But there she was, and there I was, and I couldn't just crouch there waiting for somebody to haul me off to the loony bin.

I stood up. The little lady saw me towering over her like that and her shrieks went all high and squeaky like an old swing. She got up and flapped away toward the bar, but you could tell something was wrong. She'd get airborne, six inches off the nasty wooden floor, and fly about a foot before going *splat*. It was pathetic. After the fourth try she stayed down. She crawled under a barstool and collapsed on her stomach, sobbing.

"I'm not going to hurt you," I said in the singsong voice you use for kittens. I was on my hands and knees now. *What am I doing?*

The little lady/bat went absolutely still, listening. She sat up, said something I couldn't hear. She gulped in air, calming herself down. *"Turpina es?"* Her voice sounded as if she were in a tin can in Providence, Rhode Island.

"Uh, hello. My name is Mellie Turpin." *You're talking to her? She's not real. Fairy Fat, Fairy Fat.*

The lady flung her arms open wide. "Turpina!"

Fidius called me that.

Excuse me? Fidius. Was. Not. Real.

The lady pulled herself together. She tucked her bare feet under her skirt and straightened her back. Her nose went up in the air. Like Fidius, she looked almost human, quite pretty, but her face was pale and pointy and unusually blank. Her light brown hair was pinned up in what probably had been a fancy hairdo but now looked like a squirrel's nest.

Don't panic. Fairy Fat. The little lady said something else I couldn't understand.

I couldn't help myself. "Do you speak English?"

"*Lingua Latina* better is. You speak *lingua Latina*?"

"Sorry."

"Ogier did speak Latin." Ogier was Grand-père's first name. He pronounced it Oh-shee-yay. So did the little lady.

She was dressed in something out of Cinderella, like a painting by this guy Watteau. *Facts. Think facts. Jean-Antoine Watteau, 1684–1721.*

Fact: The Louvre Museum in Paris has 35,000 works of art and 60,000 square feet of exhibition space. Fact: Andy Brown made a portrait of Queen Elizabeth out of one thousand tea bags.

She was still there.

"I speak English well," she said. "I am educated." She

reached over her shoulder to grab the top part of a wing and pull it through her hands, grooming herself the way Fidius used to. She was calmer. Her wings began to look more like wings, not so limp and pale.

I leaned in to watch the oily puddle effect, but she flinched and squeaked, so I backed right off. "It's okay," I said. "I really won't hurt you."

"I am jumpish," she said. "And sickish. It is this nectar you drink here, this bourbon, named for *nos anciens amis.*"

"For nose what?" I asked. She pronounced "bourbon" almost the way Grand-père said "Turpin." As if she were about to throw up: "Boorghh-boh."

She said, "Ai-yi-yi-yi!" Or something like that. Anyway, she was horrified. "*Nos anciens amis!* Our old friends! You are not speaking *la langue des Bourbons?*"

"Lah long day boorghh-boh?"

"*Français*, you warm dolt! The language of our favored kings, the Bourbons."

"I only started French this year," I said, although I didn't see why I should justify myself to a figment. "And I had a lousy teacher."

"Ogier spoke French."

"Oh yeah? Well, instead of speaking French and Latin all the time maybe he should have cleaned out the refrigerator."

I decided not to worry. A bit of sunshine and fresh air, and she'd turn out to be an albino bat. Easy-peasy. *Fact: Vincent van Gogh sold exactly one painting in his entire life, and now he's sold nine hundred and they're worth millions.*

"I desire food and drink, warm dolt."

"My name is Mellie."

"Mellie, Mellie," she said, making my name sound like a swear word. "It is having no dignity. Is this all the name you have?"

"Melissa Angelica, if you must know."

"Ah! Better. This is a name of lineage."

That's what Fidius used to say. *Fact: Édouard Manet was born in 1832 and died in 1883. Fact: The Museum of Modern Art in New York hung a Matisse painting upside down for forty-six days.*

"My name is Durindana, also of lineage. I desire food and drink. The great seeds are no more." She gestured toward the top of the bar.

I stood up and found a bazillion empty nip bottles of bourbon, plus a million-bazillion empty packets of salted peanuts. Which reminded me. "Hey, who's Salty May?"

"I do not understand your words."

"When you saw me you yelled 'Salty May.' Is that a person?"

She snorted. "*Servate me.* This means 'save me.' A natural reaction to a great warm dolt advancing when one is infirm. And in dreadful need of food, as I have said before."

I never had to feed Fidius. He helped himself from what I had on my plate. How was I going to get food for this little lady without tipping off my parents?

Will you please *stop pretending she's real?*

"Help me back to my bed, warm dolt." She pointed to the chandelier, where a fluffy pink slipper nestled among the dirty crystals.

I hesitated. *If you put your hand down, a baby bat will scuttle away. If she's not a bat, she'll get on your hand. And you'll know you're nuts.*

I put my hand down. Durindana clambered aboard and sat down.

COLD!! I almost dropped her. Her dress protected me some, but her bare feet were right on my skin. You know how an ice cube starts to burn if you hold it in your hand? That's what it was like. I surged to my feet, flung my hand up as high as I could. "Go! You're freezing me!"

She lunged for the chandelier, almost didn't make it. She climbed the rest of the way to the fluffy pink slipper, toppled over the side, and disappeared.

I'm nuts. I bolted for the door.

By the time I got back upstairs, though, my hand had stopped tingling. A store-bought chicken pie was in the oven. My mom was putting groceries away and Dad was pouring frozen green peas into one of Grand-père's fancy cooking pots. "Never been allowed to touch these before," he said, as if it were Christmas morning.

"Frozen green peas probably never touched them either," my mom said. "Definitely not up to his standards." They were being so normal.

I tried to open a box of cereal without attracting attention. Being a great warm dolt, however, I ripped the liner open and a geyser of oat flakes spewed all over the floor.

"Nice one, Mellie," Dad said. "We don't have enough mice, so let's throw cereal everywhere."

"Sorry. Where's the broom?" This was all right. I'd sneak cereal into my sweatshirt pouch while sweeping.

Mom saw my last handful going into the pouch. "What's this, a snack for later?"

I put the broom away. "There's an albino baby bat in the pub." I kept my head in the closet, making a big deal of putting the broom back exactly where it had been. I don't lie well, at least not to my parents—they look at me, they know what I'm thinking. *But I'm not lying, am I? It's a baby bat, right?*

My hand hit the broom handle just the right way, and it stung. "Ow," I said, and there they were on my palm: two tiny red prints from two freezing little bare feet.

She was not a bat. She was real, with freezing feet. *No, no, no, no, no, no, no . . .*

"You're feeding a bat?" my dad said. "Mellie, there's an army of mice in this place. Start scattering food around and . . . Ohhh." I emerged from the closet and he got a look at my face.

"What is it, Roly?" my mom said. Then she looked at me and said, "Oh. Dang it."

"We've got a Small Person with Wings," Dad said.

Chapter Five
The Curse of the Turpins

"IN LATIN, THEY CALL THEMSELVES PARVI PENNATI, Mellie," Mom said. "Parvi for short. A female is a Parva, a male a Parvus."

"What are you two talking about?" I said. But they're not the only ones who can read faces. I looked at them and my brain opened up like a sea anemone in a plankton storm.

Fidius was real. And my parents knew it.

I wasn't nuts. I had a frostbite handprint on the end of my nose. Squash *did* turn into candy corn. I had a friend who tried to mend my jeans. He left me a present. I was fine, thank you.

Fidius was real.

Fidius was real! I wanted to sing, sing, sing!

But . . .

My.

Parents.

All the time I'd been counting stuff and organizing stuff and keeping King Kong under control, I could have been reading Roald Dahl.

"You KNEW!" I slammed the broom closet door as hard as I could. "You let that woman smile like a horse at me and everybody called me Fairy Fat and I thought I was a freak and they threw slush balls at me. And you . . . KNEW!"

I flopped to the floor and buried my face in my hands. The clock was bonging its head off upstairs. What kind of people would lie like that to their own daughter? Mom sat down in the toasted oats, tried to put her arm around me. I shrugged it off.

"Mellie." Dad pulled up a chair. "Honey, look at me. Look at . . . Okay, don't. Honey, what could we do? If we told her, she'd have thought *we* were nuts, they'd take you away from us."

"We didn't know what to do, sweetie." Mom's voice wobbled. "You were so young when he was here, we thought maybe you'd forgotten him. We didn't know what you'd been saying at school until that Appleby woman called us."

"Oh god, Mellie, I wanted so much to talk to you about it," Dad said.

"We were protecting you," Mom said.

That got my head up. "Nice work, Mom. You protected me right into freakhood." I wiped my nose on my sleeve, even though I was not, not, not crying.

Mom managed to give me a squeeze. "We were definitely going to tell you when you got older, sweetie."

Dad pulled out his handkerchief and blew his nose. "I didn't know they called you Fairy Fat. Why didn't you tell us?"

The Curse of the Turpins

"Oh, Roly," Mom said. "They threw slush balls at her, horrible, *horrible* kids. Now I see why you didn't have any frien . . . Well, not that you didn't have *any* . . . I mean, there was Girl Scouts and . . . Oh, dang it." She gave me another squeeze. "This is the curse of the blasted Turpins. Excuse me, the blasted *Tooghh-pehs*."

"There's a curse of the Turpins?" I wasn't sure how much more I could take.

"Oh, now." Dad surged to his feet with an air of putting the bad times behind him. He stuck a hand down to haul Mom off the floor. "Calling it a curse is a bit strong. It's more of a legacy, really. A lineage."

That word again. I sniffed, hoping I wouldn't smell anything and therefore would know I was dreaming. I smelled chicken pie and bleach.

The peas came to a boil. "Let's eat," Mom said. They were pretending everything was normal, but neither of them would look at me.

"Hang on though," Dad said. "I gather our little guy needs fodder?"

"It's a little lady," I said. "She's been drinking bourbon because she can't get nectar. And eating bar peanuts." *Oh my god she's real.*

"We'll have to do better than that," Dad said, all jovial. "Especially if we know what's good for us. Parvi are uppity. Although if there's only one there's not much she can do to us."

Do to us? I didn't want to know.

Mom got out the chicken pie, and Dad put half a teaspoon of it on a doll-sized plate he found in the cupboard. He grabbed one of the half-inch-tall bottles that were up there too.

"I wondered what those were for," I said.

"Oh, I knew exactly what they were for," Mom said. "I didn't think we'd need them so soon."

Dad mixed sugar and water in a salad dressing cruet and dripped a few drops into the tiny bottle. "It ain't nectar, but it's close enough. Better for her than bourbon, anyway." He shook his head. "Ogier. Sheesh."

When he came back up from the pub, he was grinning the way he does when my mom tells him off with extra dang-its. "We've got a tartar this time. Called me a warm dolt."

I sank into my chair, exhausted. I wasn't even sure I could eat. "Are you going to tell me about the curse?"

"Legacy," Dad said. "Lineage."

The tale he told me then was like nothing I'd ever expected to come out of my dad's mouth.

Apparently we're descended from this guy Archbishop Turpin, one of the Twelve Peers of Charlemagne, the King of the Franks. "Franks" is what the French were called before they were French. The peers were Charlemagne's favorite knights.

"I don't know that much detail," Dad said, shoveling chicken pie into his mouth and talking anyway, which Mom wouldn't let me do in a million years. "Ogier and my mother never told me anything. But we had Parvi when I was a kid, and I picked up some stuff. A long time ago, 775 to be exact, Archbishop Turpin met a bunch of little people calling themselves the Parvi Pennati."

"Elbows off the table, Mellie," Mom said. "Parvi, by the way, is a diminutive—that's a shortened, sort of affectionate version of a longer name, in this case *parvi homines*, meaning 'small persons.' *Pennati*, of course, means 'with wings.'"

"Right." Dad swallowed his mouthful. "Anyway, Parvi like to live underground, but they'd been rousted out of their home by . . . I think it was a mole or something, I don't remember. So the Parvi offered Turpin a small moonstone—that's a kind of gem—in exchange for sanctuary. The moonstone enables you to see the truth, so nobody can lie to you. You can drink an elixir made out of it, and that does the same thing."

"Making the Turpin family the scourge of used car salesmen everywhere," Mom said.

Dad ignored her. "Anyway, Turpin took the stone, had it set in a ring so he could wear it. He pledged himself and his descendants to provide a home to the Parvi, individually or as a group, any time they needed one. The pledge is called the Obligatio Turpinorum, the Duty of the Turpins."

I couldn't believe this. We had a thousand-year-old pact with a bunch of fairies. We believed in magic moonstones. And my dad was sitting there eating chicken pie and saying "I guess" and "probably" as if nothing was all that critical.

"Uh, Dad, where is this moonstone?" (He shrugged. Great.) "Did you ever see it? What does it look like?" (Another shrug.) "And why couldn't the Parvi make themselves another hole and move into that? I mean, they're fairies, right? They can do magic, right?"

"Don't call them fairies." Mom sounded furtive. "They hate that." She fingered her earlobe, wincing, and saw me notice. "It's nothing, sweetie. A touch of frostbite."

I had a flash of memory: Fidius, hands curled into claws. *"Fairies! Figments!"*

"You ask good questions, Mel," Dad said. "All I know is that we have to take them in when they ask. I've gathered over the years that their magic is all about making things look good, and it fades if they're away from home for too long. That's why our little lady is so messy. Parvi like to live well, but they can't fend for themselves at all."

He swallowed three rapid bites of chicken pie. "Last I knew, Ogier did have the moonstone, being the official head of the family. There's supposed to be a parent-child chat sometime before the head of the family dies, telling the new owners the full history of the Obligatio and where to find the moonstone if they need it. As you know, Grand-père and I didn't spend a lot of time together in recent years."

"You let that happen?" I said. "You knew we could

be infested with fairies . . . I mean, Small Persons with Wings, and you let Grand-père die all by himself in this pigsty without explaining anything?" I threw down my fork and burst into tears.

"Bed," Mom said. "Tomorrow's another day." She was in Model Mom mode, which drives you up a wall but you can't argue with it.

I'm not saying she was wrong. I did go to bed, in a sleeping bag on an air mattress because the moldy bed in my new room had been chucked out in the backyard. But first I took my little china guy out of my backpack and set him on the windowsill. I fell asleep looking at him silhouetted against the light from the street, wondering where Fidius was now and if he'd ever forgiven me for wanting to take him to kindergarten with me.

In spite of everything I slept right through the night. And when I woke up in the morning it was, in fact, another day. I went down to the kitchen, where my parents were eating cereal.

"So these fairies . . . I mean, Parvi . . . how long do they stay usually?" I asked, getting myself a bowl. Fidius had been with us four years, I figured.

Dad shrugged. Didn't he know anything? "However long they need to, I guess. When they're by themselves it means they've left the Domus, and not for a happy reason."

"Domus?" I said.

"Latin for 'home.' Five hundred or more Small Persons with Wings, living together under the ground some-where near the Turpins. There'll be one right here in the neighborhood."

He said this in his "Fascinating Facts from the World of Nature" voice. As if we were discussing penguins in Antarctica instead of an alternate universe in the cellar.

"So are we going to look for the moonstone?" I asked. "Any idea what it looks like?"

Guess what. He shrugged.

Chapter Six

Burgess Wright

I WAS GETTING DURINDANA'S BREAKFAST READY when somebody rapped on the downstairs door and started up the stairs before we'd even thought about inviting them up. I hid the tiny sugar water bottle and bowl of cereal in the cupboard.

Mom tightened the belt on her bathrobe. "Guess we have to lock that door," she muttered.

Dad stepped into the reception area. "Hello?"

"Who's that?" said a deep voice.

"Who's asking?" Dad sounded pleasant and jokey, but his voice had an edge.

The footsteps kept coming up the stairs. "Where's Mr. Turpin?"

"I'm Mr. Turpin. I ask again, who are you?"

"You must be the son." A tall, square guy in a police uniform pushed past Dad into the kitchen. He had a belly like rolling foothills, but he looked so big and strong Mom and I instinctively backed up. Dad got between us and the guy, but he still made me nervous.

I circled around him, intending to hover in the door-way to the reception area in case I needed to phone for help. I almost bumped into someone already there—the boy from the day before. Close up, he was so coated with freckles that he looked even scrawnier, and he had these weird bluish gray eyes with a thick black rim around the iris. He had one foot on the threshold, one on the floor behind him, as if he too wanted a head start to book it out of there.

"Perhaps I'm not being clear," Dad said to the policeman. "Who are you?" The boy turned so red his freckles disappeared, and he gave me this sad half grin. *He's pathetic*. I felt braver.

The big man stuck out his hand for Dad to shake but didn't smile or anything. "Wright, Burgess Wright. Police chief. Live next door. My boy here saw you arrive yesterday. We were curious what was going on."

Dad shook the hand but didn't smile either. "Can we help you with something?"

"Guess we shouldn't have barged up like this," Chief Wright said.

Dad smiled in a polite way that meant he agreed. His chin was jutting out.

"Sit down for some coffee, Chief Wright." Mom isn't usually the family diplomat, but Chief Wright was awfully big. She smiled at the freckled kid. "And can I get you something?"

The kid opened his mouth, but his dad spoke first. "My boy, Timothy Oliver. Timmo, we call him, except I call him Spaceshot. He doesn't need anything." The kid sketched me a *Parents, what can you do?* shrug.

Totally pathetic.

"I'd take a cup of coffee, if you've got it made." Chief Wright didn't sit down; he thrust his head forward like a turtle and peered at Dad. "Your name's Roland, right?"

"Roly. This is my wife, Nick. Our daughter, Mellie."

"You two must be the same age." Chief Wright looked at me, jerked his head at his son.

"I'm going into the eighth grade," Timmo said to me while Mom bustled around getting Chief Wright's coffee, and Dad stood there with his chin out.

"Me too." *With any luck, we'll be in different classes.*

"Cool. We got Mrs. Anderson next year."

Oh, yeah, this is the sticks. Only one eighth grade.

"She's nice," Timmo said. "She's really fat."

My face got hot. I fought an urge to stretch my T-shirt down over my hips. "What's that supposed to mean?"

He shrugged. "She must weigh two hundred and fifty pounds."

"Yeah? So?"

The weird eyes widened as he sized up my mom and me and realized what he'd said. "Sorry. I mean, your mom's not fat. You either. Okay, you're not skinny. But, geez, you're not—"

"My mother has grandeur," I said. "And I . . ." *I what? Aced Science Fair?*

"Yeah," he said. "I mean, sure."

"Just because we're not emaciated—"

"Yeah, I said yeah. Sure."

We watched Mom try to persuade Chief Wright to sit down. He wouldn't, just stood in the middle of the floor taking up too much room. Mom was not actually looking all that grand at the moment. Her hair was dirty and she had a gimongo bleach stain on her bathrobe.

Timmo leaned in and whispered, "The heavier you are, the better it is for your bones."

I had nothing to say to this kid.

"Really," he whispered. "Astronauts lose bone calcium being weightless in space. The more weight your bones carry, the better."

"Spaceshot," Timmo's dad said. "Can it, will ya? I can't hear myself think."

I pushed off from the doorjamb and edged around Chief Wright to stand next to Mom.

Chief Wright sipped his coffee and smacked his lips. "Nice for Mr. Turpin to have some visitors. Where is he, by the way?"

We all stared at him.

"Well," Mom said, then changed her mind.

"Huh," Dad said.

"He's dead," I said.

Chief Wright froze, coffee to lips, then lowered his mug with extreme care. "Dead? When did that happen?"

"In April," Dad said. "Two months ago. April twentieth."

Chief Wright glanced at his son. "I thought you said there were lights on out back." He gave Dad a *Kids, what can you do?* look. "Timmo's room has a bay window in back and he sits in it with his telescope, stargazing like a spaceshot."

That's what Timmo's eyes reminded me of—in the Hubble Telescope book at school, a blue-gray swirling galaxy with a black rim. *Spaceshot,* I thought.

"And there was that lady, Dad," Timmo said. "I told you about the weird lady." His dad gave a rhinoceros sigh, so Timmo addressed himself to my dad. "I saw this blond lady and some guy come out and the door locked behind them and she started whamming on it, all ticked off. She had these high, high heels and she almost fell off the doorstep. And then she . . ." He glanced at his father's face and shut up.

"Nobody I've ever seen around," Chief Wright said to Dad. "Never heard of this blond lady except from Space-shot here." Timmo got interested in his sneakers.

"But . . . who could she be?" I asked. Timmo looked up. *I'm not on your side, kid. I'm only curious.*

"I said, I've never seen anyone like that around. Before or since." Chief Wright squinted into his coffee like Benny trying to fart. We waited for him to say how sorry he was that Grand-père was dead. "How did Mr. Turpin die?" he asked instead.

"Heart attack," Dad said.

"Awful quiet heart attack. Something like that happens in a town this size, people usually hear about it. Nobody called an ambulance?"

"I guess not. He probably was alone."

"That's an unattended death. You're supposed to call in the coroner for an unattended death, do an autopsy."

"Sorry," Dad said, although he clearly wasn't. "We didn't know."

"You seem to have heard about it quick enough. Who told you?"

"His lawyer called."

"Who's the lawyer?"

Dad went pinkish around the neck and jowls. "I beg your pardon, but this is your business . . . how?"

"Somebody dies mysteriously, it becomes my business. Nobody called an ambulance, nobody knows who found the body, nobody saw it leave the house. Pretty suspicious, wouldn't you say?"

"Dad," Timmo muttered. "Geez."

"Chief Wright." Mom was trembling with suppressed laughter, which made me feel better. "Are you making some sort of accusation?" The clock upstairs chose this moment to start bonging, fifteen o'clock this time.

Chief Wright had no trouble talking over the noise. "No, ma'am. But I would like to know who told Mr. Turpin here that his father was dead."

"His lawyer called," Dad said, every word an icicle. "And then she wrote, with the keys. I don't remember her name. The letter's in our stuff on the moving van. It'll be here this afternoon."

Chief Wright loomed over Dad, who held his ground.

The kitchen shrank. "You heard from a lawyer that your father died, and you can't remember her name? Didn't ask questions? Find out where the body was? Inform the authorities?"

"Look. I was going to call her when we got here, go over his will, figure out what to do with his ashes. She was his *lawyer*, for Pete's sake. I figured she'd tell whoever needed to know, and I'm sorry she didn't, but—"

"And you can't remember her name."

Dad took the kind of deep breath that means you're about to scream.

"Chief Wright," Mom said. "We'll get the lawyer's name to you tomorrow. This is simply a misunderstanding."

Dad was not calming down. "If you're so interested, how come you haven't noticed Ogier's been gone for two months? And *some*body must have carried him out of here."

Otherwise this place would be even stinkier, I thought. Timmo caught my eye and held his nose with thumb and forefinger. *Oh yeah, really mature, kid.*

Chief Wright was pinkish now. "Mr. Turpin kept to himself, and my son saw lights on. And you're right, I'd be very interested to hear how that body got out of here. If it did."

Mom clamped her hand on Dad's elbow, so hard he winced. "We'll do our best to find the letter, Chief Wright," she said. "Anything else we can do for you? More coffee? It's French."

"Find that lawyer, ma'am. Thanks for the coffee."

Timmo raised one hand to say good-bye. Then he was out of there, feet tip-tapping down the stairs. We listened to Chief Wright thump down, open and shut the outside door. Then we listened to the faucet drip. Something skittered behind a wall. At least the clock had shut up.

Two days ago, I'd had the comfy notion that my parents were on top of things. "Can we go home if we don't like it here?" I asked. All of a sudden, Boston seemed like home.

"Everything will be fine, Mellie," Mom said. "Roly, I can't believe you forgot the lawyer's name."

"Hey, there's been stuff going on, you know?" Dad banged his coffee mug down on the table and sank into a chair.

"It is odd, don't you think, Roly? How *did* the body get out of here? And how'd the lawyer know, when the police chief didn't?"

Dad frowned. "You think the lawyer's crooked? Something to do with the will, maybe?"

"Who knows." Mom sat down too. "I've never dealt with a lawyer. How do you tell if they're crooked?"

"We should find the moonstone ring," I said, since I wanted to find it anyway. "Then you could wear it and tell if she's lying."

Dad gave a half smile. "That's not a bad idea, hon."

I remembered what I'd been doing before Timmo and his father came. "I'm going to feed Durindana."

The pub was chilly and silent except for the gentle snores coming from the chandelier. I stomped to the bar and set Durindana's breakfast down sharply, hoping to wake her. I scraped a stool across the floor and sat on it, kicking a foot against the bar.

"Warm dolt," a sleepy voice said. "Have you feet or hooves?"

Durindana crawled onto a filigreed prong, positioned herself, and did a swan dive that turned into a series of swoops, like a chickadee heading for a feeder. I'd seen Fidius do that too. My heart lifted, began to sing.

At least it did until she crash-landed on her dirty dishes from last night.

Unfazed, she pulled a golden spoon from a pouch that hung from her waist and settled down to eat, bare feet tucked under her dingy skirt.

I watched her, looking for Fidius in the way she moved, the way her wings folded. Seemed to me her face had more expression than his did—the corners of her mouth had gone up, making her look almost happy.

"Why do you stare, warm dolt?"

"Do you have to keep calling me that?"

"Melissa Angelica Turpin, why do you stare? *Valde rudis. Très gauche*. Rude."

"It's Mellie, thank you." I stopped looking at her, and picked at a hangnail instead.

"Ai-yi-yi! You expect me to eat while you tear large pieces from your body?"

"Sorry." I took an interest in the liquor bottles on the opposite wall, some of which had cool labels. Durindana finished her cereal and took a swig of sugar water.

"This does not caress the throat like nectar," she said. "I prefer bourbon."

"It's not good for you. You couldn't even fly last night." But this wasn't what I wanted to talk about. "Hey, did you ever know somebody named Fidius?"

"You know Fidius?" She pressed her hand to her bosom, as if her heart were pounding. "Where is he?"

"He lived with us in Boston when I was little, but he left a long time ago, eight years, and we haven't seen him since."

"I have not seen him for twelve, no, fourteen years. My mother says this is the blink of an eye, but she is one hundred and ninety-three years old and to me it is . . . forever. His parents' shame drove him from us, also the jeers of his year-mates. He fought with the *magi* too, of course."

He told me he was popular. "These *magi*. They're like scientists, Fidius said."

"I do not know what is 'scientist.' The *magi* work to understand our magics. Fidius was to be a *magus*, being adept in the Magica Artificia. But then he left." She heaved a great sigh.

"What is Magica Artificia?"

"You do not know? You are a Turpina! Puh. Ogier Turpin. A man of taste, but besotted with his nectar. It is unforgivable that he neglects the Obligatio in such a way."

"I know about the Obligatio. But this Magica Artificia—"

She raised a hand to shut me up. "*Bien, bien.* I will teach, although it is not my place. Magica Artificia is our second magic, the one we value most." She sounded bitter.

"What does it do?"

"It changes the appearance of a thing. But not only the appearance." This seemed to be a point of pride. "The feel of the thing, as well, even its use. If we enchant a window to look like a door, you may use it as a door."

"Fidius changed squash into candy corn, but it still tasted like squash."

"We do not taste anymore, and many of us can no longer smell, so those senses matter little . . ." Her mouth dropped open. "Turpina! You say Fidius changed this squash when he was with you? In the city he did this? So far from the Circulus?"

"Um, I guess. What's the Circulus?"

She rolled her eyes. "The Circulus, Turpina, fuels the Magica Artificia. Without it, this magic would not exist. It requires the very best Parvi Pennati, taking their turns to fly around and around in joy. The power diminishes as one moves away from the Circulus. A Small Person using the Magica Artificia alone, so far from home . . . this is an extraordinary achievement indeed."

"He couldn't make anything last."

"Some would be pleased with half so much." She brushed at a spot on her skirt but only smudged it more. I watched her work at the smudge, wanting to ask what she meant. Obviously, it was a sore subject.

"If you must know," she said, like I'd asked, "the humiliation of Fidius's parents is also mine. In us, the magics may work against one another."

"That's . . . that's too bad."

"The Parvi's first, true magic, the Magica Vera, gave us skills we needed to live, but also it protected us from spells. We saw through all lies and illusion. This was our salvation when sorcerers were everywhere, so many centuries ago. In your year 453, the last of them helped us invent the Magica Artificia, but our native magic prevented us from seeing the beauties it created. We cast the Magica Vera out of ourselves, transferring it into the Gemmaluna so we would have it at need. But we rarely used the Gemma, and three hundred years later we were giving it to you, the Turpini."

"Is the Gemmaluna the moonstone?"

"Gemmaluna, moon-jewel, of course, of course, a stone of power. And yet, five generations later, tinges of Magica Vera remain in some of us, resisting the Magica Artificia. Sometimes we cannot *see* the illusions, to say nothing of making them ourselves.

"And we are clumsy." Her voice rose into a whine. "Ah! At times I cannot even fly, it is as if a great hand pulls me from the air." She sniffed, rubbing at her skirt. "Those more skilled than I are not kind. They call me Inepta, a terrible name for a Small Person of uncommon beauty."

Inepta, I figured, meant something like "inept." *Better than Fairy Fat.* "So what was the humiliation for Fidius's parents?"

"They had skills befitting the Magica Vera: Sylvia bred crickets, Glaucus made walls that kept out the damp. But they wished to be elevated to the Circulus. They tried to win favor by hosting a ball, but the food was ugly and Sylvia's headdress fell apart as she danced."

"Was Fidius around then?"

"Yes, yes, and one's soul wept for him. He did not share his parents' affliction, was the best of the young, sure to become a *magus*. This did not change after his parents' ball, but his friends . . . ah, they were not kind. Even Rinaldo, his closest friend, made fun of Sylvia and her headdress."

"What happened to his parents?"

"They lived with the horror for several weeks, then faded into death."

"They *died*? Because they gave a bad party?"

"It was a very bad party, Turpina."

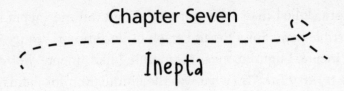

Chapter Seven

Inepta

I WAS SPEECHLESS. That doesn't happen often, and it didn't last long. "Giving a bad party doesn't *kill* a person."

"Everyone left before the first star! Next you will say that one's attire matters little, the arrangement of one's hair . . ." Durindana took in my sweatshirt and pillow hair. "You and I do not share a view of life."

"No kidding. But no wonder Fidius left you all."

"Yes, yes. He left within the year. He fought with the *magi*—the precise reason I do not know, but his parents' fall could not but reflect upon him."

"They didn't just fall. They *died*."

"Yes, yes, very sad, very sad."

Tough crowd. "So did something like that happen to you?"

"Ah!" She pressed her wrist to her forehead dramatically. "I cannot talk of it, too, too tragic, an embarrassment beyond bearing."

"Did anybody die?"

"No, no. But I wished to sink into the floor."

I almost tried to cheer her up by telling her about the tampon incident. Instead, I used Mom's method, which is to highlight your strengths when you're freaked out about your weaknesses. "I bet you do some things better *because* you have strong Magica Vera. You see things as they are."

Durindana didn't look as if she bought that. "Why would one wish to undo the Magica Artificia, to see the slug behind the *coq au vin*? Although"—she brightened—"sometimes one encounters an enchantment worth undoing. When that Gigantea visited Ogier, I saw she was a *pupa magna*, a large walking doll, very frightening. And I knew enough to hide."

"A Gigantea? What's a Gigantea?"

"You are a Gigantea. A large, warm female."

"Somebody visited Ogier? And she was a *doll*?"

"Yes. A shabby one also."

It seems weird, considering that I was talking to a three-inch-tall lady with wings, but I found it hard to believe in a giant doll walking around pretending to be a human.

Durindana yawned. "You will fetch my bourbon, Turpina."

"I don't think I'm supposed to—"

"Warm dolt!" Durindana stamped her bare foot on the bar. "I . . . desire . . . bourbon!"

Obviously, we have mixed feelings about alcohol in our family. Mom drinks wine now and then, and Dad used to. But then he took a good look at Grand-père and gave it all up. "I don't know if I have a problem," he said, "and I don't want to know."

One of those bottles on the wall behind Durindana might be bourbon. Last night, though, Dad didn't seem to think much of feeding the stuff to Parvi. I decided to ask him. "I'm going upstairs," I said, heading for the door. "I'll be right back."

"Aaayyyiii!" She landed on my head, burrowed into my hair, freezing my scalp. I reached up to haul her out of there and she grabbed my finger hard, freezing it, too, until I yanked it away from her. She pulled out one hair, then another.

I shrieked, and shrieked some more. I shook my head. I shook my whole body. I danced around the room, stomping and waving my hair, which only made the pain worse.

The pub door slammed open. "Mellie!" my dad yelled.

Someone grabbed me by the head. "Hold still, Mellie," my mom said.

She messed around in my hair a second, and the pain and freezing stopped. When I straightened up, she was dangling Durindana from her thumb and forefinger, holding on to the back of her skirt. Durindana was writhing, punching, kicking, her wings dark brown. Mom had a grim smile on her face.

"Never hold a Parva by the wings, Mellie," she said. "We don't wish to harm her, no matter how uncouth she may be."

"Uncouth!" Durindana lapsed into French. I caught the word *chien*, which I think means "dog." I didn't know which of us she was talking about.

"Now hear this," Dad said, louder and sterner than I've ever heard him. Durindana stopped wriggling. "You hurt my daughter again—hurt any of us, in fact—and we don't feed you."

"You must care for me," Durindana said, quite haughty for someone dangling by her skirt. "Fail to honor the Obligatio and your lives are cursed."

"I don't care," Dad said, although you could tell he had doubts.

"A Small Person pulling your child's hair out counts as a curse in my book," Mom said.

That stiffened Dad's backbone all over again. "Do we have an agreement?"

Durindana dangled there, thinking. She nodded. Mom let go of her skirt without any warning, and Durindana almost hit the floor before her wings kicked in. She flitted up to the chandelier and disappeared into her pink slipper.

I wondered if I really wanted a Parva around. This one was a cross between Janine and . . . well, me. One of me was enough, and none of Janine was just fine, thanks.

"What did you do to tick her off?" Mom asked.

"She wanted bourbon. I was coming upstairs to see if it was okay."

"It's not good for her," Dad said.

"Who are we to decide?" Mom said. "She's not a pet, after—" A wail from the chandelier cut her off. "Oh dear."

Durindana was sobbing and talking to herself. I couldn't understand what she was saying, probably because it was in French but also because she was crying so hard.

"Aw," Mom said, in one of her typically bizarre turnarounds. She hates wasps, but she never squishes one when it gets into the house—she captures it in a glass and takes it outside. She says they have an important place in nature, just not in our house. She's a cockroach killer, though, and they have a place in nature too. Sometimes it's better not to look for logic.

Durindana obviously was in the wasp category. "Roly," Mom said. "Get a ladder."

Dad hauled a dusty, rickety stepladder out of a storeroom behind the bar. Mom climbed up until she was eye-to-slipper. "Hello, dear."

"Go away."

"We can't go away, we live here. And we're perfectly happy to have you live here too. For . . . you know . . . for a while."

"I am in a nasty hole all by my suh-suh-suh-self." A new round of sobbing commenced.

"It *is* nasty," Mom said. "I'm sure it's not what you're used to. We'll fix it up eventually, although I'm afraid the cellar isn't our first—"

"I want to go ho-ho-home."

"Can't you?"

"No."

"Would you prefer to move upstairs with us?"

"No. I am uncomfortable sleeping aboveground."

"Fidius slept with us," I piped up. "We were on the fifth floor."

A disheveled head peeked over the side of the slipper. "I am not Fidius."

"Whatever you say, dear." The ladder gave a serious wobble. Mom started down.

Durindana craned her neck to watch Mom's progress. "If I drank more of the nectar of Ogier Turpin, I would feel better."

"It's not good for you," Dad said again. "You couldn't even fly yesterday."

"Flying is not everything."

"Perhaps if you drank just a little," Mom said, reaching the floor. "And sipped it slowly."

"Yes, yes, this I will do."

Mom looked at Dad. Dad's forehead wrinkled up. "I don't know. I'm not sure where my responsibilities lie."

"Sometimes you have to let people be what they are," Mom said.

He gave her a sharp look through his wire rims. "You're right, of course." He went behind the bar and peered at the bottles. He blew the dust off of one, opened it, and dribbled some brown stuff into last night's water bottle.

Durindana swooped to the bar before he finished dribbling.

"Hey, take it easy there," Dad said when she grabbed her bottle and took a swig. "You said you'd sip it."

She curtsied to us, bottle in her arms. "I thank you, Turpini." She swooped back to her slipper with the bottle.

"I don't think this was a good idea," Dad said.

"We'll take it as it comes," Mom said. "Think it over. Ponder the wisdom of our actions. Come on, we have work to do." She loaded Durindana's used dishes onto the palm of her hand and headed upstairs, shutting the door behind her with a crisp *thunk* that said she was already developing the chore list in her head.

Dad gave a heavy sigh and stared up at the ceiling, hands in pockets, pondering Life the way he does sometimes.

"Hey, Dad," I said. "What happens if we give back the moonstone? Do we become Parva-free?"

"Probably we can't give it back. Where magic is concerned, I bet what's done is done."

"The Turpini can give back the Gemmaluna," a tinny voice called from the pink slipper. "But all Parvi Pennati and all Turpini must be present for the ceremony."

"How do you know that?" I asked.

"I am educated." Durindana began to sing to herself in French.

"I suspect the chances of us getting all the Parvi together are pretty slim," Dad said. Durindana giggled, then hiccupped. "Let's find the thing first, then weigh our choices."

"We'll want to use it on the lawyer, anyway." I was looking forward to us being super truth-detectors.

The door opened and an elegant blond lady stuck her head into the pub. "Hello-o," she trilled at Dad. "You are being the new Mr. Turpin?" She said it the French way, which told me she probably had known the old Mr. Turpin. She sounded foreign herself.

She had the most bizarre voice I'd ever heard—strained, sort of, like she was shouting at us from the far end of a tunnel. From the chandelier, Durindana gave a cry that almost pierced my eardrum. I hoped the lady hadn't noticed and that Durindana would shut up now.

The lady minced down the steps on these really high heels and handed Dad a card. "Gigi Kramer, real estate," she called out, head swiveling back and forth, looking the place over. "I welcome you. You prepare to sell, I believe."

"Uh, yeah," Dad said. "We need to fix it up first."

She leaned forward, staring into his eyes. "*Tiens, monsieur*, where will you locate the money for this renovation? You will seek a loan from a bank?"

I thought she was pretty nosy. I also thought it was rude not to acknowledge that I was standing there. The third thing I thought was that I'd never seen anyone wearing elbow-length green cotton gloves at the end of June. They looked nice with her fancy black suit, but still.

Doesn't anybody normal live in this town?

Oddly, Dad didn't mind that a stranger was asking him such personal questions. He looked as if someone had hit him over the head with a dusty bourbon bottle. "We've got money set aside," he said, eager to please. "We can invest that in renovations. We'll make it back, maybe double it."

This was the first I'd heard of using money we'd set aside. The only set-aside money I knew about was my college fund. "Hey, wait a minute."

The lady whipped around and gazed into *my* eyes this time. Hers were absolutely dead, like a shark's. I thought briefly that this was even more bizarre than the gloves. But it was only a flash of a thought, followed by the absolute knowledge that she was the most beautiful woman I'd ever seen and that I would do anything in my power to please her. "Can I get you something? Coffee? Bourbon?"

"*Zut*, what an adorable child. No, I thank you, my dear." She turned back to my dad, causing me great sorrow. "You will be making the renovations yourself?"

"Mostly ourselves." Dad slurred his words. "Unless you think it's best to hire someone."

"No, no. You will be wise to keep such things inside the family. And on such a project you must work slowly and carefully. Haste is making the waste." She gave a hollow laugh . . . literally hollow, with a slight echo. "You will be needing a building inspection first, of course."

My head cleared and I saw that the lady was staring past Dad to the bar, where today's tiny bottle of sugar water was still sitting. I got all tingly, the way you feel (a) jumping into an ice-cold sea. Or (b) when you've knocked over an easel with someone's wet painting on it.

Or (c) when a lady with dead eyes might find out about a Small Person with Wings. "Oh!" I said, hustling to the bar. "There's my dolly's bottle."

I hadn't had a doll since I was six, and even then we all called her what it said on the box: Female Anatomical Model, Fully Articulated. FAMFA. Fammie, for short. Mom used her for a figure model when she painted. We shared her.

"Adorable," the lady said. She narrowed her shark eyes at me as I rejoined her and Dad. I didn't want to leave Dad alone with her. He was looking stupider by the minute.

"My dolly gets very thirsty," I said, waving the bottle. A drop of water flew out and hit the lady on the cheek. She didn't notice. It didn't dribble off.

As she returned her attention to Dad I stepped closer. The water stayed on her cheek, dull rather than shiny, not running, not even flattening out. As she talked—I don't remember about what—it fell off her cheek as if it were solid.

She and Dad headed for the door. Her heels sounded like tap shoes. I poked at the water droplet, still intact on the floor. It actually was solid.

In fact, it was ice.

Chapter Eight

Parvi Pennati

"THIS IS A COMMUNITY OF MUCH LOVELINESS," Gigi Kramer was saying when I joined her and Dad on the sidewalk. "You will be happy here."

"Loveliness," Dad said. "Happy."

She smiled at him and you could see his knees buckle. "Be keeping me informed of your progress. I shall be most enchanted to advise you as the renovation proceeds."

Dad stared after her as she sashayed her high heels to a fancy black car with tinted windows. She got in and took off, hanging a left to drive up Oak Street.

"Think that's the lady the kid next door saw?" I asked as Dad opened the door to go upstairs. "She is one weird lady."

"What lady?"

"Dad. You've got her card in your hand."

"Oh. Huh." He put the card in his pocket.

By the time we got up to the kitchen, Dad was his regular self again, apparently not bothered by the fact that some lady with shark eyes seemed to be stalking us. *I'll talk to that kid again,* I thought. *Maybe he can tell me more about her when his dad isn't around.*

"So," Dad said, rubbing his hands together as if he'd

never been reduced to a zombie by a real estate lady. "Let's start looking for that moonstone."

"And the note," I said. "Let's hope there's a note telling us how to use it."

You'd be surprised at all the hiding places a pair of shop teachers can come up with, and they never even made it up to the guest rooms.

Mom unscrewed the covers from the electrical outlets and took down the wall sconces and ceiling lights, shining a flashlight into the maze of wires to see if anything sparkled. She looked for letters taped in, on, and behind the plumbing. She turned the water off so she could gross me out by searching the toilet tanks.

Dad took up every floorboard that seemed loose or had newish nails in it. He took apart every picture frame on the walls and made me shake out every single book in the family quarters.

They took the top off the stove. Took the back off the refrigerator. Took apart Grand-père's ancient television set.

Frankly, I couldn't see Grand-père going to that much trouble to hide something. So once I'd finished the books I decided to start in the guest rooms on the fourth floor and work my way down, checking more obvious places. I poked into every closet, ran my finger across the top of the doorjambs, looked under carpets and mattresses. I found a whole box of whiskey nip bottles in one closet and held every bottle up to the light. Nothing.

Being up there by myself creeped me out. I kept feeling I *wasn't* by myself. Somebody was breathing the same air, but I couldn't hear or see or smell who it might be.

I got through the two floors of guest rooms anyway. The mattresses needed to be explored further, but I decided I'd leave that to my parents since they were so good at taking things apart.

I made the same decision about the bonging grandfather clock, which turned out to be on the third-floor landing. I couldn't figure out how to open the clock face, and the door looked to me to be fake, painted on. It looked like something the artist Vanessa Bell would have done in 1917—she painted on everything, including chairs and people's walls.

She went to a party once and danced so hard her dress fell off.

I must have jostled the clock, because the thing went nuts. *Bong,* it said. *Bong, bong, bong, bong . . .* It went on and on and on and I couldn't see any way to stop it. Finally I gave it a good whack and yelled, "Cut it out!" It wheezed, gave one more unhappy *bong,* and shut up.

Stupid thing. It said four o'clock and it was only one in the afternoon.

I was starving. I went downstairs to find my parents sitting in the kitchen like a pair of depressed trash bags, eating cheese and crackers.

"Nothing?" I said, cutting myself a hunk of cheese.

"Worse than nothing," my mom said. "We just realized we have to go through all that moldy stuff in the backyard."

"Plus the mattresses in the guest rooms," I said.

Dad groaned. "Bloody old man. Why couldn't he make this easy?"

"When did he ever make anything easy?" Mom said.

The moving van distracted us by rumbling up to the front door and honking. The sun was low in the sky by the time we got our possessions moved in and set in place.

Moving my stuff into my new room felt like starting my life all over again. I forgot all about Chief Wright and his freckled son and the weird real estate lady. Even though my genes were against me, I resolved to (a) play sports, (b) eat less, (c) become thinner and cooler. I was going to (d) have friends in this place. I would (e) wear blue eye shadow, and (f) walk into school holding hands with someone—a taller and smarter version of Benny who liked Degas.

Listing things doesn't necessarily mean you're being rational. Particularly when the only boy I'd met so far was Timmo the weight-bearing space-nerd.

I stuck my china guy in his regular spot on my dresser and danced him around the way I used to when I was little. I wished Fidius would turn up. I wanted to apologize for trying to show him off to the kindergarten. When I became popular, I wanted him to know about it.

My stomach growled. I was wondering if anyone was

going to make dinner when an alarm bell went off in my head.

We'd forgotten Durindana for eleven hours. Eleven and a half, to be accurate.

Mom and Dad were in their bedroom, swearing at each other in an affectionate and jocular fashion as they tried to hang her still life with poppies.

"Hey," I said, running in and almost killing myself when the scatter rug . . . well, scattered. "Anybody feed Durindana?"

The swearing got un-jocular in a hurry.

"We'd better go down there together," Dad said as we bustled around the kitchen tearing bread and cheese and tomatoes into small bits, all we could think of at short notice. "She's not going to be happy."

We were pretty tired and the stairwell was dark, which must be why we didn't notice the change of wallpaper on the way down to the front door. Later, when we had it together, we discovered that the wall closest to the pub had broken out in striped silk. It must have oozed through the plaster like some eighteenth-century mildew.

Having made it to the sidewalk without noticing anything unusual, Dad reached for the pub doorknob and stumbled backward in surprise. There was a new door, a stunning blue one with a fancy gold handle. Light and tinkling classical music poured out the mail slot, which had never had a flap.

I could tell Dad didn't want to go in there, but we aren't

descended from a warrior archbishop for nothing. He took a deep breath and opened the door. The three of us huddled in the doorway, aghast.

Parvi were everywhere, and I mean EVerywhere. You could barely see the chandelier for all the ornately dressed little ladies and guys sitting on the prongs, swinging it slightly. More of them were sitting on the windowsills, all over the grimy tables, on the wall sconces, on the bar.

Six feet above the floor, fifty small figures were flying around in a circle, all packed together and moving so fast I couldn't distinguish one from another. *The Circulus*, I thought. *Powering the magic that makes illusions.* Now and then, a beautifully dressed figure would fly up from the floor and ease into the circle, while another would emerge from it and float blissfully downward.

As they circled, stuff kept happening in the room until it was covered with marble, gold filigree, and silk. The top of the bar and the tables turned into glass. Brocaded and tasseled wall hangings unfurled themselves from the ceiling. The windows grew heavy velvet drapes.

The only thing that stayed the same was the chandelier, except it was sparkling clean.

On every surface, matchbooks and other bits of debris were turning into Parvi-sized tables and chairs and sofas and beds.

"Aw, dang it," Mom whispered.

Dad looked at the bread and cheese and tomatoes in

the palm of his hand. It had been a pitiful offering to begin with. Now it was an embarrassment. "Here, Mellie," he whispered, "put this on the stairs next door. Quick, before anybody sees it."

"*Turpini!*" Two small figures made a beeline for us, joined us on the sidewalk. Hand in hand, they hovered in front of Dad's nose. Dad didn't brush them away like wasps, but his fingers twitched.

The lady wore a gown of some shiny, gold-colored cloth, ruffled and flounced and so encrusted with jewels I couldn't see how she stayed in the air. Her white-powdered hair was piled high, with white plumes bobbing around in it. She had a fancy necklace and a bunch of bracelets so brilliant it hurt to look at them.

Her gentleman was in a purple satin suit with knee breeches, a pink brocade vest, and his own bunch of ruffles. He had big jeweled buttons on his coat and powdered hair tied back with a black velvet ribbon. Totally looked like they came out of a Watteau painting.

The gentleman nodded to the lady and dropped her hand. He swept off his plumed hat and bowed to us in midair, face expressionless.

"Er, how do you do?" Dad said as the little man settled his hat back on his head.

"*Rinaldo sum,*" the little man said in that tinny Parvi voice.

"*Linguam Latinam non loquimur,*" Dad said, meaning that we didn't speak Latin. Then he said the same thing in French. "*Et nous ne parlons pas français.* Do you speak English?"

"I speak very, very well. My naming is to be ..." He got the fish eye from the overdressed lady, and tried again. "I ... am been ... I am being ... I *am* Rinaldo, gubernator of the Parvi Pennati. This is being ... This is the Lady Noctua, my consort and *domina* of the Circulus." He indicated the circling figures under the chandelier.

Rinaldo. Fidius's former best friend. Who made fun of Fidius's parents. He didn't look like a bad guy, although it's hard to tell without cues from a person's facial expression.

"How do you do?" Dad said again. "I am Roland and this is my, uh, consort, Veronica. Our daughter is Melissa Angelica."

"Names of lineage," Rinaldo said, beaming. "Such as mine."

I kept forgetting to ask what that meant.

"*Alors,*" Lady Noctua said. "To business, Rinaldo. Roland Turpin, we are to be imposing upon the hospitality of this house. We invoke the pact of our ancestors."

"I can see that," Dad said. "May I ask why?"

"Please enter and be seating of yourselves in comfort." Rinaldo gestured like a head waiter.

"Yeah, Dad," I said. "Better get in there and shut the door." A car slowed down behind me. They probably couldn't see into the pub. But still.

Thanks to the Parvi's natural chill, we could see our

breath. The breeze from the whirring Circulus didn't help. I hoped we wouldn't stay long.

Rinaldo shooed some ladies off three human-sized chairs around a table and invited us to sit. Lady Noctua curtsied to us in midair before gliding down to the table next to ours, where a bunch of ladies and gentlemen were making merry.

Mom was unnaturally quiet, her eyes practically rolling around in her head as she sized up the miniature population. I guess she hadn't seen so many Parvi in one place before. You couldn't keep tabs on them all.

If there's only one of her, there's not much she can do to us, that's what Dad had said. My scalp was still sore from that "not much." What could a group of Parvi do to us?

Rinaldo landed on our tabletop. He sat down in a miniature chair, swept off his plumed hat, and set it on a tiny round table, fluffing the feather. "Ah." He put his feet up on another chair. "*Melius*. Better."

"If I may ask again," Dad said, "why are you here? Not that we're not delighted to have you, of course."

His voice boomed over the chatter, which dimmed immediately. A thousand eyes focused on Rinaldo.

Rinaldo stood up, putting his hat back on so he could sweep it off again in a bow. "It is been—bah, this English—it *is* my duty to announce that the Parvi Pennati, children of the Larger Gods, wish to regain the Gemmaluna, gem of insight, which our forebears in happier times have entrusted to the esteemed family of Turpini."

The crowd murmured. We Turpini looked at one another sideways. I zipped my lips, in case I blurted out that we had no idea where the stupid moonstone even was.

Dad assumed the role of family spokesman. "May I ask why you want it back?"

"We taste no food!" a little lady shrieked from the floor.

"We cannot smile or frown!" a little guy in a scarlet coat shouted. It was true—now that I looked around, the Parvi did seem awfully Stoic. Unlike Durindana, who almost had real facial expressions. Where was she, anyway?

"Bah! *Crétin!*" A little guy in green tackled the guy in scarlet and they rolled around on the floor, punching and hair-pulling. All over the room, little ladies and gentlemen unfurled their beautiful wings—*fwap!*— and started shoving and shouting. Here and there, wings began to darken.

"Peace! Peace, my Parvi Pennati!" Rinaldo beckoned to us. We bent in close. "As you see, many of the Parvi Pennati do not want the Gemma to return. Even my dear Lady Noctua." He bowed to Lady Noctua. She gave him the cold shoulder and turned her attention to the guy next to her. *Nice marriage*, I thought.

"If we have the Gemmaluna," Rinaldo continued, "we shall make from it an elixir to regain the Magica Vera, our true power, which makes real objects for our comfort and support." He gestured toward a small table covered with a silk carpet. Displayed on it were a miniature plow, a bunch of tiny pots and pans, some earthenware pottery, and a collection of tweensy tools: mallets and shovels and things.

Dad looked puzzled. "I know a little about the elixir. But why would you want pots and plows instead of . . ." He waved around at all the brocade and gold and marble.

"*Exactement*!" yelled the guy next to Lady Noctua, brandishing his fists at Rinaldo. Rinaldo shook his head sadly. "We love our comforts," he said. "But the magic that creates the beauty you see around us, the Magica Artificia, it has developed . . . how do you say this . . . a side effect."

"And what is that?" Dad asked.

Rinaldo loosened his lacy neck-cloth while Lady Noctua's table glared at him. "Since the time of my grand-père, we have watched our senses die. No one now living is remembering the taste of food. Few can smell the spring air. We cannot use our faces to express what we feel. Those most adept at the Magica Artificia are the ones least able to smell or smile."

"Why is that happening?"

"We do not know. Our *magi*—myself and Noctua among them—have tested and tested, trying to identify the difficulty. And now we . . . that is, most of the Parvi Pennati"—Rinaldo slid a glance at his wife—"we believe we shall lose all our senses if we continue with the Magica Artificia. Our hearing, our sight, perhaps speech, even the sense of touch."

"Wow," Dad said.

"Pah," said Lady Noctua.

"Yes, Roland Turpin, it is very wow," Rinaldo said. "Our remaining senses are being dear to us. We admire the look and texture of food because we cannot taste it, the sound and feel of a breeze because we cannot sniff the air. We must act before all such pleasures leave us."

"Will you get back the other senses?" I asked. "I mean, once Fidius got away from the Circulus, he could smile a little."

"Fidius?" Rinaldo said. Was it my imagination, or did his wings darken? "You know Fidius?"

"Yes," I said. "And Durindana is even more—" The gentlemen and ladies at Noctua's table broke into raucous laughter. "Inepta," one of the ladies said, and the others cracked up.

"Inepta," Rinaldo repeated. "This is how we call her. Always she stumbles in the dance, bespills herself with food. She falls from the air and disrupts the Circulus. Even now she sleeps as a besotted one. Puh."

"Oh," my mom said, the first words out of her mouth since we sat down, "here she is now."

Durindana stood in her pink bed, barely keeping her balance as the chandelier swung gently back and forth. Surrounded by opulence, she looked even more disheveled than before. I hoped she wouldn't embarrass herself by trying to fly.

As she wobbled there, her pink dress turned bright blue and her hair tidied itself.

"She's fixing herself up," I said. "The Circulus must be helping her."

"The least she could be doing," Rinaldo said.

"Ho, Inepta," shouted a gentleman at the next table, waving his hat.

He yelled something I couldn't understand, and his friends shrieked with laughter. Lady Noctua slapped him with her fan, but in a flirty way, not really angry.

Durindana shouted something back. "*Something-something-pupa-something*," I heard. She gestured at Dad and me, gabbled some more Latin.

The room went silent. The music faltered. Every face turned to the chandelier. "Ha!" yelled the hat-waving gentleman. "*Inepta-something-something-pupa-something!*"

Every little being in the room started to yuck it up, doubling over, slapping one another on the back. Lady Noctua covered her face with her hands, shoulders shaking. Rinaldo said something none of us could hear. Dad bent down to him.

Durindana retreated into her pink-slipper bed, mouth contorted like a mask of tragedy. This proved exactly what I'd been trying to say about her facial expressions, but nobody noticed that.

"She says she saw a giant walking doll," Dad told Mom

and me as the laughter began to die down. "*Pupa* means 'doll.'"

"But of course she has not been seeing a giant walking doll," Rinaldo said. "Mademoiselle Inepta is besotted by the nectar of Ogier Turpin."

"When did she see this giant doll?" Mom asked.

"This very morning, she says. Durindana was in her bed and a giant walking doll was conversing with Roland and Melissa Angelica Turpin." Rinaldo bowed to Dad and me as if we were royalty.

"She means the real estate lady," I said.

"What real estate lady?" Dad said.

"Try your pockets. She gave you her card."

He stood up and fished around. He came up with a quarter, six pennies, a bunch of nails, three postcard stamps gummed together, an unwrapped throat lozenge with fuzz. And, stuck to the lozenge, a bent and grimy business card.

"*Gigi Kramer*," he read. "*Real estate*. And then there's a street address, phone, fax, and e-mail. Huh. Don't know where I got this."

"She came this morning, when Durindana was in bed with the bourb . . . Well, in bed," I said. "She sounded like she was shouting in a tunnel and she had dead-looking eyes like a shark. She looked at me and I got weird, but mostly she looked at Dad. And now he doesn't remember her."

"Mellie, this isn't like you," Mom said. "Are you feeling all right, sweetie?" She reached for my forehead, but I evaded her.

"She kept asking what we were doing with the inn. And she turned Dad into a zombie."

"I'm not a zombie." Dad rubbed his hands together to get the circulation going. "For example, I'm freezing. It's a known fact that zombies don't freeze."

Rinaldo wagged his finger at me. "You are making up a story, Melissa Angelica Turpin."

"Why would a giant doll care what we do with the inn?" Mom asked, the voice of reason.

Durindana shouted something from her slipper. Lady Noctua's delicate hand flew to her mouth in shock. The Parvi on the floor murmured and milled around.

"She says this giant doll has a Small Person with Wings inside of it," Rinaldo said. "How can this be?"

"Her voice did sound sort of hollow," I said.

Dad shook his head. "Why don't I remember this dame?"

Rinaldo frowned. "Melissa Angelica, you say she looked in your eyes and you—how did you say this . . ."

"I got weird. I wanted to please her. And Dad turned into a zombie."

Lady Noctua's gentleman friend strode to the edge of his table and cried out, "Magica Mala!" Rinaldo leaped from his chair and unfurled his wings to their most impressive; the other guy unfurled back and gabbled in Latin. An ocean of murmurs swelled up from the floor.

"What's Magica Mala?" Dad asked.

Rinaldo patted the air to shut the other gentleman up, then slip-slapped his bare feet to the edge of his table to address us. "This is our third magic, discovered many years after the Magica Artificia. This is forbidden, except for study by the *magi*."

"Forbidden? What's wrong with it?"

"You must understand . . . the Lady Imprexa, a *maga* of great renown, invented the Magica *Artificia* with the help of a sorceress. It is part sorcery—not like Magica *Vera*, our true magic, which was in our bodies when we sprang from the earth. Magica *Mala* was developed by rogue *magi* long after the death of the Lady Imprexa, and is a stronger magic, with more sorcery in it. Magica Mala makes a deeper illusion, controlling the actions of an object, even other creatures, other Parvi. This offends nature, this befuddling of others."

"So you made it illegal," Dad said.

"Yes, yes. We named it Magica Mala, as I have said."

"*Mala* means 'bad,'" Mom said.

"So . . . I guess Inepta's right about seeing a giant doll," I said. Rinaldo stiffened. *Score one for the downtrodden.* "And you think whoever's inside might be using Magica Mala."

"This cannot be true," Rinaldo said. "Although I admit, our plight does breed desperation. When we were possessed of our native magic, we lived under woods and fields, each of us a Small Person alone in nature. The

Magica Artificia requires that we live together, sharing the power of the Circulus. This makes great beauty but also, as you have seen, great irritation. And, perhaps, illicit behavior."

He swept us an especially low bow. "Another reason why we wish you, the esteemed family of Turpini, to return to us the Gemmaluna, our stone of insight."

"We don't know where it is," I said without thinking.

The room went utterly, freaked-out, frozen-up silent.

A shriek rose from the floor, and so did the five hundred Parvi Pennati. The air was solid with fancy little figures, expressionless but menacing, frigid fingers curled into claws, wings beating in fury. Lady Noctua's gentleman friend was an inch from my nose, claws reaching, wings muddy brown.

I clapped my hands over my eyes. The beat of a thousand brown wings filled my head, whirring, whumping, whirring. Cold fingers pricked at me—I pressed against Dad, waited to be chilled unconscious, frostbitten to death.

Nice one, Mellie.

Chapter Nine

The Fluff in the Wind

MY DAD HAS HIS AWE-INSPIRING MOMENTS.

He lurched away from my side—I was afraid the Parvi had somehow carried him off. But then he bellowed so loud I almost jumped out of my cold-pricked skin. "GET AWAY FROM US! NOW AND I MEAN NOW!"

The cold prickings stopped. I peeked between my fingers and saw Dad standing next to me, three feet of empty space between us and a crowd of angry, fluttering Parvi.

Dad wagged his finger like a schoolteacher. "That's enough of this. You calm down RIGHT NOW and we'll explain."

"How can you make us calm down?" yelled a furious little guy in yellow. "What will you do to us, you Turpini, hey?"

Dad folded his arms over his chest like some Turkish pasha, chin jutting out. "You need us. Without us, no Gemmaluna."

"But you do not have the Gemmaluna," Rinaldo said, fluttering forward and landing on our table again. "Melissa Angelica Turpin has said this."

"I believe my father hid it somewhere in this house," Dad said. "We will find it."

"The Parvi Pennati will help," Rinaldo said. I was relieved to see that his wings were lightening, the iridescent color returning.

"The Parvi Pennati will do no such thing," Dad said. "You may search this cellar if you wish, but we will do the rest of the house. This is your place, that is ours. Is that clear?"

"*Bien*," Rinaldo said. He turned to the fluttering, overdressed crowd behind him. "*Pacem*, Parvi Pennati. Peace." He talked soothingly in Latin and his people drifted away, back to the floor and the bar and the chandelier. The music started up. I breathed again.

Rinaldo invited us to stay for dinner. The menu turned out to be slugs in truffle sauce. We declined, pointing out that we were too big to get much out of a slug. Also too grossed out, but we didn't say that. Also too freakin' cold.

Also too freakin' freaked out.

"I suppose a slug is pretty much the same thing as a snail," Dad said as we trudged up the silk-lined staircase.

"I think slugs are squishier inside," Mom said.

"Can we stop talking about this?" I'd never eaten snails and never intended to.

Mom had run around the corner to the store again and bought spaghetti and a bottle of sauce. We put on sweaters and socks and ate the spaghetti with more peas, everything piping hot.

The Fluff in the Wind

There's something about spaghetti that radiates calm from your stomach to your whole body. I think it's an amino acid or something. Anyway, I was feeling all right. I almost forgot that we'd faced death by a thousand frost-bites.

"Now," Dad said, "we have to decide whether to give back the moonstone."

"Finding it would be a nice first step," I said, yawning.

"Right," Dad said. "Tomorrow we hit all that stuff in the backyard, and maybe some of the mattresses up-stairs."

Mom groaned and buried her face in her hands. The end of her rope was in sight.

"C'mon," Dad said. "It'll be fun."

"When did you turn into Susy Sunshine?" Mom asked through her fingers.

"I'm employing a positive attitude," Dad said. "Some-body has to."

Mom dropped her hands and gave him a look that could have fried his liver. My parents don't fight that much, but you can always tell when the atmosphere's about to de-cay. "I feel sick," I said.

"Oh, sweetie," Mom said. She reached out to feel my forehead, and I let her do it. "You don't feel hot, but it's been quite a day. Why don't you go up to bed?"

They forgot about bickering and I got out of doing the dishes. Good deal.

I woke up the next morning with an ice cube on my

chest and something tickling my nose. "Warm dolt," said a tinny voice. "I wish you awake." She tickled my nose again.

I opened my eyes. Durindana tucked an ostrich plume back into her hairdo and fluttered up to my bureau. She landed next to my china guy. "This pretty man is—"

"China," I said. "He's not alive."

Durindana looked much better: Her hair was powdered white and done up in an intricate knot with plumes. Her blue dress was silky and flouncy and exquisitely clean. Jewels sparkled here and there.

"Listen," I said. "I'm sorry they were so mean to you down there."

"It matters little. Parvi Pennati never have admired me. No one dances with me."

"That's too bad."

"They remember my shame."

"I'm sorry." I was curious, but didn't think I should ask.

She muttered something. I caught "skirt" and "gubernator."

"I didn't catch that."

She unfurled her wings, and flapped over to hover in front of me. "If you must know, Turpina, my skirt disappeared when I danced with the gubernator."

"I'm sorry."

"I was in my drawers!"

"I'm sure it was awful."

"Everyone laughed! This was a deep, deep humiliation, never to be forgotten!" She flung herself onto my pillow and curled up the way Fidius used to. Something happened to my heart—it warmed up or lifted up or maybe both.

"Isn't there some way to train yourself?" I asked. "I mean, take a class or something? Organize your brain?"

"In my youth I tried this," Durindana said, a dispirited lump of silk. "In the Gigantes year 1880, my poor mother asked the Lady Noctua to school me in secret."

"Lady Noctua? Rinaldo's wife, with all the jewels and flounces and things? She seemed kind of ill-tempered. Not to mention overdressed." It would be like me asking Janine how to kiss boys.

"This is to show her skill at the Magica Artificia. The Lady Noctua is very well regarded among the Parvi Pennati."

"And did it help you, having her teach you stuff?"

Durindana assumed her mask-of-tragedy look. "The effort was a dismal failure. As was seen when my . . . my skirt . . ." She wailed and flung herself facedown on the pillow.

I let her have her cry, and when she quieted down I told her the Tampax story. I wasn't sure she'd know what a Tampax was, so I described it as "an object even more secret than underpants."

She was upright in horror. "How can you be laughing at such humiliation?"

"I've moved away now. Nobody knows me here. I can start all over again."

Her shoulders sagged. "I moved away, but I did not find him."

"Him who?" I had one of those flashes of inspiration you get sometimes. "Fidius?"

Her pale cheeks took on a greenish tinge, which I found out later was the Parvi equivalent of blushing. "Fidius alone was pleasant to me in my darkest days. He was kinder when he returned from his ordeal."

"His ordeal?"

She shuddered. "He left the Domus by himself and was caught by a Giganteus boy."

I felt like she'd doused me with ice water. "I know about that! He was in a glass jar." I fingered my frostbite handprint, remembering what Fidius had made me see the day before he left me.

"Yes, one cannot imagine a greater torment. He came home strange, both angry and kind. He feared the Gigantes, would not leave the Domus by himself, said small creatures such as we must protect ourselves, travel in groups. After his parents had their calamity, however, he became more angry than kind, almost—how do you say this—unhinged. He fought with the *magi* and all his friends, then to my horror he left alone, and now who knows where he is?"

"Well, he was with us eight years ago. A blink of an eye to you."

"This is so. Thank you, Melissa Angelica." She unfurled her wings, and I thought I'd cheer up pretty fast if I had something that gorgeous attached to me. She took off and bounced slowly around the ceiling in that wasp-like fashion I remembered from Fidius. When she returned to my pillow, the subject had changed.

"This room is being very clean," she pronounced.

"We did a lot of dusting and stuff when we got here."

"Ogier was a pig."

"No joke. Do you have any idea where he hid the moonstone . . . the Gemmaluna?"

She tucked her feet under her skirt, smoothing it just so on the white pillow. "He showed it to me once, but then he put it away."

"Really? Where did he put it?"

"I do not know."

"Why didn't he wear it, in case somebody lied to him?"

"I do not know."

"Okay, try this. What does it look like?"

"This I know." She held her hands up to form an oval. "It is such as this, white as milk unless held to the light, when it has many colors inside. The ring fits Ogier's smallest finger."

Well, that was something. Time to get up and start looking again.

"How on earth did she get up here?" Mom asked when I walked into the kitchen, Durindana flitting around my head like a deerfly. "Last I knew, they couldn't go through walls."

"We have made a Small Person's door into your grand staircase," Durindana said.

"Oh," Mom said. "Great."

I went down and peeked while Mom got Durindana a bowl of cereal. Sure enough, halfway down the stairs to the street door, one of the vents near the ceiling had turned into a set of six-inch-tall white double doors. I suppose when you have wings a door near the ceiling makes sense.

When I got back to the kitchen, Durindana was perched on the toaster, eating. Mom had made a cup of coffee and was sitting at the table, watching her. I sat down too.

"Well, well, well, well, well!" Dad marched in from the stairway. "Good morning, Mellie. Good morning, Durindana. Lovely day."

He poured himself cereal and ate it like someone who didn't have a morning of cushion-and-mattress innards ahead of him.

"How are they all?" Mom asked him.

"Sound asleep. Apparently there was a ball last night." Durindana gave a milky sob. "Rinaldo woke up long enough to urge me to find the moonstone with no unseemly delay. Had absolutely no suggestions as to where it might be."

"They have a door into the stairway now."

"So I see. Oh well, one big happy family."

Mom snorted into her coffee.

"Is that the French stuff?" Dad said. "It's kind of bitter."

"I'm scared of the Turkish stuff. Besides, who knows how long it's been in there. At least the French stuff has a date on it."

"I don't think coffee goes bad in the freezer. Especially Turkish coffee."

"Roly, feel free to make Turkish coffee if it means so much to you."

"No, no." Dad poured himself a cup of what she'd already made. "This'll be fine." He sipped it noisily and made a face. Mom—still at rope's end—blew air out of her nose.

"What are we doing today?" I asked.

"Oh, it's going to be a jolly day," Mom said. "We're going to tear open everything out there in the yard and sift through the stuffing. Personally, I plan to wear a dust mask and I want you to wear one too, Mellie. I don't want any of that stuff in our lungs."

"I'll wear one too, if anyone cares," Dad said. Mom walked over and gave him a great big kiss on the lips. They are so strange.

We spent a gruesome morning in the backyard, ripping open sofa cushions and mattresses and poking around in the innards. The breeze picked up about mid-morning and pretty soon the yard had moldy cushion stuffing all over it, mostly this whitish fluff. It looked like the cotton plantation in my fifth-grade social studies book.

"We'll rake it up later," Dad said.

Which was a great idea except that the breeze gradually turned into a wind. Soon our yard and the Wrights' yard were in their own private blizzard.

"Maybe we'd better start raking now," Dad said.

"Hey!" a lady yelled from an upstairs window next door. "What is this stuff?" She didn't actually say "stuff" but as I mentioned before, I can't use biological swears until I'm eighteen.

The lady disappeared from the window and we knew she was on her way down to raise holy heck. (Now, why is *that* okay? Beats me.) Dad started raking to show he was doing his best. Mom combed her hair with her fingers and smoothed her T-shirt, preparing for battle.

The lady was short, tidy, and Mrs. Wright, of course. She was ticked. Turned out they had a swimming pool and now it had white fluff all over its entire surface and that would clog the filter and cost thousands and thousands and what kind of idiot makes all this fluff on a windy day? And why did we have masks on? Was it dangerous, this fluff?

Mom said no, it's just moldy and we didn't know the wind was coming in so hard and of course we'd clean everything up right away and were so, so sorry and new in the neighborhood and from Boston and how do you do, Mrs. Wright, I'm Veronica Turpin and this is my husband, Roly, and my daughter . . . where did she go? Mellie? Mellie?

I was next door, where the freckled kid, Timmo, came out and handed me a scoop thing for the pool. He took a rake and pushed the fluff in my direction and I scooped it out. Being wet, it stayed where it was while we used yard rakes to clean up the fluff that was all over their grass.

More fluffs kept wafting over the fence but Dad actually was making progress on his side, so they got to be fewer and fewer.

"Sorry," I said to Timmo. The galaxy-gray eyes weren't so obvious in full daylight. You wondered why the wind didn't scoop him up like fluff, he was so scrawny.

"No big deal," he said. "Mom gets a bit overwrought."

"Overwrought" was a fat word for a skinny kid. Nevertheless, I was not there to make friends. I had enough troubles.

A tall blond girl came out. She looked like she was in high school. "Where's the evil mom-creature?" she asked Timmo. He jerked his head toward our yard and kept raking. The girl leaned against the house, watching us.

"Don't help or nothing, Eileen," Timmo said.

"Okay, I won't."

"Don't help or *anything*," I said.

Eileen snorted. "I heard about you."

I stopped raking to look at her. She had perfect purple eye shadow. I felt doom coming on.

Eileen smiled. "My friend's cousin goes to your school in Boston."

I waited for it. *Fairy Fat. Tampax.*

But Eileen didn't say any of that. Her smile broadened. "Yup. I heard all about you."

I couldn't rake anymore. My whole new life turned to slush on a playground.

"Eileen doesn't know nothing," Timmo said. "Nor does she know *anything*." He kept his head down, raking, but the corners of his mouth quirked up.

The adults arrived to check out the damage. Mrs. Wright didn't know what to say when she saw that the pool was fluff-free, so she pointed to the pile of wet stuff and said, "Timmo, get that junk" (again, not what she really said) "off the custom pavers."

"I'll get it," said Dad, who had a trash bag in his hand.

"How are you, Timmo?" Mom said, smiling.

"Good 'n' you," Timmo said. Which turned out to be a question, because Mom said, "Fine, thanks."

"How do you know Timmo?" Mrs. Wright asked.

"He and his father . . ." Mom paused, and I guess we Turpins all remembered at the same time that we hadn't even thought about looking for the lawyer's letter.

There was an awkward pause, which Eileen finally broke. "Oh, that's right. And they found out Mr. Turpin's dead."

The Fluff in the Wind

We waited for Mrs. Wright to say she was sorry for our loss, but she didn't. She gestured at Eileen. "My daughter, Eileen."

"Pleased to meet you, Eileen," Mom said.

Without warning, Eileen transmogrified herself into Miss America. She extended her hand to Mom and said, "And how lovely to meet *you*, Mrs. Turpin." Mom shook Eileen's hand and Eileen extended it to Dad, palm down as if she expected him to kiss it. He shifted his rake from right hand to left and grasped her fingertips, giving them a bit of a shake before dropping them like dissected earthworms.

Timmo blew out his breath and came to take my rake away. He leaned it against the fence, along with his own rake.

"You study the stars, Timmo?" Dad said. "Mellie's got sort of a science bent too."

"I'm going to be an astronaut," Timmo said.

"I'm going to be the Venus de Milo," I said. It came out more snide than I'd intended.

Predictably, Eileen snorted and Timmo turned red behind his freckles. His mom said, "Nice to meet you, Mellie," and opened the sliding glass door to her house.

"I guess we'll be going," Mom said, giving me her *How did I ever end up with a kid like you?* look.

"No, no," Miss America-Eileen said. "Please come in for coffee." She ignored the hairy eyeballs everybody was giving her. Her mother's had death rays in them.

Pause.

"Yes," Mrs. Wright said. "Please come in."

Mom aimed a despairing look at Dad, easily interpreted as "Think of an excuse not to do this." Dad inspected his rake, buying time. "Uh, we have a lot of, um," he said. *Smooth, Dad.*

The look in Eileen's eye was oddly familiar . . . beady, bright, out for a good time. *Fidius, turning slimy squash into slimy candy corn.* I didn't trust Eileen. "Oh, you can take a minute for a cup of coffee," she said.

"Very kind of you," Mom said mournfully. Dad leaned his rake on the fence next to Timmo's.

There was a neat row of shoes inside the sliding glass door. Mrs. Wright, Timmo, and Eileen slipped off their flip-flops and sneakers and added them, neatly, to the row. Mom gave Dad and me the fish eye, and we took off our shoes too. Dad's big toes were sticking out the ends of his socks, which were speckled with paint like everything else he owns.

"Please sit down," Mrs. Wright said and disappeared into the kitchen. Mom and Dad pulled out chairs from the dining table—we all eyed the pale satin-covered seats and our own filthy jeans. "We'll stand," Mom said. "We've been sitting all day."

"You've been raking all day," Eileen said. "Take a load off." She smirked into the kitchen, where her mother probably was planning to burn anything we touched.

There was plenty of furniture to spare, all of it gorgeous. The house was about a hundred years old, with shiny wooden floors and sparkling clean windows. It had art on the walls in rich, calm colors, and big pottery and lamps that did not come from our favorite shopping emporium, Goodwill.

"You have a beautiful house," Dad said.

"Thanks to Amalgamated American," Eileen said.

"What American?" Mom said.

"Eileen," Mrs. Wright said in a warning tone, coming in with a tray of coffee mugs. She smiled at Dad. "I had a lucky hunch in the stock market. I'm an investment manager."

"Dad says she could sell seashells to a shrimp," Timmo offered.

"That'll be enough of that kind of talk, Timmo," Mrs. Wright said. "Please, Mr. and Mrs. Turpin. Sit down." Mom and Dad perched themselves unhappily on the very edges of a couple of chairs.

"My work here is done," Eileen said. She waved her hand airily at us all, and legged it through the living room. Obviously, Eileen had what Mom called "an impish streak." The thought of her knowing all about Fairy Fat and the Tampon Incident made me want to throw up.

"Computer's upstairs," Timmo said to me. Terror prickled at me. I'd never gone upstairs in any kid's house, let alone a galaxy-eyed boy's. *He's nothing special*, I reminded myself. Plus, maybe I could ask him about that blond lady he saw.

"We don't own a computer," I said as we went up the stairs. "Dad says they suck your soul." I'd used them at school, though, and my soul was intact as far as I could tell.

The Wrights' computer was in a narrow room full of clean laundry and cardboard boxes. To get there, you went past a closed door with a poster of some handsome guy dressed like a doctor, which I figured was Eileen's. Next to the computer room was a bedroom with paper airplanes and starship models dangling from the ceiling.

"Ooo," Eileen said from behind the handsome doctor. "Timmo has a *girl* upstairs."

My face started to warm up, but Timmo wasn't bothered. "You have to get used to Eileen," he said. *I'd rather not, thanks.*

I stuck my head into the airplane room. There was a telescope in the bay window, and star charts and nebula posters all over the walls. "Guess you do like space stuff," I said.

"I designed this plane, look." Timmo squeezed past me and detached one of the paper airplanes from its string. He handed it to me, and it turned out to be thin cardboard rather than paper. It had sharp wings like something you'd see on the cover of a comic book, and a nose that hooked down in front.

"The space program has selected three hundred and twenty-one astronauts since 1959," Timmo said. "I figure designing planes might be a way in."

"The Renaissance artist Leonardo da Vinci made more than a hundred airplane drawings," I said.

"Yeah, one of them had wings like a screw," Timmo said. "He wanted to run it with a wound-up spring."

"He was one of the first to use oil paints instead of egg tempera, which was—"

"He designed retractable landing gear."

"Egg tempera," I continued, "is pigments mixed with egg yolk and it dries too fast, so oil paint is much more flexible."

"Leonardo did not invent the telescope."

How do you shut this kid up? I waggled the cardboard airplane at him. "Does this thing fly?"

He grabbed the plane out of my hand. The next thing I knew it had sailed smoothly down the hall and hooked a right to disappear down the stairs. There was a *thunk* below, followed by the tinkle of something fragile falling on something hard.

"Oh, man," Timmo said.

"Timmo!" Sharp footsteps marched up the stairs. Mrs. Wright appeared, cardboard plane in hand. "What did I say about flying these things in the house?"

Timmo stared at his white socks.

"What did I say?" his mother persisted. I couldn't believe she was doing this in front of me. She was treating him like he was ten.

Timmo muttered something.

"I am a woman of my word," Mrs. Wright said. She

marched past us into a room at the front of the house, rumbled around in there a bit, returned, snapped the door shut. "That plane is no longer yours."

After she left I didn't know where to look. Not that it mattered, because Timmo appeared to be counting the threads in the carpet.

Eileen stood in her doorway, watching her brother. She tiptoed past us into the front room and came back with the plane in her hands. "Here. Take it."

Timmo took it. "What're you, nuts?"

"I keep telling you, she puts the stuff in her closet and she forgets about it. I took back my curling iron and she never said a word."

"Eileen melted the shower curtain," Timmo said. He looked uncertain.

"C'mon." Eileen gave Timmo a smirk that was pure mischief. I wanted to tell him not to do anything she said. "She doesn't even know what this thing looks like. It's the same as any other stupid plane."

"That's how much you know," Timmo said. He shoved past me, went into his room with his plane, and shut the door, leaving me out in the hall with Eileen and no chance to ask him about the blond lady.

"Little wimp," Eileen said. She kicked Timmo's door and stalked back into her room as if I didn't exist, which I was perfectly happy not to.

I'd had it. And I wasn't the only one, judging by the way my parents jumped up as soon as they saw me downstairs.

They thanked Mrs. Wright very much for the lovely cup of coffee, and we beat it the heck out of there.

Dad retrieved his rake on our way back to our yard, but once we got there he leaned it up against the house. "I could use a break," he said.

"You can sing that in three-part harmony," Mom said.

And we still hadn't found the moonstone.

Chapter Ten

Art Appreciation

WE HAD LEFTOVER SPAGHETTI FOR LUNCH. There was a ton of it and we ate it all, and Mom said not one word about how food should be for sustenance rather than for comfort.

No sign of Durindana. Maybe she went back downstairs.

"Well, that was filling." Dad unbuttoned his waistband. "Wish we had decent coffee."

Mom got the Turkish coffee out of the freezer and plopped it in front of Dad. "Live it up."

Dad started water boiling and got down Grand-père's French press. He opened the sack and inhaled. "Ah. Ambrosia." He came over and made Mom and me sniff it too.

"I guess I'll have some after all," Mom said.

We all heard the coffee scoop hit something that crinkled. Dad froze as if the coffee was talking to him. "That crazy old jackass." He dug his fingers in and hauled out a plastic bag with a piece of paper in it. "Anybody could have found this."

"Took us a day and a half and we live here," Mom said. "We're lucky I didn't throw that out."

Art Appreciation

Dad fished the note out of the plastic bag. Something fell, clanged onto the counter. We all stared at it like dummies.

A small gold ring. Set with an oval, milky stone.

The moonstone, the Gemmaluna. Created by sorcery, a millennium and a half ago. It probably knew Charlemagne and half the kings of France. And here it was in our freezer.

I slipped the ring on my forefinger. I didn't feel a thing. The gold was worked into a laurel wreath, so fine you yearned for a microscope. I held my hand up to the light and the stone went translucent, shot with reds and blues and greens.

If I'd had this on, would I have known that Mina Cardoza wasn't my best friend? That a hug from Benny didn't mean anything?

That my parents knew Fidius was real.

"Hey, lie to me," I said.

"Get that off, Mellie," Mom said. She was watching Dad unfold the note.

"Roland," Dad read aloud. *"You are a blot on the name of Turpin, you with your little apartment and your little job and your little life with that little yet overbearing woman."* He stopped reading.

"You're ten times the man he was, Roly," my mom said.

"I'm fine," Dad said, although anyone could see he wasn't. "To continue: *You have no sense of grandeur, no* sense of style, no joie de vivre, as the common phrase would have it. You have abandoned your talent in order to teach ruffians—this I never will forgive."

"Says the drunken innkeeper," Mom said. "Did you know he started out as a painter, Mellie?"

Dad kept reading: "Be that as it may, you are my heir. You and your plump sparrow of a daughter. So I leave you the inn and our family treasure, our Gemmaluna. Guard it well and never forget the Obligatio Turpinorum, the Duty of the Turpins.

"When it became clear that all contact between us had ended, I wrote down some particulars about the Gemmaluna. I put the note where you will find it if you appreciate art, act like your elders and betters, and look beyond the end of my nose. All I will say here, worthless boy, is that I know you will want to return the stone and end the Obligatio. This is more complicated than you imagine. Sadly, you do not have the brain power to make it work."

"Why would it be complicated?" I asked.

"He's probably making that up," Mom said.

"A father's blessing on you, by which I mean something weak, mean, and abandoned by all. I leave no . . ." Dad stopped reading and slapped the letter down on the table. "Well, no point in reading the rest."

Mom gave the note a once-over, and laughed. "I leave no message to Veronique, and the child is too dim-witted to understand anyway. Ogier." She patted my hand.

"Coming from the right place, sweetie, an insult is as good as a compliment."

"Yeah, I know." It was bad enough being called a plump sparrow. But dim-witted? "I'm glad he's dead."

Dad grabbed my shoulders. "Don't ever be glad of a death, honey. Even a nasty-minded old drunk has a right to live out his life."

"I know, I know." Of course I knew that. Couldn't a person say anything off the top of her head without another person having a hissy about it? I shrugged his hands off my shoulders.

"She knows that, Roly, calm down," Mom said. "Mellie, get that ring off your hand until we're sure what it does."

"Lie to me first," I said.

"Take it off."

"Give it to me, Mellie," Dad said. "I'll put it in my pocket for safekeeping."

Mom and I looked at each other. We didn't want to insult him right now but, honestly, he could lose a small hippo in those pockets.

"I'll get that silver chain Gramma gave me and hang it around my neck," I said, meaning my mom's mother, the normal side of the family. "I can wear it under my T-shirt."

"I don't think anyone should have it on them," Mom said. "We don't know what the Parvi will do if we walk in there with it on. Let's hide it again."

So we reburied the ring in the coffee and stuck it all back into the freezer. Dad got out one of the other sacks of Turkish coffee, slamming the freezer door shut as if Grand-père were in there.

Mom picked up Grand-père's note. "Appreciate art. Look beyond the end of Ogier's nose. Is there a portrait of him somewhere?"

"Not that I remember," Dad said. "Who'd want it around?"

"What does 'act like your elders and betters' mean?" I asked. "Does he mean himself? What did he act like, anyway? He *was* a painter once, right?"

"A long time ago, before I was born," Dad said. "Anyone seen any painting supplies?" None of us had.

"Durindana might know something," I said. "She saw him after we did."

"Yeah," Dad said. "Where is she, anyhow?"

She turned out to be sound asleep on one of the guest beds upstairs, nestled into the pillow with a washcloth for a blanket. Next to her was a half-empty nip bottle of bourbon.

"Where'd she get that?" Mom asked.

"I found a box of those tweensy bottles in that closet over there," I said. "I forgot."

"This has to stop," Dad said. "She could have nectar downstairs now."

"Would you go down there, if you were her?" I said.

We left her to sleep it off. Dad carried the box of nip

bottles down to the dining room and sealed it with about a hundred layers of duct tape.

"I don't know if duct tape will stop someone who can turn a vent into a double door," I said.

"I'm moving it down here so we can keep an eye on it," Dad said. "To be honest, the tape's more for me than for her. I've never wanted a drink so much in my entire life."

After a brief silence so we could all forget he'd said that, Mom announced that it was high time we got on with Real Life and she would go food shopping. She probably wanted to get away from the inn and have a think, which she finds easier when Dad and I aren't around.

Dad said he'd go to Town Hall and see what we had to do to get a building inspection.

"A building inspection?" Mom said. "Why do we need that now?"

"You will be needing a building inspection first, of course," Dad said. Which (a) didn't answer Mom's question and (b) was a direct quote from Gigi Kramer, the fake real estate lady.

"Where'd you hear that?" Mom said.

"Everybody knows it." Dad sounded vague.

"By the way," I said, "what are we using for money to fix this place up?"

That changed the subject. Mom and Dad traded a Deeply Significant Look. "We'll try for a loan," Dad said. "And if we can't get one . . . well, we'll cross that bridge when we come to it."

"We're not using my college fund," I said.

"No," Dad said. "Of course not. Although—"

"Of course not, sweetie," Mom said.

I was not reassured.

They left on their errands and I went up to my room to unpack some more. I was filling my last bureau drawer when a weird, guttural cry floated in through the open window, followed by a door slam. I poked my head out and saw Timmo down on the sidewalk, hugging himself. He was right outside the door to the pub.

Uh-oh.

I scrambled down two flights of stairs and burst through the outside door to see that Timmo had cracked open the pub door again. He was tense and poised to run. Music tinkled out.

"Hey!" I said. Timmo jumped a foot and I ran out of things to say. What *can* you say when someone opens your cellar door and finds five hundred Small Persons with Wings?

"Hey," he said weakly.

"You're probably wondering."

"Yeah."

The door swung open on the breeze. The music got louder. Rinaldo fluttered out and opened his arms wide. "Melissa Angelica Turpin! Come in! And be bringing your friend!"

"It's wearing clothes," Timmo said. "It knows your name."

"Well," I said, "I guess you'd better be going now. See you around."

"See me around? Are you nuts? You think I'm going to walk away from this? This is huge."

"You can't say anything to anyone," I said.

"Says who?"

A car turned the corner. Rinaldo hovered between us, politely following the conversation. The music sparkled and danced.

"Get inside." I pulled Timmo into the pub, Rinaldo fluttering behind. I slammed the door and locked it. Timmo squeaked like a sneaker on floor tile, but I figured, *Hey, you got yourself into this, neighbor boy.* Maybe I'd have to lock him in there. I didn't know what to do.

With much bowing and fluttering, Rinaldo ushered us over to the bar, where we got up on stools. The air, of course, was freezing. I looked at Timmo and found out that freckles don't fade even when someone has gone pasty white and is shaking like a paint mixer.

"Rinaldo, Lady Noctua," I said, when she fluttered over. "This is Timothy Oliver Wright. Timmo, Rinaldo is gubernator of the Parvi Pennati. That's a diminutive of the Latin for Small Persons with Wings. A diminutive means a shorter, sort of affectionate version of a longer—"

"I know what a diminutive is," Timmo said shakily. He nodded to Rinaldo and to Lady Noctua, who curtsied haughtily.

Rinaldo swept off his hat and bowed. "Oliver is a name of lineage. Are you of lineage, dear sir?"

Timmo swallowed hard. "I don't think so."

I remembered what I kept forgetting to ask. "Excuse me, Rinaldo, but when you say 'of lineage,' what exactly do you mean?"

Rinaldo shook his finger at me. "Ogier has not been telling this to you?"

"I barely knew Ogier."

Rinaldo shook his head, disgusted by human families. "The lineage does extend from the glorious king Charlemagne and his aides, called paladins. Turpin was one such, and his descendents take their names from the old tales. Roland was another, of bravery unmatched upon his heroic death at Roncevaux. Oliver was his cousin and friend, of equal valor upon that bloody field."

"I'm named after my uncle Ollie," Timmo said. "He's an insurance adjuster."

"Why are my names of lineage?" I asked. "Durindana's too. I can't see them letting a girl be one of these paladins, somehow."

"*Zut!*" Lady Noctua said. "Some ladies were warriors—Bradamante, for example, she of the white plume and shield. But Mademoiselle Durindana is named for the *sword* of the mighty Roland. Your names, Turpina, honor Melissa, priestess of Merlin the enchanter, and Angelica, a princess of Cathay beloved of Roland. Generations of Turpini have named their daughters in this way." Rinaldo bowed to her for talking, and to me for having the same name as a princess of Cathay.

The Parvi had been busy. Durindana's chandelier now hung from the inside of a dome painted with cherubs floating around on clouds and making goo-goo eyes at one another. They weren't wearing much and they were embarrassing to look at, especially with a freckled kid you hardly knew sitting right next to you.

Every single surface in the pub now was foofed up except for the dusty, spidery liquor bottles behind the bar. They looked even worse compared to the gilt and marble everywhere else.

Rinaldo saw me looking at them. "We are leaving the bottles in tribute to Ogier. They were dear to Ogier."

"I bet."

"Some are very old and Ogier took pleasure in drinking of them because they too are of some lineage."

I could almost hear Dad saying, "Ogier. Sheesh."

"When I would visit Ogier he would make his joke. He would say, 'Time for art appreciation, Rinaldo.' And we would admire the bottle and he would drink of it. Sometimes I would drink of it too, although this nectar makes one fly crooked."

I scanned the rows of bottles. Some of the labels were plain, but the ones on the top shelf were gorgeous. They really were works of art, with portraits of pirates and monks and farmers and barmaids, landscapes, even a horse or two.

One of the portraits was of a guy wearing a tall whitish cap with a cloth hanging down to cover his neck. You could just see a desert scene behind him. The name on the bottle was "The Legionnaire." I remembered that Grandpère had been in the French Foreign Legion.

"Can I get a closer look at that one?" I said, getting off my stool.

"We shall fetch it, Melissa Angelica." Rinaldo gave a screeching cry and a bunch of gentlemen and ladies joined him on the bar. They gabbled at one another in Latin, pointing and waving their arms, then fluttered over to fetch the bottle in a mass of tiny bodies.

Very cool, that dusty bottle wobbling toward us on flapping iridescent wings. Timmo thought so too, because he groaned in admiration. Unless it was nausea.

The portrait was even better close up. The legionnaire had this snotty expression on his face, as if his mustache smelled of old soup. His head was turned haughtily, probably so he could watch an insurance adjustor inspect his camel.

He looked like a young Grand-père. At the end of his nose, there was a square bump under the label.

Exactly as if someone had shoved a note under there.

Chapter Eleven

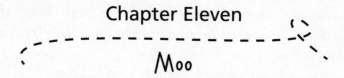

Moo

"APPRECIATE ART," DAD SAID when he got home. "Ogier. Sheesh."

The bottle of Legionnaire stood in the middle of the kitchen table. All of us, Timmo included, sat and stared at it. Timmo knew as much as we did now. I didn't think that was a good idea, but my parents figured since he'd seen the Parvi he needed to hear about everything.

"He needs to know enough to stay away from us if things get weird," Mom said.

"Stay away?" Timmo said. "Are you nuts? This is like the world's greatest video game, except less realistic." His skin was normal color and he'd been breathing easy ever since my parents came home. Before that, he told us, he'd been afraid he was going to get turned into something.

"People don't get turned into things," I said, making it clear who was the knowledgeable one. "That's so Brothers Grimm. But you better not tell anyone about this."

"I won't," Timmo said. "I swear. Really." I didn't believe him.

"Well," Dad said. "Let's get this note." He slid his penknife in between the label and the bottle to loosen the glue, then pried the note out with a pair of tweezers.

"We'll see what the old man thinks of us now." He unfolded the note and read out, "*My Worthless Descendants.*"

"You're worth ten of him, Roly," Mom said.

"*I may have given you the Gemmaluna. If not, it is hidden where you will find it in the unlikely event that you wish to wake up.*"

"He put it in the coffee," I explained to Timmo, in case he didn't get it.

"*The Gemma is the basis for the Obligatio Turpinorum, the Duty of the Turpins. It contains the Magica Vera, the Parvi's original magic. It therefore offers the gift of insight, which the Parvi did not value once they had their newer magic, the Magica Artificia.*

"*The Parvi love a good appearance. It was only recently that they realized their illusions were sapping their senses.*

"*I don't know what you learned from the Parvi we harbored in your childhood—not much, I suspect. So I will tell you that the Magica Artificia is only as strong as the Circulus, which generates the power for it. The Magica Mala, the Parvi's forbidden magic, also requires the Circulus. If the Circulus should stop, the illusions it has empowered will fade slowly. When the Parvi drop the Gemmaluna into water to make the elixir, any remaining illusions will disappear in that instant.*

"*Gubernator Rinaldo has approached me about returning the Gemmaluna. They have to ask nicely, you* see—when the ancient magi transferred their magic into the moonstone, they added spells that protect the Gemma from theft. It is ours now, and will work for another only if given directly by us, its true owners. The Parvi may take it back only at midnight of the full moon.

"I have not made up my mind about returning the Gemma. Rinaldo says their original magic, the Magica Vera, gives them the power to manipulate solid objects, with results better than any human craftsman—he says they helped to build Rome in its heyday. If they have the Gemmaluna back, they will repair this inn. But the moonstone ring has power for us too. It enables us to see through all illusions, not only those created by the Parvi. One senses lies, an obvious benefit in this age of falsehood.

"For a more permanent insight, or if more than one person needs to see the truth, you may drop the moonstone into a cup of water, say 'cupio videre,' and drink the elixir."

"'Cupio videre,'" Mom said. "I think that means 'I wish to see.'"

"That makes sense," Dad said. "But be warned, Roland: One must not drink the elixir lightly, for its effect on humans is intense and difficult to control. Some illusions are beneficial and you will regret their loss. I drank it and survived, but I am strong. My own père was the last before me to drink the elixir, with disastrous results.

He was weak. You are too—of this I am depressingly certain.

"*If you are reading this letter, I am gone and the decision whether to return the Gemma is yours. Do not forget that you are Turpins—the stone is your burden but also your birthright. Our association with it and with the Parvi elevates us above the cattle we call our neighbors.*"

"Moo," Timmo said. Mom patted him on the back.

"*For once, try to live up to your heritage. Ogier.*" Dad handed Mom the note. "Yeah, thanks, old man. Some heritage." I could tell he was bummed by more than Ogier.

"How'd it go at Town Hall?" Mom said, doing her mind-reading trick.

"Not good." Dad dug his fingers into his forehead, hunting a killer headache. "They know this place pretty well. There's a whole list of stuff we have to do to sell it for any decent price. Replacing the foundation sill, that's probably the worst. Means somehow keeping a four-story building from falling down on us while we do it."

"How did Ogier run an inn without fixing this stuff?" Mom asked.

"The inn's been closed for years," Timmo said.

"Three years, to be exact," Dad said. "There are plumbing issues too. And mold."

"No kidding," Mom said. She gave his hand a squeeze.

"Why don't we give back the moonstone and let the Parvi fix it for us?" I said.

Dad chewed his lip. "I dunno, hon. They say they can use this old magic, but I bet they haven't tried for thirteen hundred years. They could bring the place down around our ears. Plus . . ."

"Plus, you've never had a magic moonstone," said Mom the mind reader. "And you're not ready to give it up until you've had a chance to try it out."

"Hey, I can go out anytime and get someone to lie to me." Dad blew out his cheeks, kissed Mom's hand, and stood up. "Maybe we'll try using it at the bank—find out what they're willing to do for us. If we can't get a loan we can sell the inn as is, although we won't get much." He avoided looking at me, which was fine. I was not forking over my college money.

"For the moment," he continued, "what we're doing is cooking Roland's Big-Time Teriyaki Chicken. Timmo, can you stay and eat?"

"Why'd you do that?" I whispered to Dad while Timmo phoned his mom out at the reception desk.

"You need to make some friends before school starts," Mom whispered.

"Maybe I don't want friends." But then Timmo came back and we had to act normal.

Yeah, like that's possible.

While dinner was cooking, Mom made me get out the ring to show Timmo. I put it on and tried to walk through a wall, in case Ogier hadn't told us everything. It didn't work.

"Have you tried flying?" Timmo asked.

"Melliedon'tyoudare," Mom said.

Timmo cracked up. "Mom, like I would," I said.

"What happens when somebody lies to you?" Timmo asked.

"Let's try," I said. "What's your name?"

"Neil Armstrong, first man on the moon."

I shuddered, breaking out in goose bumps. "Brrr. That's cold."

"Awesome," Timmo said. "So it works."

I looked him straight in the galaxy eyes. "Are you going to tell anyone about all this?"

The smile left his face. "No. I told you. No."

Warmth flooded over me. "I guess that's the truth," I said.

"I don't lie," Timmo said stiffly.

I kept the ring on while we ate the utterly awesome teriyaki chicken. I kept holding the moonstone up to the light to watch it go translucent. "I can see why they named it after the moon."

"The first moon mission discovered a whole new mineral, so they named it after Neil Armstrong, Buzz Aldrin, and Michael Collins," Timmo said. "It's called armalcolite."

"The Dutch artist Vincent van Gogh had a sunflower named after him," I said. "It's called *Helianthus annuus van Gogh*." Take that, neighbor boy.

Mom wasn't paying attention. "Did you ever find that lawyer's name?" she asked Dad.

"Yeah, it's Kramer. Something Kramer. Ever heard of her, Timmo?"

Timmo shook his head, his mouth full of basmati rice.

"Kramer?" I said. "That's the name of that real estate lady. You know, Dad, the card you had in your pocket."

Dad gave me a blank look and shook his head. "Sorry. Don't remember. Oh well, I'll look in the yellow pages. I'd better talk to her soon, I guess. Get the police off my butt—sorry, Timmo—and find out what other surprises the old man stored up for us."

"Ogier isn't your average dead guy," Mom said to Timmo. "In fact, he wasn't your average any kind of guy."

"Yeah," Timmo said. "He was a scary dude. We used to dare each other to sneak up the stairs and ring the bell on the reception desk. Old Man . . . uh, Mr. Turpin caught Jacky Wallace once and Jacky let out a scream you could hear at the beach."

Timmo smiled down at his chicken, remembering the good times.

"Who's 'we'?" I said.

"My friends and me. Hanging out in the summer, you know." He gave me a curious look, and my face heated up. He probably could tell that I'd never hung out with anyone.

"Grand-père threw whiskey bottles at us." At least I had better Grand-père stories.

But Timmo wasn't finished. "Is it true Old Mr. Turpin killed his own father?" he said in an off-hand tone, like he was asking who got the D- in Earth Science.

I snorted. But then Mom patted Dad's knee under the table. Dad's face was white as rice.

Is it . . . true? How come this kid knows about it and I don't? Timmo was as still as a marble faun. I guess he could tell he'd said something ugly.

"Dad?" I said.

"That's not exactly what happened, Timmo," Dad said, fake-jaunty. He picked up his fork, then figured out we were waiting to hear more. "Oh, listen, Ogier never talked about it. Never. I only heard about it when I was a teenager, when I met my aunt for the first time. That was in Gloucester, where she and Ogier grew up." Gloucester is a couple of towns up the coast from Baker's Village.

He speared a piece of chicken.

"Yeah?" I said. "And . . . ?"

Dad gave his fork an accusing look and put it down, as if he couldn't talk and hold silverware at the same time. "And she told me about when their father took the elixir. Ogier was fifteen, was supposed to be the one watching his dad while their mother was out. But his father went to sleep and Ogier figured it was okay to go call some girl he liked. Next thing he knew his father was gone and his mother was going crazy look-ing for him. And his father jumped off a bridge and drowned."

"Oh, man," Timmo whispered.

I was incapable even of whispering.

"Ogier's mother never uttered a word of blame," Dad said. "But she didn't utter many words to him after that. She pretended he wasn't there. She wasn't the motherly type to begin with, I guess, but still . . . Angelique—my aunt—she said she tried to take Ogier under her wing, but he got more and more withdrawn."

Why had I never heard this before? *What else do I not know about my own family?* "When did Ogier take the elixir?"

"Before he went into World War II. Angelique didn't know until she heard him roaring in the attic. It was aw-ful, she said. She had to stay with him so he didn't hurt himself."

"Why did he do it?" I couldn't imagine anyone being that stupid. "And what did he see when he did?"

"We never talked about it," Dad said, his voice tight. "We never talked about much, frankly. I'll tell you one thing—it didn't do his disposition any good. I never could figure out what my mother saw in him, but she stood by him until the day she died."

"She had cancer," I told Timmo.

"And you loved him, right?" Timmo asked. He had this intense expression on his face.

Dad looked him in the eye. "To be honest, Timmo, I don't know that either."

Timmo went home after dinner, but he was back again after breakfast. It was one infestation after another in this place. My parents had gone off to Town Hall again, so it was just me and the oat flakes.

"I read up on moonstones last night," Timmo said.

"How'd you do that?"

"Internet. Moonstones are a type of feldspar. Most come from India and places like that, but some come from the Alps in Europe. Feldspar is a crystalline mineral that—"

"I know what feldspar is. And just because it's on the Internet doesn't mean it's true."

"Okay, but I didn't used to believe in fairies either."

"Don't call them fairies. They're Small Persons with Wings."

"Do you want to know what I found out or not?"

I slurped the milk out of the bottom of my cereal bowl. "Yeah. I guess."

"Well, moonstones are supposed to strengthen your intuition and make you understand things you didn't used to. I suppose you know what intuition is."

I didn't dignify that with a reply. "We know most of this stuff already."

"Do you have some kind of problem with me?"

"No. I'm being honest."

"You're being a dork."

I was, kind of. I thought about apologizing. Instead, I said, "Nobody asked you to sneak into our cellar."

"I didn't sneak. I heard music and I . . . I looked."

"You could hear the music that much?" *This could be a problem.*

"You think I'm lying? Wanna get the ring out?"

"No, I think they should turn down their music. Or at least lock the door."

"Yeah, probably."

Grumpy silence. I knew I'd been a dork, but didn't know what to do about it. Fortunately, Durindana chose that moment to whir through the door at high speed and crash into the refrigerator. She slid to the floor and lay there motionless.

"Is that one of them?" Timmo asked.

"More or less. She's an outcast. She may be hungover."

I picked her up by her skirt and carried her to the table. She lay there quivering, her blue dress rumpled, her hair a mess again.

I prodded her with a forefinger. "Hey, Durindana. Want something to eat?"

She sat up, saw Timmo, and shrieked. At first I thought she was afraid of him, but the problem turned out to be her appearance. She scrambled up and hid behind the toaster. I could still see her, but apparently that didn't matter.

I watched, fascinated, as her hair tidied up, loose ends knitting themselves into a hairdo. Her dress turned emerald green, with matching jewels and hair ornaments.

She sashayed into the open, pulling her wings through her hands.

"*Bonjour*," she said to Timmo. "And your name is . . .?"

"Timothy Oliver Wright," he said, watching her wings do their motor-oil-on-puddles act as she groomed them. "Timmo."

"Ah, Oliver! That is—"

"We know," I said. "A name of lineage."

Her nose went up. "You were to be getting food for me, Turpina."

While I got her cereal, Durindana told Timmo all about her exile from the Domus, although not about her skirt disintegrating.

"They made you leave just because you were clumsy and spilled stuff?" he said. "Geez. I spill stuff all the time." I pictured his house, with its gorgeous furniture and the neat row of shoes by the door. He grinned, as if he knew what I was thinking. "Yeah. My mom goes nuts every time."

He told Durindana how freaked out he'd been when he met the Parvi, and about Grand-père's notes and the moonstone ring. "And Old Mr. Turpin drank the elixir once and so did his father," he confided. "He wasn't sure they should give the ring back. Now Mellie and her parents want to sell the inn to make money to be artists and go to college, only they can't because it's such a mess and there's so much to fix up."

Sheesh. Tell our whole family history, why don't you.

Durindana got a beady look in her eye. "This is a good time to be giving back the Gemma, Turpina. Then the Parvi Pennati could be fixing of your house for you."

"Do you think you can? It's probably thirteen hundred years since you used the Magica Vera."

She looked offended. "Of course we can. This is our native magic."

The downstairs door opened. Dad said, "So come up and look around."

"I don't want to look around up there," a deep voice said. "I've been up there. I want to see what's flying in and out of that pub of yours."

"Oh, no," Timmo said. "That's my dad."

"Durindana," I said, "get down to the pub and tell everyone to hide or something. Quick."

"They will not believe me."

"Do your best. Hurry, or Timmo's dad will be here before you can get out."

". . . up for a cup of coffee," my mom was saying. "I assure you, Chief Wright, there's no infestation of any kind in that pub. Anyway, the building inspector is coming later today, and he'll be all over the place looking for . . . whatever he looks for. I'm sure he'll see if there's a problem."

"There's music playing down there all the time," Chief Wright said. "Have you opened that pub without a proper permit?"

"My daughter goes down there now and then," my dad said. "She's a big fan of Bach."

Great. Hope he doesn't ask me anything about Bach.

"Please come upstairs," my mom said. "We'll show you our paintings." She sounded desperate.

I'm not a good liar, so I have no explanation for what popped into my head then.

"Mom," I yelled, "are my baby parakeets still safe in the pub? I'd hate it if they got loose."

Silence at the bottom of the stairs. Then my mom yelled, "Don't worry, sweetie. They're fine. But you'd better get them back in their cages before the building inspector gets here."

"Nice one," Timmo whispered.

Chapter Twelve

Acne and Champagne

"MELLIE BREEDS PARAKEETS," Mom said over a cup of Grand-père's Turkish coffee.

"Really." Chief Wright sized me up. I'd given him my chair and was standing in the doorway in case I needed a quick getaway. "And then she sells them?"

"Yes," I said, panicking. "But I don't talk about the business side of it. I'm in it because I love birds." That could have been true. I'd never been close enough to a bird to find out.

"She got a permit to breed livestock?" Chief Wright asked my dad, which I thought was rude when I was standing right there.

"Yes, I do," I said. "Issued in Boston, though, so I can't sell any until I get a permit here."

Dad grinned at me behind his coffee mug.

"If you're so eager to keep them inside, how come I saw one of them flying through the mail slot?" Chief Wright said. "That mail slot doesn't even have a flap."

I was stumped. I looked at Mom. She looked at Dad.

"My daughter raises a special breed of parakeet," Dad said. "They're called . . . they're called tribal parakeets." Everybody digested that. "So, see, she can let them go out

145

one or two at a time and they always come back to . . . to their tribe. It's only a problem if you open the door and the whole tribe gets out at once. Then they'll never come back."

Dad slurped his coffee, staring out the window so he didn't have to look anyone in the eye.

"You find that lawyer's name yet?" Chief Wright asked.

"Nope. I've been busy."

But he did find her name. How come he's lying?

Mom gave Dad a look that said she was wondering the same thing. "We'll get right on that as soon as . . . as soon as we get the parakeets settled," she said.

"Yeah, right. The parakeets." Chief Wright contemplated Dad as if he was measuring him for handcuffs. "There a big market for those things?"

"The market isn't very good right now," Dad said, sounding savage. "International budgie glut. I'm sure you've heard all about it."

"It's nice to see a kid with some can-do spirit." Chief Wright was every bit as savage as Dad but looking at his son. Timmo, leaning against the broom closet door, hunched himself up and stared at his sneakers.

Mom went into Angry Mother Swan mode. "Savage" didn't come close to describing her tone. "We're very impressed by Timmo. He's extremely smart and person-able."

"Yeah?" Chief Wright said. "Seems to me he spends

all his time on the Internet looking at constellations like a spaceshot. Don't know what police academy will make of him."

"He's going to police academy?" Mom said. "I thought he was going to be an astronaut."

"There's been a Wright as police chief in this town for three generations."

"What about Eileen?" Mom said, Mother Swan wings up and flapping.

"She wants to be a doctor."

Timmo gazed at his shoes, as if he'd heard all this before. When his dad finally left, Timmo told him he'd be home later to mow the lawn.

My mom drained her coffee. "That was awful. Timmo, I'm so sorry to get you involved in lying to your father."

"S'okay. It's not the first time and it won't be the last."

"I think you'll be a very good astronaut," Dad said. "You seem to get along fine in zero gravity, which is what we've got going on in this house right now."

"Roly, why didn't you tell Chief Wright the lawyer's name?" Mom asked.

"I don't know her name."

"You told it to us last night. Kramer, you said."

Dad squinted at Mom, shook his head. "Nope. Don't remember any Kramer."

Mom raised her eyebrows at me. Dad saw her do it and

set his coffee mug down sharply. "I'm going downstairs to visit the parakeets. I'll tell them we've got the moonstone, ask them to undo the pleasure palace and hide for an hour. The building inspector's coming after lunch and he'll want to see the cellar."

"You're kidding. You're going to tell them to unfoof the cellar?" I thought of all those sharp, cold little fingers.

"They'll understand," he said.

When he came back upstairs he had the worst case of acne I'd ever seen in my life. His pimples had pimples, bubbling up on every visible inch of skin. Probably every non-visible inch of skin too.

Mom shrieked and sat down hard. "Roly, what in tarnation did they do to you?"

"What do you mean?" Dad reached for his coffee cup, caught sight of his hand and dropped the cup, splashing coffee on his pants. He ran his ravaged hands over his equally ravaged face. "Those friggin' little creeps!" (He did not actually say "friggin'." He used the only English swear word that I'll never be old enough to use in front of my parents. It was very exciting.

Dad pelted back down the stairs.

"Roly! You'll make it worse!" Mom pelted after him.

"Mom!" I yelled, and followed.

"Wait for me!" Timmo yelled. I could hear him pounding down the stairs behind me.

We all tumbled into the pub at once like a bunch of

cartoon characters. Mom missed a step and had to grab Dad's arm to keep from falling on her face. I stopped short on the bottom step so I wouldn't smush a bunch of Parvi on the floor. Timmo crashed into me and we both fell backward, me on top of him. That was embarrassing in ways I couldn't begin to count.

We were a big hit with the Parvi. Every single miniature lady and gentleman was cracking up. It did sound like a parakeet farm.

"Now hear this!" Dad thundered. "Put me back to normal or else!"

Or else what? I asked myself.

Either the Parvi didn't ask themselves that question or they thought enough was enough. Rinaldo nodded at Lady Noctua, who shrieked something in Latin. The Circulus speeded up, and Dad's pimples bleached out and shrank, one by one by one. It was cool to watch.

"We are sorry for our joke." Rinaldo ushered Lady Noctua forward until they were fluttering in front of Dad's nose. "But you must not be telling us to undo our beauties."

"As I attempted to explain," Dad said, in a tone that could have earned him a few pimples back, "if humans— Gigantes—see you, it will be bad for you. And a man comes here today who must see this cellar."

"*Tiens*, why is this Giganteus to be coming here?" Lady Noctua asked. Parvi crowded around to listen.

Dad explained about ordinances, occupancy permits,

and building safety codes, the inn's various structural problems, and our need to fix it up before we sold it.

"If we have the Gemma, we can be fixing up your inn," Rinaldo said. "Without the Gemma we can only make it pretty."

"So we understand," Dad said. "But—"

Lady Noctua gave her husband a good shove. "Rinaldo! It is not being your place to make such an offer all by yourself. Those of us with taste and intellect wish to retain the Magica Artificia for all time."

Rinaldo took his hat off. "This will not be possible, my love. We are losing our senses."

"*Zut.* We have lost no further senses for a hundred years. I have studied this, and—"

"Excuse me," Dad said. "There's still the problem of the building inspector, who will be here in"—he looked at his watch—"two hours."

"Pah." Noctua dismissed Dad with an airy gesture. "Do not worry, Roland Turpin. We shall hide ourselves cleverly when this Giganteus comes. I lived among the Turpini in my youth, and know well how to be outsmarting Gigantes. But we are not to be undoing our beauties."

"You will explain our beauties to this Giganteus," Rinaldo said.

"Really?" Dad said. "How?"

Rinaldo bowed, feathered hat in hand, and ushered Lady Noctua away to watch a minuet.

"At least I have my skin back," Dad said as we trudged back upstairs.

"We should tidy up," Mom said, with a noticeable lack of enthusiasm. "Make the place look as nice as we can before the inspector gets here."

"We cleaned three days ago," I said.

"Is your bed made?"

She had me there.

Timmo went home before the tidying started, demonstrating that he did have a brain. We Turpini made our beds and put our underwear in the laundry hamper. We tried to come up with explanations for a dingy old pub turning into an eighteenth-century pleasure palace. Not to mention why anyone would redecorate *before* a massive renovation.

"We did it so our daughter wouldn't be homesick," Dad said. "She has exquisite taste."

"We did it because a real estate lady told Dad the inn would sell better that way," I said.

"Ogier did it before he died, because he'd gone nuts," Mom said.

We chose that one. Then we went down to the kitchen to eat lunch.

Correction: We went down to the silk-lined boudoir we once called the kitchen.

Our first glimpse of the problem was on the stairs from the family quarters, which now were marble. Correction: The bottom half was marble. As we stood at the top, stunned, the marbleizing crept toward us, tread by tread. The stairwell was papered in ivory-colored damask with candles flickering in sconces.

"This can't be good," Dad said.

"Be careful going down," Mom said. "Marble can be very slippery."

The kitchen still had all its appliances, but they were covered in marble, ebony, crystal, and gold filigree. The room looked like a tent because of the rose-colored silk draped from a chandelier in the middle of the ceiling.

The kitchen table was marble, as were the front desk out in the reception area and the tables in the breakfast room, which had gold place settings. The walls were varying shades of rose-colored damask, with cream-colored moldings and more candles in sconces.

The new decor was too much for us. Dad sank into a gilt chair at the kitchen table and stared straight ahead. Moving like a robot, Mom got cold cuts out of the refrigerator, ignoring the gold-filigree door handle. She made sandwiches on the marble countertop and served them to us on golden plates from silk-lined cupboards.

"Can we still say Grand-père did this?" I asked.

"I don't see what else we *can* say at this point," Mom said.

Durindana flitted in. "Ooooo," she said, making for the chandelier. "Look what the Parvi Pennati are making for the Turpini, from the goodness of our inner selves."

"Thank you," Dad said in the voice he used when Mom gave him socks for Christmas.

"I thought you couldn't see this stuff," I said.

Her little back stiffened. "I am seeing it most of the time, warm dolt."

We offered her cold cuts, but she said she preferred slugs. She settled down in the middle of the table to watch us eat.

"So," Dad said, "where are you all going to hide when the building inspector comes?"

Durindana tittered. "This will be a big surprise for the Turpini." Her mouth turned down ever so slightly. "Lady Noctua says I may not participate. I must hide in my bed."

"Why is that?" Mom asked, Mother Swan wings rustling.

"The Circulus will stop while your Giganteus is here." Durindana unfurled her beautiful wings, I guess to console herself. "I cannot hold an illusion under such circumstances."

"And the rest of them can?" Dad said.

"Yes, yes," Durindana said irritably. "Some can store the power of the Circulus in themselves. But even they begin to lose their power after a time. The Turpini must not dawdle with this inspector."

"Interesting," Dad said. "The Circulus is like a power generator."

"And the better you are at the Magica Artificia, the

farther away you can tap the power," I said. "Right, Durindana? Fidius could use it miles away in Boston, and you were right here in town and couldn't . . . um . . ."

Durindana's mouth quivered. Before any of us could say another word, she flitted out of the room. We heard her wailing as she flew down the stairs.

"Nice, Mellie," Mom said. I did feel bad, in spite of being a warm dolt.

"Never mind," Dad said. "Let's do the dishes." The tap water turned out to be champagne, but Dad washed the dishes anyway, figuring alcohol was at least cleaner than mayonnaise. I tried to dry them, but the dish towels were silk and didn't absorb much. Fortunately alcohol dries fast when you wave a plate around in the air.

"Going to be interesting brushing our teeth," Dad muttered.

The building inspector was a doofus. His name was Bruce McCarthy. He was really skinny, hunched over at the shoulders, with thick glasses, grayish skin, and chin stubble. His hair was greasy. His teeth were bad. He kept tripping over bare marble, and when you talked to him he didn't seem to be listening with his entire brain.

The oddest thing about him was that he didn't see anything odd about us. He walked into the kitchen, said, "Ooo, nice," and just stared around. I didn't know what he was supposed to inspect, but it seemed like his main concern was that we met the gold filigree requirement.

He had this blond-haired lady with him. She had on a ton of makeup and a black linen pantsuit, which she wore with green gloves and stiletto heels that sounded like tap shoes.

"This is . . . uh," Bruce McCarthy said.

"Gigi Kramer," she said in that far-end-of-the-tunnel voice. "*Moi*, I am the plumbing inspector."

You probably saw that coming. I didn't. Even though I completely remembered her visit in the pub that day and completely remembered her name, she didn't look familiar to me.

Dad, of course, had forgotten her all over again. "Plumbing inspector? Dressed like that?"

She looked deep into his eyes. His face went soft like cheese in a microwave. "Whatever you say," he murmured. "Whatever you say."

"We shall start in the cellar," she purred.

"We shall start in the cellar," Bruce McCarthy said.

"Let's start in the cellar," Dad said. "Watch your step." He was a zombie again. I figured I'd better stay close to him so he didn't give the inn away or promise anybody my college fund.

Bruce McCarthy jostled with Dad for the privilege of opening the door at the bottom of the stairs for Gigi Kramer. Dad lost that encounter but got to the pub door first. Now, if it had been me, I would have opened it a crack and peeked in to make sure the coast was clear. Dad threw the door open and stepped back to let Gigi Kramer sweep past him.

"*Zut alors*," she said. "What a lovely collection."

Mom and I hustled past Dad. The pub was freezing cold and still decked out like Versailles, the palace of the French kings. But it wasn't the temperature or the furniture you noticed first.

What you saw first was that the place was knickknack heaven. Every single surface had china figurines on it. There were hundreds of them, some in court clothes, others dressed as milkmaids or shepherds and shepherdesses. None of them had wings, and each had the same stupid smirk, nothing like real Parvi.

But just like my little china guy upstairs.

Chapter Thirteen

The Frog

MOM NUDGED ME. "Why is the plumbing inspector inspecting the liquor bottles?"

This was a good question. I didn't know where the plumbing was, but my guess would have been in the ceiling or walls. Definitely not in a bottle of whiskey.

At first I was afraid Gigi Kramer was eyeing the bottles because she knew about Grand-père's note. But then I realized she was patting her hair and admiring herself in the mirror *behind* the bottles. She really enjoyed being Gigi Kramer, plumbing inspector.

She noticed Mom and me staring at her and rolled her dead-looking eyes at us. I thought about that drop of water turning into ice on her skin. The tiny yet shouting voice. Durindana saying she was really a Small Person with Wings inside a doll.

Enough fooling around. I wanted answers.

"Mom," I whispered, "I'm going upstairs for a minute. Don't look Gigi Kramer in the eye."

Time to give the moonstone a real test. And while I was at it, see if my china guy really was china.

Thanks to Mom's shopping trip, the freezer was crammed full of food and the sack of coffee was buried.

I was so intent on finding it and digging for the ring, I never heard the slow footsteps on the stairs.

I put the ring on. I turned around. I dang near fainted.

The moonstone was working. To my eyes, the kitchen was back to normal—no more pink silk tent, no more gold filigree or damask. Standing in the doorway, however, was . . . well, it was dressed like Gigi Kramer the plumbing inspector. But it was no longer a she. It was an it.

To be precise, it was a department store mannequin with a cheap yellow nylon wig. She—it, I mean—had seen better days. Its fiberglass skin was pitted and peeling, with a spiderweb of cracks where the head attached to the neck.

The face was frozen in a Mona Lisa smile, the shark-like eyes painted on. Each eye had a hole in the middle, so somebody could peek out.

"*Tiens*, you wear the Gemma," the mannequin's left eye shouted. "By the expression of your face, I believe you see me as I am."

I couldn't think of anything to say. I mean, what could you say? "Love the neck cracks"?

"Do not be concerned, Turpina," the mannequin said. "I cannot hurt you while you wear the Gemma. Illusions are my weapon. At this moment you have none."

I went frigid, goose bumps rising. There was a lie out there somewhere. But what was it? I had no idea. *Gee, thanks for the help, Gemmaluna.*

The mannequin teetered to the kitchen table, used

both hands to pull out a chair because its fingers wouldn't bend. It sat down, creaking, and pulled one leg up, bent stiffly so it could cross over the other. It waggled its foot in a flirty way, painted eyes staring.

I needed to hear my own voice. "Who are you?"

"I have told you. I am Gigi Kramer, plumbing inspector." Somebody tittered behind the frozen Mona Lisa face.

"Who's that inside there? Are you a fair— . . . a Small Person with Wings?"

"This is not being your beeswax. Do not change the subject."

"We don't have a subject."

"Yes, yes, we do have a subject. You wear it on your great gigantic finger."

Has to be a Parva. Who else would call a human finger great and gigantic? "Durindana?"

"Puh. Our good lady Inepta. No indeed."

"Why are you riding around in a fiberglass dummy?"

"Do not call me a dummy, *moi*. Why do you suppose? I want the Gemmaluna."

That didn't make any sense. "We're probably going to give it back to you. Give us a chance to discuss it some more and then—"

"You misunderstand," the mannequin said. "I do not wish that you will give back the Gemma, at least not to Rinaldo. I wish that you will give it to me."

I made a fist so the ring wouldn't slide off my finger.

"What good would it do you all by yourself? I thought the Parvi had to get together and drink the elixir."

"This is what I do not wish. If I have got the Gemma, Rinaldo has not got it. All stays as it is. Give me that ring."

I tightened my fist. "Why should I?"

"I could make you pretty," the voice said, wheedling. "Beautiful, I could make you."

I'm smart. That's enough.

But . . . "Would I be thin?"

"As if you starved. With long, shiny hair of any color you desire. And a figure . . . how do you say this? . . . a figure to die for."

I went warm. She was telling the truth. *I'll be prettier than Janine. I'll wear a push-up bra, and so what if Timmo knows about Fairy Fat. She won't exist anymore.* "What will you do with the moonstone?"

"That would be my affair."

I took the ring off. Gigi Kramer became a gorgeous blond lady, panting with her tongue between her teeth like I was a chocolate layer cake. "Do me first," I said.

"No. Give to me the ring."

"You were lying about something before."

The downstairs door opened. "Mellie?" Mom called up the stairs. "Are you okay?"

"Yeah, Mom. I'm fine." But she woke up my brain, my stupid, inconvenient brain. "I wouldn't really be pretty," I said. "It would be fake."

"*Zut*, Turpina. We are as we look."

I couldn't tell if that was a lie or not. "Are not," I said, putting the ring back on. The neck cracks and nylon wig reappeared.

"Fine," the mannequin said. "I will be making you so hideous your own parents will not know you."

"You said you couldn't hurt me with the Gemmaluna on." I had a nasty feeling I'd identified the lie.

"I will not *hurt* you." The mannequin started laughing so hard its head jiggled. I looked at my hands—they weren't breaking out in anything. But I'd had all I could take of Gigi Kramer.

"Mom!" I shouted, and hurtled out the door.

When I burst into the pub—and thanks to the moonstone ring I did see it as a pub again—Mom yelled and jumped behind Dad, who yelled and jumped behind Bruce McCarthy.

"What the heck is that?" Bruce McCarthy yelled, looking for somebody to jump behind.

"What the heck is what?" I looked around too. The china figurines now were live Parvi standing absolutely still with frozen faces. They were wearing the most disgustingly filthy and raggedy rags I'd ever seen, but I didn't have time to worry about that.

"Mellie." Mom shoved my father and Bruce McCarthy out of the way. "Is that you?"

"Of course it's me. What's the matter?" But before I'd even finished the question, I knew the answer. Something had happened to me after all, something I couldn't see because I had the moonstone ring on.

"Here, Mom." I pulled off the ring and handed it to her. "You can wear this for a while."

The moonstone off my finger, the pub sprouted marble and damask and crystal all over again, like ink soaking through a paper towel. The Parvi turned into china figurines.

And my hands were green. I ran to the bar, climbed up on a stool so I could see into the mirror behind the liquor bottles.

Staring back from the mirror was . . . a giant frog. Wide-mouthed. Drooling. My body was its normal shape and I still had my brown eyes, but they looked weird surrounded by all that waxy green skin. I had nostril holes instead of a nose.

The frog's mouth opened wide. It drooled. I screamed.

I kept telling myself to look at something else, anything else—as if that would solve it—but I couldn't stop staring at this frog-person shrieking at me from the mirror. *Isn't me, can't be me, not real, can't be, can't be, can't be, can't be—Timmo will tell all his friends and his dad and his mom and his dad and his mom ohmygodohmygodohmygodohmygod . . .*

I screamed and screamed and screamed. Someone grabbed me and held me. *Mom, makethisgoaway.* She crooned, telling me to calm down and it was all going to be okay and looks didn't really matter. *She says that all the time.* I shrieked into her shoulder.

The Frog

My dad patted me on the back, the way he does when he wants to help but doesn't know what to do. "Is this really Mellie?" he asked my mom. *What do you think, Dad, some monster stole my clothes?*

"Here," Mom said to him, not letting go of me, "put the ring on a minute."

"Or, if you wish your daughter to be herself once more, you will give that ring to me," said Gigi Kramer, standing in the doorway in stiletto-heeled glory.

At least that was what I saw. Dad, however, had the ring on. He made a gargling sound and staggered backward a step or two. He was seeing the fiberglass mannequin with the nylon hair.

"*Tiens.* Be getting a grip," Gigi Kramer said. She turned her full, shark-eyed attention to Bruce McCarthy, and in seconds he was gazing at her in zombified adoration.

"Can I do anything for you at all?" he said. "Waive an ordinance? Fake a permit?"

"You could be seizing that ring for me," Gigi Kramer purred.

Bruce McCarthy grabbed Dad's hand, tried to break off his fingers.

"Hey!" Dad caught Bruce McCarthy's wrist. "You're breaking my fingers."

Mom let go of me and kicked Bruce McCarthy in the lower abdomen. Nobody breaks my dad's fingers when my mom is around. Bruce McCarthy went *oof* and doubled over, releasing Dad's hand.

"That won't work anyway," Dad said, flexing his fingers. "We have to *give* it to you."

I felt like I had a fever, all sweaty and unreal. I was dizzy from hyperventilating. *Give her the ring, Dad!* I wanted to shriek. But here's what I really said: "Dad, there's a Parva inside that dummy and she wants the moonstone for herself. Not a good idea." *Why the heck did I say that?*

"Better not give it to her, Roly," Mom said.

Dad took the ring off. He got an eyeful of me, turned the color of that school paste you can eat, and put it back on. "Nick, we can't sentence our daughter to go through life like that."

"Roly, I don't trust this . . . this . . . whatever she is. Who says she won't take the ring and leave Mellie exactly the same?"

"I would never do such a thing," Gigi Kramer said.

Dad shuddered. "You're lying," he said, surprised. He had the moonstone on, remember.

"*Tiens,*" Gigi Kramer said. "I feel that I am intruding. You must be talking this over as a family. I shall leave now and return for your decision. Come, Mr. McCarthy." Still hunched over and breathing funny from Mom's kick, Bruce McCarthy hobbled to the door and held it open for Gigi Kramer. She sashayed out, and he hustled after her.

"I guess we'll hear from you about the inspection results," Dad called after him.

The Frog

"Did he ever inspect anything other than Gigi Kramer?" Mom asked.

The door closed behind Bruce McCarthy. "Gigi Kramer?" Dad said. "Who's she?"

Mom turned to me, intending to exchange a *men!* look. But a fly buzzed by my nose and, without thinking about it, I flicked out my tongue and caught it. My tongue was nowhere near as long as a real frog's, but it turned out to be agile and a bit sticky.

Flies taste like sausage. My mom whimpered.

"Rethinking your 'looks don't matter' position?" I asked her.

"A little." Her voice wobbled.

"Take the ring back for a while," Dad said.

I seemed to be breathing all right again. Not staring into the mirror did help—made it all theoretical, you know? Except for the green hands and the expressions on other people's faces.

Something was weird, though. I mean, weirder than usual. This was more than an illusion. I was sort of *acting* like a frog.

"Oooo," said a tinny voice from the bar. "Look what has been done to our Turpina." Other voices sniggered.

The speaker was Rinaldo, dressed as a shepherd but no longer a china figurine even to those of us not wearing the moonstone. He was standing on the bar surrounded by other Parvi in shepherd and shepherdess outfits, all of a silken silliness that would have put a real sheep-herder to shame. They were pointing at me and giggling behind their little hands.

I reminded myself that what they were seeing wasn't the real me. That was no comfort.

Their laughter died when I told them about the Parva inside the mannequin. Durindana stood up in her chandelier bed, but if she thought anyone was going to admit she'd been right about that giant doll, she was sadly mistaken.

"This giant doll has a bad, bad Parva Pennata inside," Rinaldo said, as if he'd known all along.

"Can you undo whatever she did to me?" I asked him.

He shook his head. "The magic is not mine to undo."

"Can't you create another illusion on top of this one?" Dad said.

"It is not good to make illusion of illusion," Rinaldo said. "Perhaps I would make her look even more like a monster of the earth."

"Oh, thanks." A glance in the mirror and my breathing went funny again. He wasn't wrong.

My stomach hurt. I wanted it to be last week. Or next week. Anytime except now, when I looked like a frog and I was freezing cold and surrounded by blank-faced fairies and mildew.

Slush balls and Tampax. Child's play.

Chapter Fourteen

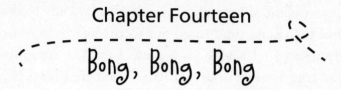

Bong, Bong, Bong

MOM WAS PULLING ME TOWARD the pub door—she seemed to think everything would be okay if she just got me upstairs—when Lady Noctua flew in through the mail slot. Rinaldo embraced her in midair, the first time I'd seen a Parvus exhibit any real enthusiasm.

"My Lady Noctua," Rinaldo said. "Wherever have you been?"

She did not seem to be returning his hug. She hovered there, arms by her side, the two of them bobbing up and down with their wing beats. "I was beside the sea," she said. "I . . . I forgot the time." The hem of her dress was wet and sandy, totally out of character.

"But our trick, the turning of us into china Parvi Pennati . . . this was your idea, *ma chère*. Without you, all was very nearly lost."

"For this I am sorry. Excuse me, consort. I am *fatiguée*." Noctua turned her back on him and flitted off to drink nectar. Rinaldo watched her go, and I wished I could read an expression—any expression—on his pale face.

Something was fishy.

"Let's get out of here," Mom said. "I need a Parvi break."

As we climbed the stairs, I wondered why Lady Noctua chose that exact time to go out to the beach, to return only when Gigi Kramer was gone. I tried to remember what Gigi Kramer sounded like. Could that have been Noctua inside the mannequin?

I needed to talk this over with my parents, but I never got the chance.

"Here's a question for you." Dad dove for the refrigerator's gold-filigree door handle as if he were honey-ham-deprived, stuck his head in so the door was between us. My own father didn't want to look at me.

Mom, who still had the moonstone on and could look anywhere she wanted, gave me a chocolate chip cookie. I took it in my green hand and felt absolutely no desire to eat it. I handed it back to her. "Oh, lovey," she said, her eyes teary.

"Remember that china guy Fidius left behind?" Dad said, emerging from the refrigerator. "Think he's really china?"

I'd been wondering the same thing, but Gigi Kramer and my frog face had driven it out of my mind.

If that little guy was actually Fidius, I was hurt and ticked off for reasons I couldn't even count. Sheesh, just a year ago I'd started imitating Peter Paul Rubens's fat naked Venus in front of the mirror.

Rubens (1577–1640) was Dutch and loved fat ladies with cellulite. The Venus is a cool picture because you think she's looking at herself in the mirror when she's really looking at you. It is not, however, a picture you imitate in front of a small guy with wings.

"Give me that ring, Mom," I said. She took it off, got a load of what I looked like, and buried her face in her hands. Dad rubbed her back, averting his eyes.

"Thanks, guys," I said. "Way to make me feel better."

"Oh, Mellie." My mom started to cry. I figured the least I could do was get out of sight.

I raced up the stairs, which went marble-free the minute I shoved the ring onto my finger.

My china guy was standing on my dresser, looking completely normal. I pulled the moonstone off, put it back on. Still china.

I would have been irate if the guy turned out to be Fidius. Now that he wasn't, I was ridiculously disappointed. I sat down on my bed, blinking hard. Something landed on my shoulder, chilling my ear. *Durindana?* I wanted to say hi, but I didn't trust my voice.

"The clothes are right," a tinny voice whispered in my ear. *That isn't Durindana.* "But the frog face? Not my little Turpina. Not my little Turpina at all." He took off from my shoulder and hovered at the end of what used to be my nose. "What happened to you, Turpina?"

"Fidius," I whispered, reaching out to touch him. He looked the same, except thanks to the moonstone ring I could see he was dressed in a torn, filthy burlap tunic and breeches.

He backed away from my hand. "Careful, Turpina. You

don't need any more frostbite. Remember my hand on your nose?"

A tear ran down my cheek, although I wasn't sure why. Joy at seeing Fidius? The memory of when he froze my nose and left?

Oh. Or maybe not having any nose at all. "Fidius, a Small Person in a mannequin turned me into a frog."

His face showed no expression—less than I recalled, even. But his wings missed a beat. "A Small Person in a *what*?"

"A mannequin. A human-sized . . . uh, doll that you see in store windows. She can walk and talk, and she looks like a woman unless you have the moonstone ring on. Then you can tell it's a mannequin with a Small Person inside."

Fidius sucked in his breath. "This is Magica Mala, Turpina. Do you know what that is?"

"Rinaldo told us. When this mannequin lady looks you in the eye, your brains turn to mush and you do what she says."

Fidius's wings darkened. I instinctively pulled back. "Rinaldo knows nothing of the Magica Mala," he snapped. "Rinaldo is an imbecile."

I remembered what Durindana had told me, about Rinaldo making fun of Fidius's parents. "He was your friend once."

"You were my friend too. Friends betray."

My tears welled up again. "I didn't mean to, Fidius. I didn't understand."

He whirred closer, patted my cheek but not enough to freeze me. The color returned to his wings. "I know, Turpina. I didn't understand back then either. You're all so big . . . I forget how young some of you are."

"What do *you* know about Magica Mala?" I asked

"The *magi* study it and so did I, when I thought I would be a *magus*. Magica Mala gives one unnatural control of others. But to master a lifeless object . . . that takes deep study, remarkable talent." Fidius flew to my bureau, settled down next to the china guy. "You see, Turpina, Magica Mala is a stronger version of the Magica Artificia. This big doll of yours—Magica Artificia makes it look like a Gigantea, but making it move and talk, this requires illicit power beyond what even the *magi* permit themselves to study."

"She wants us to give her the moonstone, and not give it to Rinaldo."

"What did she offer you for it? She must have offered something."

I discovered I was ashamed that I'd almost given up the moonstone for blond hair and a figure. "She didn't offer me anything," I said, and goose bumps rose all over me. *Hunh. The moonstone tells me when I'm lying too. Isn't that handy.* I shivered and changed the subject. "Fidius, why would she want the moonstone all for herself?"

Fidius shook his head slowly. "This is a puzzle for you, I must admit. If she drank the elixir, she would kill the Magica Artificia." His eyes widened. "Oh. Maybe . . .

sheesh, as your *père* would say. Maybe she thinks she can use Magica Mala as a bridge between the other two, achieve the Three Magics? Sheesh indeed, Turpina."

I still felt shivery. "What do you mean, *achieve* the Three Magics? You mean combine them?"

"This is complicated, Turpina. The Parvi began with the Magica Vera, a simple magic that helped us make things and resist other enchantment. A sorceress taught the Lady Imprexa to make the Magica Artificia, but that was only a teaspoon's worth of sorcery, and some who worked with Imprexa wanted more. Working in secret, they manipulated the Magica Artificia, creating a third magic with deeper powers. They had the purest of motives, hoping to protect the Parvi Pennati in a world of Gigantes. But the *magi* in their wisdom deemed this power *mala.*" He shrugged. "Just as well, I suppose, since the stronger power would have eroded our senses even faster."

"But what's this bridge thing you were talking about?"

Fidius whirred over to my shoulder so he could talk softly into my ear. "Here is the thing, Turpina. Some believe combining the Three Magics would give us the full powers of a sorcerer, the power to change reality to whatever we wanted, without eroding our senses. Over the generations, some have argued that we should take back the Gemma and experiment with the Three. But the *magi* always say no."

He sounded sad. I thought I could guess why he'd fought with the *magi*. "Did you want to do that?"

He hesitated. "Yes, I admit it. But I was young and I was frightened of the world. I see my mistakes now."

I shivered again. "Yes, Turpina," he whispered. "That's a bad, bad walking doll." He took off and hovered in front of my face. "But we will stop her, no big deal." Goose bumps. Did that mean he was lying, that we *wouldn't* stop Gigi?

"Let's change the subject," he said. "Did you enjoy the china Parvus I left for you?"

"Not much. Fidius, where have you been all these years? Why did you leave me that way? Why can't you smile? And—"

He chuckled, face immobile. "One question at a time, Melissa Angelica. I have been many places all these years, but often with you. I hid from you, that's all. For reasons best kept to myself."

"Durindana says you got put in a jar when you were little."

"As if the Parvi are ever anything *but* little. Inepta should mind her own business."

"Don't call her that." *Huh. She said he was nice to her.* "Fidius . . . you thought I'd take you to school and they'd put you in a jar. I'm sorry."

He moved closer and briefly stroked my cheek. "Do not be concerned, my Turpina. I know you meant no harm." I basked in warmth. *He's telling the truth. He does forgive me.*

"You've been here all this time?" I asked him.

"Some of the time." His eyes went beady. "Didn't you suspect, when the small Gigantes turned to piglets in the slush?"

"That was you! I . . . I didn't know what to think."

"They called you Fairy Fat," he said softly. "Why was that?"

I hadn't wanted him to know about my social status. But then I remembered that he too was an outcast. "They made fun of me because I didn't bring you in to school that day, and they didn't believe me when I said you were real."

"I am sorry I caused you distress, Turpina. You are a loyal friend. Loyal to a fault!" He took off, laughing, and swooped around the room, bouncing against the ceiling, ricocheting off the walls.

"Why did you leave me that little china guy?"

"So you would not forget me." *Bounce, bounce, bounce.* "I found it in the basement of your building." He did a somersault in midair and landed neatly on the bureau. "And now the others pretend to be china. How rich."

"They were all in rags when I had the moonstone ring on."

He gave me a sharp look and inspected himself. "All I see are my nice clothes, the illusion. Am I at least decent?"

"Sure, yeah, you're fine. A bit tattered, that's all."

"You have the Gemma on, so you are seeing us as we

are. We have made nothing real for thirteen hundred years." His wings darkened and he kicked suddenly, savagely, at the china guy, knocking it over. "At least I have my own face. What are we going to do about that frog face, Turpina? I don't enjoy looking at it."

I wasn't hurt. Not. At. All. *He's saying mean things to make me face facts, that's all.*

"I guess we'll figure something out," I said.

"Brave Turpina," Fidius said, and I watched his wings return to normal. "It's not *such* a bad face. It is a frog of . . . of great gentility. We will get your face back, I promise."

I went cold all over, because he definitely was lying this time. It was a very bad face, and we both knew it.

My parents walked in, looking solemn. Dad nodded at Fidius, who swept a bow.

"Give me the ring, Mellie," Mom said in a voice that meant business. I gave it to her and she dropped it into a glass of water. "*Cupio videre.*"

"Hey, Mom, no!" I lunged for the glass. "Grand-père's note, he warned us . . ."

Mom held me off with an elbow. The water in the glass was giving off a vapor—not a foggy kind of vapor, though; it made things clearer, somehow. I could see through it to the doorknob, which was like . . . I don't know, the essence of Doorknob, as if I'd been wearing someone else's glasses all my life and just took them off.

Mom drank half the water and handed the glass to Dad. "*Cupio videre*," he said.

"Dad," I pleaded. "Don't do it. Remember what Grand-père . . ."

He drank up the rest of the water and set the glass down on my desk.

"We know what Grand-père said." Mom burped. "Excuse me. We've had a talk, your dad and I, and we don't see any way to get you back the way you were. So we're drinking this stuff. Maybe we'll feed it to everybody we know, put it in the water supply or something. It's not a perfect solution, but we figure—" She broke off with a gasp. "Oh. Oh, Mellie."

"What, Mom? What? What do I look like now?"

She was turning whiter by the second. "You look fine, dear. But . . . oh, Mellie."

My dad groaned.

"What?" I said. "What, Dad? What?"

He slumped against the door frame. "You don't respect us at all, do you?"

"Respect you?" I said. "Of course I do. I love you."

"You love us but you think we're idiots," Mom said. "I never thought I'd have a child who felt this way about me. It's as if I'm my mother."

My insides had dropped out. I wanted to take back every time I'd ever thought how stupid they . . . *no, no, I don't mean that.* "Mom. It's just—"

She burst into tears and ran from the room. Her sobs

echoed in the stairwell to the third floor. Dad made for the door too.

"Dad," I said.

"No, Mellie. Leave us alone now." He went out, his shoulders curled over as if he were carrying something heavy, and trudged up the stairs after Mom.

Bong! Mom must have jostled that old clock on the third floor. *Bong! Bong! Bong! Bong! Bong! Bong! Bong!*

"What a noise!" Fidius said, hands over ears.

"Mom! Dad!" I fished the moonstone out of the glass, shoved it on, headed up the stairs. The clock stopped bonging. Instead, someone was yelling, "Help me, you benighted fools! Help me! Help me!"

Oh great, I thought. *Now I really* am *going nuts.*

On the third-floor landing, my parents stood frozen, staring at the place where the grandfather clock had been. It wasn't a clock anymore. It was a skinny, pale, whiskery, glaring old man trussed up like a Thanksgiving turkey, the rope anchored to the wall behind him.

I hadn't seen him for a long time, but I was pretty sure it was Grand-père.

"Are you the clock?" I said.

"Am I speaking words? All I hear is bonging."

I nodded. He grimaced at the sight. "What in blue blazes are you, anyway? You sound human."

"I'm Mellie. I don't normally look like this. I've been cursed."

"Crossed Gigi Kramer, hey? Well, happens to the best of us. How come you can see me?" I held up my hand. "Ah. You found the Gemma. Every fool has his day."

Dad gurgled. Mom walked carefully over to the wall and slid down it to sit on the floor.

"What's the matter with them?" Grand-père asked. "*They* can't see me, can they?"

"They drank the elixir."

"Blast. Blast, blast, and blast. They'll be worthless until the next full moon. And we'll have to run around after them, making sure they don't do themselves in before it wears off."

"Worthless," Dad said. "That's a good word for me. Worthless." He too sat down on the floor. He stared at the threadbare carpet, rocking slightly.

"After all these years, finally he listens," Grand-père said. "So, my gorgeous granddaughter—think those funny green fingers of yours can untie a rope?"

I looked closer. "I don't think anybody's fingers could undo those knots. I need a knife."

"There's one attached to my belt around back," Grand-père said.

To my surprise, the knife cut the first rope I tried. "These must be real ropes."

"Brilliant child," Grand-père said. "So observant."

"Well, they could have been an illusion."

"In which case you wouldn't be seeing them with the Gemma on, would you?" He was right, but he didn't have to be so obnoxious about it. My mother's voice came into my head, from years back. *I know Grand-père is a bit testy sometimes, Mellie, but it's not easy being old. Be respectful, and we'll go home soon.* Probably being a clock was no picnic either.

I was trembling so hard I could barely hold the knife. Here's the emotional tally from the previous, what, three hours? (1) I looked like a frog; (2) My parents had gone nuts; (3) My grandfather was alive, so nobody could say my father was a murderer; (4) My grandfather was a jerk; (5) We didn't own the inn anymore, which was just as well because it was a wreck and infested by Small Persons with Wings; (6) Some walking mannequin was trying to take over the world; (7) I ate a fly.

"Our Lady of the Painted Eyes entranced the building inspector into tying me up," Grand-père said. "Using, as you so intelligently noted, real rope. Then she transformed the whole package into a clock, ropes and all, right in front of him. He probably doesn't remember a thing."

My dad groaned and buried his face in his hands.

"You say that elixir wears off, Grand-père?" I sawed at another rope.

"When the next full moon rises. Tide chart next to the refrigerator will say when that is."

My mom gave a sob. I sawed some more. "Your dad jumped off a bridge."

"Dad. What a disheartening thing to call someone. But yes, you are correct. I allowed my male progenitor to jump off a bridge." He said this without any emotion at all.

I wanted to forget the stupid rope and hug my mom, then my dad, then my mom again. But I kept hacking away, trying to ignore the tears that were starting to run down my cheeks.

"Your tears are the color of phlegm, do you know that?" Grand-père said. *It's not easy being old. It's not easy being old.*

The last rope fell away. Grand-père collapsed onto the floor like a bunch of pick-up sticks.

"Can you walk?" I asked.

"Give me a minute. I'm eighty-four years old. I just spent two months as a clock."

"Aren't you still a clock?"

"Interesting point." He held out his hand. "Am I holding out my hand?"

"Yeah, your hand's right there. You can't see it?"

"No." He looked down at himself. "All I see is a clock. And it's standing up, even though I know I'm sitting down. Curious."

A fly buzzed by, but I managed to keep my tongue in my mouth. My stomach gurgled. "It's dinnertime. Can you eat?"

"I don't know. I've been alone with my memories for two months—an experience that would madden a weaker man, by the way. I haven't felt hungry or thirsty, no need to pee, none of the usual urges. Perhaps it's a side benefit of being a fake clock."

"I'm a fake painter," Dad said to the carpet. "If I'd wanted to be a real painter, I should have devoted my life to it."

"I'm a fake painter and the school hired me as a shop teacher to fill an equal opportunity quota," my mom replied. "Plus I'm dumpy-looking. And a terrible mother. Other people's children respect them."

"No, they don't," I said.

"Well, let's see if I can walk." Grand-père got up on his knees and reached for my arm. I helped him stand, his joints popping, and leaned him against the wall. He stretched out his arms, massaged his neck, wiggled his feet—all the things you'd do if you'd been tied up for two months.

In the interests of science, I took off the moonstone ring. My hands turned green and there, leaning against the wall, was . . . a clock, quivering as Grand-père continued to work out his kinks.

"Can you walk?" I asked, feeling like an idiot for talking to a quivering piece of furniture.

Bong, the clock said. It rose an inch and floated forward. Then it stopped, trembled, and tipped over backward against the wall. I put the ring back on. The old man was leaning on his arm, glaring at me. "I could use some help, Froggie-face," he said.

I turned to my parents, trying to sound cheerful. "Let's all go downstairs. We can have a cup of tea and I'll make dinner." My syrupy tone reminded me of my third-grade teacher, who told me skinning my knee on asphalt would make me a big, strong girl as long as I didn't cry.

"Why would she make us tea?" my mom said. "She doesn't even like us."

"Now wait a minute," I said. "Okay, so I think your plans might be unrealistic sometimes and I don't want you spending my college fund. But I respect and love you. L-O-V-E love. Love, love, love. You. Both of you."

"You think we're behaving badly right now," my dad said. "You think we were stupid to drink the elixir."

"Will you please come downstairs and have a cup of tea," I said through clenched teeth.

"Do they know what you look like?" Grand-père said as we all started down the stairs. He was behind me, hands on my shoulders, leaning heavily.

"That's why they took the elixir, so they could see the real me."

"Ah, the real you. And what is that, exactly?"

Now he was the one who sounded like a teacher. "I'm not in the mood," I said, trying to sound respectful yet firm. "Sir. Concentrate on walking down the stairs, okay?"

When we got to the kitchen, my parents sat down and stared at the tabletop. Grand-père flung himself into a chair and gazed around as if the kitchen were Mammoth Cave. "*Mon Dieux*. This is beautiful. Is that gold filigree on the refrigerator?"

Thanks to the moonstone ring, I'd forgotten about

Sleeping Beauty's Dream Kitchen. "Oh, yeah. The Parvi did that. They're living in the pub."

"Did you promise to give them the Gemmaluna?"

"No."

"So why did they improve your surroundings?"

"It's all fake. They were trying to impress the building inspector."

"This is exactly what I wanted," Grand-père said. "Except it was going to be real. I was going to give them the Gemma and they would fix this place up for me."

"They've offered us the same deal. But now Gigi Kramer wants the moonstone."

"I know. That's why she turned me into a clock."

I was pouring hot water into the teapot when someone behind me said, "Gah!"

It was Timmo, standing round-eyed in the kitchen doorway. He gaped at me, then at Grand-père. Then at the room, which he saw all done up in pink silk. Then at me again.

I didn't want Timmo seeing me as a frog, although why I should care I didn't know. "It's me, Mellie. A walking mannequin turned me into a frog, but underneath I'm still the real me."

"Awesome," Timmo said. "Why is there a clock on the chair?"

Chapter Fifteen

Behind the Clock Face

"I CAME TO INVITE YOU TO MY HOUSE for supper," Timmo said. "But, uh . . ."

"Maybe some other time." I took off the moonstone ring. "Here. Put this on."

As soon as the ring was out of my hands they turned green. The pink silk and gold filigree oozed back into view and my crabby old grandfather turned back into a clock. He did look bizarre, stuck up on a chair like that. Where his legs should have been, there was nothing.

Timmo put the ring on his finger and looked at Grand-père. "Hunh." He looked at me, and somehow the fact that he could see the real Mellie made me feel better. Not that the real Mellie is any thing of beauty.

Bong, bong, bong, the clock said.

"Yessir, I'm Timmo from next door. Timothy Oliver Wright."

Bong, bong.

"Nope. Named after my uncle. He's an insurance adjustor."

Mom roused herself from contemplating the tabletop. "You respect your parents, Timmo?"

Timmo sized up Mom's red eyes and Dad's rounded

shoulders. "That all depends. My dad erased our computer's hard drive twice in six months. Once I could handle. Twice, I'm not so sure."

"You're not telling the complete truth," Dad said, "but who cares."

"We don't have a computer, because we are bad parents," Mom said.

"We're worthless," Dad said. "We don't even paint well."

Timmo wrinkled his forehead at me.

"They drank the elixir," I said. "Turns out it takes away all your illusions and makes you really, really depressed."

Timmo nodded. "Like that guy who jumped off the bridge."

Bong, bong, bong.

Timmo blanched. "Sorry. I forgot that was your dad."

Bong! Bong!

Timmo sidled closer to me. "What's wrong with calling someone 'dad'?" he whispered.

"Don't worry about it," I whispered back. A fly buzzed by. I snapped at it. Got it.

"That was gross," Timmo said. "Cool, though."

My male progenitor stood up. "I suppose I should be glad to see you," he said to the clock. He turned to me, eyes desolate. "I'm going to bed."

"Me too," Mom said.

"Don't you want tea?" I said. "And we've got Roland's Big-Time Teriyaki for supper."

"That's not really so special." Dad schlumped to the door. "We only think it tastes good because it's so salty."

"It's better than anything *I've* ever cooked," Mom said, following him.

We listened to them trudge up the stairs.

Bong, bong, bong, bong, bong. "What's he saying now?" I asked Timmo.

"He says bed's the best place for them because at least they'll stay off bridges. And he thinks magic suppresses the appetite."

"I'm hungry," I said. "And I've been magicked." I was hungry for flies, but nobody had to know that.

Bong, bong, bong.

Timmo turned bright red and refused to translate.

"Give me that ring," I said. The clock turned into a scrawny old man who was supposed to be dead but wasn't.

He gave me a sour smile. "I said, for some people appetite suppression is not a bad thing."

I don't care how hard it is being old. This guy's a jerk.

"Are your parents going to be okay?" Timmo asked, sitting down at the table.

"I don't know."

"Must be weird."

"Yeah. They usually respect themselves a bit more than they do right now."

"I mean for you. Being the only kid and all."

"Yeah." *I'm all they've got. Sheesh.*

"I hope they're okay." Timmo's right toe prodded a curl of torn rubber on his left sneaker, letting it spring up, flattening it again. It was mesmerizing. "I like them. They talk to you like you're a human being."

"Instead of a frog, you mean."

He flushed. "No, before this. And I don't mean 'you'— I mean 'us,' everybody. Kids. They really like you. Meaning me."

Okay, I'm confused. "Are you saying your parents don't like you? Because I'm sure they do."

"A fatuous response if ever I heard one," Grand-père said. "*Fatuous.* Heh." Fortunately, I had the ring on and Timmo only heard a series of bongs.

"What do your parents say you're going to be?" Timmo bent the curl of rubber backward until it broke off. "When you grow up, I mean."

"Fat," Grand-père said. *Is it okay to hate a relative?*

My parents and I hadn't discussed my career that much—getting me through middle school was hard enough. "I think we all assume I'll be a scientist. Dad said I'd make a good accountant, but I don't think he was serious." I pondered. "I could write art books maybe."

"My dad's waiting for me to get tall so I can play basketball with the guys at the police academy. I'd rather play baseball and be an astronaut."

"Your mother's not that tall—what if you take after her?"

"I bet I do. Just my luck."

"Every time your dad talks to you," I said, "you stare at your shoes."

Timmo stared at his shoes.

"You should look at a person when they're talking to you," I said.

Timmo hit me with the galaxy eyes. "I'll look at you," he said, "but can I have the ring back? You're drooling."

Oh, right, I look like a frog. Not my fault. So why was I ashamed? I handed Timmo the ring. "Want some Roland's Big-Time Teriyaki?"

He hesitated. "Better call my mom."

I clattered around the kitchen so I wouldn't overhear Timmo on the reception desk phone explaining why he was staying here rather than me going over there. I tried to figure out exactly how it had happened that the boy next door and I were eating supper at each other's houses. *He almost acts as if he likes me.* But then, so did Mina Cardoza when she thought I had a fairy, back in kindergarten. *He's pretending he likes me because of the Parvi.*

Timmo returned. "I told her you'd been grounded. And your parents wanted me to eat here as an example of good behavior."

"She bought that?"

"*My* mother still has her illusions." He sat down at the table.

I took the pan of Roland's Big-Time out of the fridge and stuck it in the oven, then pelted frozen corn into one of Grand-père's fancy saucepans. Timmo had the ring, so Grand-père's protests sounded like *bong, bong, bong.*

"So-o-o-rreee," I said musically. "I can't understa-a-and you."

Fidius joined us. "There is a clock on that chair," he observed, settling himself on the toaster. Without the ring on, I saw him dressed in blue velvet knee breeches, vest, and jacket, with a plumed hat.

"That's my grandfather, O-gee-errr Turr-pinn," I said, pronouncing it Dad's way to annoy Grand-père, an impulse I now understood. In fact, I felt I was representing Dad, who'd had to spend his whole childhood with this guy.

"I lived with Ogier before I came to you and your parents," Fidius said. "He was a pill."

Bong! Bong! Bong!

"Now he's too noisy," Fidius said. "Old men should be seen and not heard."

Bong, bong, bong!

I introduced Timmo to Fidius. Timmo was explaining about his uncle the insurance adjustor when Durindana buzzed in. She rocketed around the ceiling, making eyes at Timmo.

Then she noticed Fidius. She just about fell out of the air, but recovered and swooped down to land on the table, showing off. She skidded over the edge and plummeted wailing to the floor.

Remembering that Fidius had called her *Inepta*, I steeled myself for what he'd say now.

But he was nice. He swooped down to the floor, bowed to the prostrate Durindana, and helped her to her feet. They flew together to tabletop height, Fidius's hat in his hand, Durindana's head at a coy tilt like a china shepherdess. He ushered her to a seat on the toaster and landed on the tabletop, only then replacing his hat.

"It is good to see you, Monsieur Fidius," Durindana cooed down to him.

He bowed to her again. "My lady Inep— . . . er, Durindana."

"Want something to eat?" I asked.

The downstairs door slammed and heavy footsteps started up the stairs.

Timmo turned pale and freckly. "That's my dad!"

"Get out of here," I ordered the Parvi. Fidius instantly turned himself into a china figurine. Durindana flitted up to sit on my shoulder.

"Change!" I told her.

"Hide!" she told me.

I remembered I had a frog face. "You win."

As Chief Wright's footsteps reached the top of the stairs I squeezed myself into the broom closet, Durindana still on my shoulder. I left the door open a crack so I could see and possibly breathe. The closet smelled like bleach and three kinds of cleaning fluid.

The footsteps stopped in the reception lounge. "Where the heck did all this fancy stuff come from?" Chief Wright said.

"Hi Dad." Timmo looked as if he'd rather be anywhere else.

"Spaceshot? I thought you were cleaning the garage."

Timmo backed up so I couldn't see him anymore. "Hi Dad," he repeated.

I imagined Chief Wright standing in the kitchen doorway, taking in the pink tent and the gold filigree. "How the heck did they do this so fast? I was just up here this morning."

"Fairies did it," Timmo said.

"Don't sass me."

"We are not fairies," Durindana whispered in my ear. "We are—"

"Shhhh."

"Geez." Chief Wright stepped into the kitchen. "There's a freakin' grandfather clock sitting on a freakin' chair." Which was when I realized Dad wasn't out of the woods as a murder suspect. As long as Grand-père looked like a clock, nothing would convince Chief Wright that he wasn't in an urn someplace.

Bong! Bong! Bong!

"Mr. Turpin's trying to fix that clock," Timmo said. "It bongs when it should *just shut up*." This was clever of

191

Timmo, I had to admit. To my surprise, Grand-père did shut up.

"Oh yeah? Where *is* Mr. Turpin? Where's everybody, for that matter?"

"They . . . went to the store," Timmo said. "They needed milk."

"All of them? And they left you here?"

"Somebody had to watch the corn." Timmo came back into view, turned down the flame under Grand-père's fancy pot. "I'll do the garage tomorrow. I swear."

Chief Wright swooped down on Timmo. I flinched, but all he did was grab Timmo's hand and hold it up. "What's this? A ring?"

Timmo pulled his hand away. "It's not mine. I only—"

"You only what? You sneak over here so you can wear RINGS?"

"I didn't sneak, Mom knows I'm here. I was trying it on—it was Mellie's grandfather's."

"Oh, sharing the loot. Let me see that thing."

Timmo hesitated. His father lunged for his hand again. Timmo gave up and handed over the ring. "*Servate me!*" Durindana whispered.

"Very pretty," Chief Wright said. "You could wear it to police academy. Guys would be so impressed." He stuck the ring on the end of his pinky.

He snatched it off again, pressing his hand to his heart.

The kitchen must have turned normal for an instant,

with Grand-père sitting where the clock had been and a raggedy Small Person with Wings playing statue on the table.

Timmo, pasty white behind his freckles, got a knowing smirk on his face that made me wonder if he'd gone over the edge. "You okay, Dad? You looked like you saw a ghost."

"Is there a drug on this thing?" Chief Wright whispered. "There must be a drug."

"A drug on a ring? How could that be?" Timmo took the ring, put it on. "See? I'm fine."

"Yeah, but . . . but I . . . all this stuff . . ."

"Yeah. Um. Here's the thing. Dad. It's just that . . . the human mind can't take in too much pink, I read that online. Too much pink'll shut you down, especially when somebody's been working too hard, like you."

"Pink," Chief Wright said in a wispy voice. He let out a breath and sat down hard on a chair. I could see only his feet now. "I don't want you hanging around here, son. These people worry me. There's something strange going on and I don't want you mixed up in it."

Timmo examined his shoes. "I like them. Mom said I could stay for supper."

"I don't share your taste," Chief Wright said. Timmo didn't respond. "Listen, Spaceshot, I know you can't see it now, but I only want what's best for you."

"Dad," Timmo said wearily. "I keep telling you, I don't want to be a cop."

"I didn't think I did either. But now I wouldn't be anything else."

"Can't Eileen be the cop?" Timmo's voice trembled. I hoped he wouldn't embarrass me.

"Eileen wants to be a doctor."

"I want to be an astronaut."

Chief Wright let out a long, slow breath. "That's a hard road, son. I want you to try something we know you can succeed at."

"I'm good at math," Timmo said in a small voice.

"I know you are, boy. That's why I think you'll make a great cop." Chief Wright stood up, came back into view. "You coming home for supper?"

"I told you. Mom said I could eat here."

Chief Wright peered around at all the foofiness, as if it could attack him. "Yeah. Well. Come home right after. And tomorrow let's do something, maybe go fishing. How about it?"

"I have to clean the garage."

"Oh. That's right." Chief Wright turned from his son and walked out of my sight. The floor creaked in the reception lounge. "Keep that ring off you, boy." Heavy footsteps hit the stairs.

Timmo held up his hand and waggled his forefinger with the ring on it, almost a rude gesture.

I emerged from the broom closet, Durindana clinging to my sweatshirt. Some ancient, buried, nicer Mellie arose unexpectedly. "You were amazing. I freaked when he put the ring on and saw everything. That stuff you said about pink was brilliant."

My face went hot. My body was not used to me giving people compliments.

But Timmo wasn't looking at me. "Dad only believes what he already thinks."

Fidius turned back into himself. "To answer your question, Turpina, I will have slugs in truffle sauce."

"Crickets with thistle seeds," Durindana said dreamily.

"We have chicken and frozen corn," I said.

While a silent Timmo helped me crumble chicken onto two tiny plates, Fidius gave Durindana a brief lecture on The Brilliance of the Gigantes. I remembered how much he used to love appliances, especially the DVD player.

"This thing we're sitting on," he said to her rapt attention, "is called a toadster. The Gigantes mash grains into a large mound, bake it and slice it, and the toadster cooks it brown and crusty. This is Gigantes magic, Electricity, applied with Know-How and Can-Do Spirit." He rapped on the toaster with his knuckles. "See? As real as rock, except now that the Parvi Pennati have covered it with freakin' gold filigree."

"This object was very ugly before the Lady Noctua worked her magic," Durindana said.

"But it makes real food," Fidius said. "With a satisfying crunch."

I handed him and Durindana each a plate of crumbled

chicken with mashed corn and mashed grains, otherwise known as bread. The Parvi extracted golden utensils from the pouches hanging at their sides and settled down on the tabletop. Durindana held her tiny golden fork with her pinky up and dropped most of her chicken into her lap.

I took the ring back so I could talk to Grand-père. The kitchen unfoofed itself and the two Parvi went raggedy. Durindana had on a long tunic of filthy burlap. It was odd to see them simply keep eating, unconcerned about their change in appearance.

"Want to try some dinner?" I asked Grand-père.

"I wouldn't touch that offal you're serving."

"You're welcome," I said.

The chicken was a disappointment. It tasted dry and . . . I dunno, unflylike. And I couldn't chew it—I had to take bits that were small enough to swallow whole. *But this is an illusion—why can't I eat? I'm still human underneath, right?*

Timmo put his fork down. "Can I wear the ring again? The drooling puts me off."

I started a new tally: (1) We were infested with Parvi, plus rampant gold filigree; (2) I was a frog; (3) My parents probably were contemplating suicide; (4) My grandfather was a clock; (5) Chief Wright thought my dad had murdered my grandfather, and I couldn't prove otherwise. (See item 4.)

And, at the center of it all, (6) Gigi Kramer, the fiberglass real estate lady/plumbing inspector. Who might really be Lady Noctua, but I didn't feel like bringing that up with the two Parvi there. It would be like bad-mouthing Santa Claus.

Something had to be done about it all, though.

"Right," I said. Timmo looked up, chewing. "We have three choices: One, give the moonstone back to the Parvi; two, give it to Gigi Kramer; or three, keep it. If we give the ring to the Parvi they get their senses back and they fix up the inn, but Gigi Kramer keeps doing bad things to us. If we give it to Gigi Kramer, the Parvi keep losing their senses and probably die, but maybe she'll turn Grand-père and me back into ourselves."

"But maybe she won't," Timmo said.

"True. If we keep it, the Parvi keep decaying, my parents spend my college fund fixing up the inn, and Grand-père stays a clock and your dad arrests my dad for murdering him. Oh, and I keep eating flies. Which taste like sausage, by the way."

"If you give us the Gemma back and we stop the Circulus," Durindana said, "the bad Parva in the walking doll will lose the Magica Artificia along with the rest of us. And then the Turpini once again will look like Turpini."

Sounded good to me. "Okay, so we have to give it back. But we can't give it back until the full moon, right? Which is . . ."—I jumped up and found the tide chart, beautifully done up in parchment and gold leaf—". . . which is tomorrow night. Phew—that's not so bad. In the meantime, though, how do we keep Gigi Kramer from attacking us right and left?"

"She can't do anything real to you," Timmo said. "She didn't turn you into an *actual* frog."

"Yeah, but what if she makes some illusion that drives us nuts, forces us to do things? Jump off the roof or something?"

Bong, bong, bong, bong, bong. "Translation?" I said.

"He says, don't forget Magica Mala. That mannequin, Gigi, shouldn't be able to move, and you shouldn't be eating flies. There's more going on here than Magica Artificia alone."

"I wondered why he didn't have to pee for two months."

Bong, bong, bong, bong.

"And," Timmo translated, "whoever's driving the mannequin must be a powerful *maga*, because she visited here before the Parvi were downstairs. That means she was tapping the power of the Circulus at full strength from a distance."

I thought about what a mess Durindana had been in the same circumstances. "How do we protect ourselves from somebody who can do that?"

Bong, bong, bong.

Timmo hesitated. I raised my eyebrows at him. "Okay," he said, "but remember I'm not the one saying this. Mr. Turpin says even an amphibian should be able to extrapolate. 'Extrapolate' means using what you know to figure out what you don't know."

"I know what it means."

"Okay, so what do we know?"

I pondered the two Parvi, who had finished eating and were grooming their wings. "Well, we know Magica Artificia and Magica Mala create illusion, and the moonstone lets you see through that illusion. And if more than one person wants to see through it, they drink the moonstone elixir."

"But then they get weirded out like your parents," Timmo said.

"Yeah. I guess if we want to protect more than one human from Gigi Kramer, we have to do what the elixir does except without the elixir."

Bong, bong, bong. "He says you're not as dumb as you look," Timmo said.

First nice thing Grand-père ever said to me. Too bad he was made of wood at the time and I didn't hear the words. I did hear the tone—those bongs sounded like Grand-père: raspy, brusque, ill-tempered. You could turn Grand-père into a succession of inanimate objects and he'd be the same cantankerous old man.

I looked at the clock, thinking about what a grump Grand-père always was, and for a second I thought the clock face had eyes. I blinked, looked again. Nope. Just a clock sitting on a chair.

Bong, bong, bong. "Impossible to be as dumb as you look right now," Timmo translated.

Hard to believe a clock's chime could sound so snide.

Just like Grand-père. I contemplated the clock face, thought about the nasty notes he'd left us, whiskey bottles smashing on the sidewalk, the way Dad always said, "Ogier, sheesh."

And it happened again, that fleeting glimpse of a human face behind the clock hands.

"Timmo," I said. "Take the ring off a second. I've got an idea."

Chapter Sixteen

Grumpheads

TIMMO TOOK OFF THE RING, GRIMACING AS I turned back into Mellie the Frog.

"Listen," I said. "Is there anything about me that hasn't changed? That reminds you of what I'm really like?"

He frowned. "Well, your voice, I guess. And what you say, what a grumphead you are sometimes—it's definitely you in there somewhere."

Exactly what I'd thought about Grand-père, which was unsettling, but I couldn't let it distract me. "So keep looking at me and—"

"Do I have to? You're drooling again."

"You know, nobody asked you to butt into all this. If you don't want to help, go home and let us solve our problems without the nosy neighbors, thank you very much. First you weasel your way in here, then you—"

"Hey!" Timmo said. "You were yourself for a second. You kind of flickered."

The hair went up on my arms. My real arms, I mean—my waxy green ones didn't have hair. Anyway, I was excited. "Try to concentrate on who I am. I'm going to talk about Degas."

It's not often I have such an attentive audience when

discussing nineteenth-century French art. I talked about how Degas started losing his eyesight in his fifties and still kept working and working. And he painted a woman in a bath and sad people in bars and ballerinas and ballerinas and ballerinas, which he also made sculptures of when he was half-blind.

Fidius lay down on the table with his hat over his face.

I analyzed Degas' technique, what I'd read about it and heard my parents say. I'd never gotten to talk about this stuff before. Usually people would have walked away by now.

Timmo's eyes drooped and his chin hit his chest.

"Hey!" I said, whacking him on the arm. "I'm not talking for my health."

Timmo's head jerked up. "Could've fooled me . . . hey! You're you! Nope, nope, you're the frog again."

I hit him again. "Concentrate, dang it!"

"Are you allowed to say that?" (I hadn't actually said "dang it.")

"Who cares, you moron?"

"There you are again . . . Nope, you're gone . . . Yup, there you are again . . . Nope, you're—"

I couldn't think of what else to do, so I pinched his arm.

"Ow. Okay, that does work for a second."

"Try pinching yourself."

He did it. "Yup, it works, but not for very long."

"So think about what I'm really like. Stop your pea brain from flitting around."

He screwed his face up like a prune. "That works. But I can't spend the entire day thinking about what a dork you are."

"So I have to be nasty to you all day because you can't concentrate?"

"Be yourself, I guess."

Durindana stood up, fussing with her layers of skirt. "I see you, warm dolt."

"You see me? The real me?"

"Yes. You are grumpy but you feed me and you are respectful to me in front of Fidius."

Fidius stirred at the sound of his name and snorted in his sleep. Durindana tiptoed over and tenderly settled his hat back over his face.

"Look up at Mellie now," Timmo said. "Do you still see her?"

"Yes," Durindana said. "There she is tired and *irata* . . . how you say this . . . irritated? Angry?"

"That sounds right," Timmo said. "But I'm back to the drooling frog. I only see her when she's talking like a jerk."

"Are you not able to smell her?"

Okay, this could get insulting. "I thought you people couldn't smell things," I said.

"I smell very strong smells," Durindana said. "For the same reason that I fall from flight—I resist the Magica Artificia." She leaned forward with an air of imparting important information. "When we met, you and your *parentes* had a strong, sharp smell. I smelled it again when we hid in that smaller room"—she pointed to the broom closet—"and after that I have been able to see you."

What had a strong, sharp . . . ah. "Bleach," I said. "You smelled bleach."

"What is this bleach?"

I rummaged around in the broom closet. The bleach bottle was bone-colored damask with a gold-plated cap, but it still had its distinctive shape. I took off the cap.

"Is that it?" I held the cap out to Durindana.

She sniffed delicately and gave a little squeal. "Ooooo, yes. Bad smell. This is the one."

I turned to Timmo. "So what do I smell like to you?"

He looked appalled. "I don't go around smelling people. You don't smell like anything."

I slammed the bleach bottle down on the table. Some of the contents slopped out.

Timmo blinked. "Whoa. There you are."

I frowned. "Why would bleach work for you too? Something about bleach itself, or—"

Timmo held the cap under his nose. His face lit up. "The pool! Bleach smells like chlorine in a pool."

"So?"

"So we were standing by the pool one time when you were seriously obnoxious to me. So this smell reminds me of that, and I guess somewhere in my head that's the real you."

"The real me is obnoxious?"

"Well, yeah. What did you think?"

"So why are you hanging around, then, if I'm so terrible?" *Like I had to ask.*

"Duh. You've got fairies."

"Small Persons with Wings," Durindana and I said in unison. *Yup. He's here for the Parvi.*

Timmo sniffed the bleach, recoiled. "Gah. That smarts. Okay, I can see you. Now what?"

Bong, bong, bong.

"Oh, yeah," I said. "I know just what to do about you."

I hustled out to the breakfast room, ripped the tape off the box, grabbed a nip bottle of Scotch. I didn't bother taping the box up again. Back in the kitchen, I fixed my eyes on the grandfather clock, opened the bottle, took a deep sniff, and gagged. *Grand-père's breath when Mom made me hug him. Bottles smashing on the sidewalk, leaking stale whiskey, while I huddled in the car.*

The clock was still there. Why wasn't this working?

Think, warm dolt. My mind kept shying away, seeing the clock because that seemed like reality. I'd spent five years of my life making sure I only saw what was in front of me. Now I *needed* my imagination to see what was real.

Aw, poor Fairy Fat.

Stop that! Concentrate!

I sniffed the bottle again. *Grand-père's breath. Broken bottles. C'mon brain—work! Imagine what's real!* I sniffed again. And there he was, a scrawny old man. I shuddered, and there he wasn't—he was the clock again.

I took a deep sniff, almost puked. *Broken glass. Smelly sidewalk. Breath. Ew, do I have to hug him, Mom?*

Concentrate. Imagine what's real.

And he was back. "Give me that whiskey," he said.

"Nope." I sniffed again, held on to the memories.

"You're a little girl . . . well, a little amphibian. Too young for that stuff."

"I'm not drinking it. I'm using it to remind me of my male progenitor's male progenitor. Besides, if being a clock makes you stop eating, it'll make you stop drinking this stuff too."

"Nothing will do that." Grand-père licked his lips, staring at the bottle. I tipped it on my finger so Durindana could sniff it and see Grand-père too. To my surprise, she wrinkled her nose. "Nectar is better," she said. "Especially when hot."

Fidius sat up. His hat fell off. "You are drooling," he said to me.

"You must smell her," Durindana said.

"Inepta. I can't."

"Don't call her that," I said automatically. Durindana got her mask-of-tragedy look on and flitted up to sit on the toaster.

I wished Fidius could see the real me, but I was doing pretty well for the first day of a curse. The tally of people who could see me was up to four, including my parents, five if Grand-père wore the moonstone ring.

Timmo dripped bleach on a paper towel, wadded it up, and stuck it in the pocket of his T-shirt, within sniffing distance. "Now what?"

"I guess we have to tell Rinaldo we're giving back the moonstone. But what if Gigi finds out? Who knows what she'll do then?"

Bong, bong, bong, bong.

"Hang on." I got out my nip bottle so I could sniff it. Timmo put the moonstone ring back on so he could see Grand-père too. "Say that again, Grand-père."

Grumpy eyes appeared behind the clock face. The clock mutated into his bony old shape. "I said, what can she do to us now? We know how to see through her illusions."

"Yeah," I said. "But only if we carry the right smells around with us. If she springs something on us, what then?"

"You can handle it," Timmo said. "You've got guts."

I didn't feel like I had guts. Not when I thought about facing that mannequin again, especially without my mom. Plus . . . "What about Dad?" I said.

Grand-père half closed his eyes like an old lizard. "What about him?"

"Well, maybe he doesn't want to give back the moonstone. He was talking about wearing it so he'd know if people were telling the truth, bankers and things."

"This is not his decision," Grand-père snapped. "The head of the family has decided."

"The head of the family is a clock."

"With a frog for a granddaughter."

"That's all it takes?" Timmo asked. "One person decides for the whole family?"

"Of course," Grand-père said.

"No," Fidius and Durindana said in unison.

"The head of the Turpini returns the Gemma," Fidius added. "But he must do so in the presence of all his living descendants. At midnight of the full moon."

"Nobody said a word to me about this having to be a mob scene," Grand-père said.

Fidius put his hands over his ears to muffle the bonging of the clock. "He says nobody told him that before," I translated.

"So," Timmo said, "you and your family turn up in the pub at midnight. No big deal."

"Not if Dad doesn't agree to be there."

"He will," Grand-père said grimly. "He'll be himself again when the full moon rises, and we don't give the moonstone back until midnight. Believe me, after living with the elixir for a day or two he won't want any part of the Gemmaluna."

"*You* kept it all these years," I said.

"Yes, but I rarely used it. I'm scared of the thing. The elixir killed my father and it nearly killed me. And even now"—he swallowed hard—"I cannot forget what I learned about myself."

I was dying to ask what he'd learned, but I was pretty sure he wouldn't tell me.

"So what happens in this ceremony, anyway?" Timmo asked.

"Nobody's ever seen it," I said.

"This is true, Turpina," Durindana said, "but all Parvi know the ritual. This is important magic, and the knowledge is passed from every parent to every child."

"As I understand it," Grand-père said, "the timing is tricky: The moonstone has to drop into a bowl of water to make the elixir precisely at midnight, at which point the Parvi lose all their powers, even the power of flight. All the illusions vanish completely. They're without any magic at all until they drink the elixir and get their original powers back."

Hands over his ears, Fidius had been contemplating the ceiling the way you do when you memorize lines for the school play. Now he lowered his hands, unfurled the glory of his wings, and began to recite:

"At the twenty-third hour on the night of the full moon, then shall gather the Parvi Pennati, Circulus and all. Not one may be absent or the spell fails. The Turpini shall enter in all the panoply of their state, the head of their house bearing the Gemmaluna on a bed of purple and leading those who are his seed, not one of whom may be absent. The gubernator of the Parvi Pennati shall ask the Turpini: 'Will you part with the gem of insight, legacy of the Archbishop thy progenitor, dispelling the Obligatio Turpinorum for all time?'"

Fidius paused for breath and Durindana took over,

eyes closed, wings wide. "Each one answering 'yea,' the gubernator shall ask of his people, 'Parvi Pennati, descendants of the Larger Gods, will you take back the gem of insight, recapturing the powers of old?' And if the Parvi Pennati answer 'yea' with no dissenting voice, the Gemmaluna is theirs. The gubernator shall create the elixir at the twenty-fourth hour, and the people shall drink."

Fidius spoke again. "And the Parvi Pennati shall drink the elixir each full moon thereafter, replenishing their powers. And they shall be humble before the universe, making their way by native wit and power, until the earth does swallow them up and the world does end."

I thought about Grand-père leading us into the pub in all our panoply. I wasn't sure what "panoply" was, but it sounded like I might have to wear a dress.

"What's 'panoply'?" Timmo asked.

"A costume of gold," Durindana said. "With emeralds and much lace."

"Silk stockings of a whiteness to dazzle the eye," Fidius said.

"Bunch of folderol," Grand-père said. "Fancy duds, the moonstone on a purple cushion."

"Turpini, all foofed up," Durindana said.

Yup. A dress.

Chapter Seventeen

Circulus, Circulus, Who's Got the Circulus?

"FULL MOON IN TWENTY-FOUR HOURS, seventeen minutes," Timmo said, handing back the ring at the street door an hour later.

I slipped it on my finger, trying to think of a way to ask him . . . something. I didn't know what, only that it would come out dweebish. "I wish I could talk to my parents," I said instead. "What if Gigi finds out we're giving this thing back, and fools them into hurting themselves?"

"How can she fool them when they've drunk the elixir?"

"Okay, maybe she'll fool me. They wouldn't like that either. And when do I tell the Parvi we're giving it back? Gigi will know right away." *Especially if she's Noctua.*

This was impossible. How was I supposed to get through the next twenty-four hours and seventeen minutes without my parents? What if they jumped off something in the meantime?

I'd never felt so alone in my life.

"I'll come back in the morning," Timmo said, "and . . . I dunno, help."

To my surprise, this was good news. I rubbed the moonstone with my thumb for luck, and asked, "Why do you care what happens to me? Us, I mean."

He shrugged. "You need help. And you've got fairies. And I've got nothing better to do."

I chilled, but just slightly. Something wasn't quite the truth. I didn't need help? I didn't have fairies? He actually did have something better to do?

This truth-detecting thing probably worked better with yes or no questions.

Grand-père was alone when I returned to the kitchen, ring still on my finger. "I want to be in my bed," he said.

"Too bad. Your bed was full of mold and is now in a trash bag."

"You're a young frog. You can sleep on the floor and give me your bed."

"You're a clock. Good night." I went upstairs and dragged my mattress into the hall. I'd spend the night by my parents' door, just in case.

When I looked in at them they were sleeping like babies. I felt a rush of love, mixed with longing for the way they used to be. And a healthy dose of terror, which I firmly tamped down. I couldn't afford terror. Terror was for kids whose parents were around to make it fun.

Before I went to bed, I rooted around in my costume box and found the elbow-length black gloves I'd worn last Halloween as a vampire. I put them on. If I didn't see my green hands in the morning and avoided mirrors, maybe I'd forget what I looked like.

Something drew my eye to the moonlight outside my open window. I turned off my lamp. Black gloves on, so

tired I was almost relaxed, I settled on the window seat to breathe.

And caught my breath.

Durindana was lovely, graceful, silver light shimmering on her wings as she swooped and twirled outside my window. Fidius was with her, in his shirtsleeves, but his movements were stiffer than hers, as if he were still buttoned up in his velvet jacket.

Durindana had conjured herself a simple dress that allowed her to move her arms as her fancy clothes never could. She was riding the breeze as if it were waves at the beach, tumbling, wafting, gliding. Her dress rippled, her loose hair afloat, her face glowing with moonlight and pleasure, no more the pinched, pale Parva but a creature of the silvery air. Fidius was laughing, although his face, as usual, was impassive.

It was almost a dance between them, but hers was nothing like the stiff, formal dances of the Domus. He was the axis around which she swirled and swooped like ribbon on a breeze. Watching her cheered me up. *This is the way they're supposed to be, without all the fancy stuff.*

Durindana's eyes were closed, so she didn't see when something below caught Fidius's attention. He halted in midair, darted to where he could see the front of the inn. His velvet vest and coat reappeared.

Durindana opened her eyes and bobbed in the air, watching him. He bowed to her, plumed hat in hand. She curtsied, watched him fly toward the sidewalk. Then she flitted off to a tree out back, disappearing among its leaves. I couldn't see her face. I wondered if she was sad.

I ran to a front window and peered down at the pub door. The door was in shadow, but here and there I saw a flicker that could have been wings, catching the moonglow. What was going on? I was too tired to find out. *I'll ask Fidius tomorrow*, I thought.

In bed outside my parents' door, I didn't think I'd sleep. But it had been another busy day—chatting with a mannequin, getting turned into a frog, watching my parents go nuts, meeting my grandfather the clock. Anyone would sack out.

My parents stepped over me in the morning. I followed them down to the kitchen, where they put bowls on the table, sat down, and stared into them as if oat flakes would sprout all by themselves.

"Hang on." I ran upstairs to get dressed. They were still staring into their empty bowls when I got back, so I poured cereal and milk and handed each of them a spoon.

"Eat," I said. Obediently, they each took a spoonful or two.

"Mmmm," I said. "Good, huh?"

"Yeah." Dad put his spoon down. "Good."

Mom burst into tears and ran from the room. Her footsteps pounded up the stairs. Dad sighed and got up to follow her.

"Where are you going?" I asked.

"Back to bed."

"Dad, you only have to make it through today. Then the full moon comes and the elixir wears off and you'll feel better."

"It wears off? Won't we see you as a frog again?"

"I hope not. We're working on that."

"Okay," he said vaguely and left the room. I followed him to make sure, and he did climb in next to Mom. She had her pillow over her head.

"Mom, Dad," I said, standing at the foot of the bed, "Grand-père wants to give the moonstone back tonight. Is that okay with you? Gigi will get mad when she hears the plan, and I . . . I think she'll hear right away." *Because she's Noctua.*

"Why are you asking us?" Mom's voice was muffled. "If he wants to do it he'll do it."

"We all have to be there and we all have to say yea."

"Yay." Dad pulled the blankets up over his face.

"Look," I said. "I can't get through this all by myself. You have to rally. You have to help me. You can't just lie there."

They just lay there.

"Fine." I sat down on the end of the bed and burst into tears. Not just tears . . . I was wailing, I was hysterical. This was coming from my gut. It was like popping a zit.

Nice one, Mellie. Way to make your parents feel better. The thought made me cry harder.

When I'd calmed down to the sobbing and gasping phase, my parents were sitting up and watching me. My mom opened her arms. I flung myself at her and she rocked me, crooning. Dad patted me on the shoulder. "Worthless," he said. "We're worthless."

"Will you please stop saying that?" I bellowed into my mother's shoulder.

"I'm sorry," Dad said. I could barely hear him.

I sat up. "Mom, Dad, I know you don't believe me, but I do respect you. I like what you tell me—about growing into my grandeur and all that. You're fun to be with and I really, really listen to what you say. And I think your paintings are awesome. Really. Awesome."

"You're lying to make us feel better." Mom said. "I can tell."

I was desperate. "Doesn't that at least mean I love you?"

They looked at each other. "Okay, now she's telling the truth," Mom said.

"I know you're all depressed and everything right now. But you're going to be fine after tonight." My throat closed up. Grand-père said he never forgot what the elixir showed him.

My parents would be different. They didn't have awful memories like Grand-père, they were nicer people. So they wouldn't be tortured for so long. Right?

Mom peered at me. "You have cheekbones."

"Everybody has cheekbones, Mom."

"I mean, your face is . . . different, it's longer, more angles. You're not my baby anymore." She stroked my cheek. "I don't know why I didn't notice until now."

Circulus, Circulus, Who's Got the Circulus?

I touched my face. It felt green and waxy. "Mom, we have to focus. You guys can stay in bed all day—just tell me this one thing about the moonstone. Is it okay to give it back? That's all I want to know."

"We should give it back," Dad said.

"Absolutely," Mom said.

"Wh-what?" I'd been expecting a discussion, even an argument. A few dang-its.

"Mellie, look at us," Mom said. "You're a human frog . . . an extremely intelligent frog, but a frog never-theless. We're basket cases. Your grandfather is a clock. This stuff will keep happening until we give the wretched thing away to somebody, and my choice would be the Parvi rather than that harpy with the stiletto heels. And she can't do anything real to us."

"But . . . what about seeing through lies and stuff? And isn't the moonstone our legacy? Grand-père said it makes us special."

"We aren't special," Dad said. "In fact, we're a waste of space."

"Not you, sweetie," Mom said, her voice catching. "Us. I mean, what kind of mother lets her daughter turn into a frog and then goes to bed?" She flung herself down and pulled the pillow over her face.

"I guess we're done here," I said.

I was sitting in the kitchen feeling sorry for myself when a pair of footsteps started up the stairs. *Oh sheesh. I never locked that door down there.*

I couldn't move. All I could do was stare through the reception lounge to the top of the stairs, waiting to see a green-gloved hand on the railing, a bright blond head of hair.

Light brown hair. Freckles. And, seconds later, galaxy-gray eyes. *Never thought I'd be so glad to see someone from The Skinny Planet.*

Timmo sniffed his shirt pocket. "What's the matter with you? You're all freaked out."

"Nothing," I said. "Just . . . everything." I handed him the ring so he wouldn't have to sniff bleach all day. With my gloves on, and therefore no green hands, the world was almost normal. "Dad says it's okay to give the moonstone back, and they'll come to the ceremony."

"Can I come too?"

He's earned it, I guess. "I'll ask."

"Cool," he said, but then such a caterwauling arose from the cellar that neither of us could get in another word. The sound rose and fell in waves as we ran down the stairs to the sidewalk and tumbled through the pub door.

The place was writhing with little overdressed bodies, wings flapping, arms and legs beating the floor. Overdressed, but messed up: clothes ripped, wings bent, arms in slings.

Rinaldo flitted around wringing his hands. "What happened?" I called to him.

He hovered before my nose, wringing and wringing and wringing. "The Turpini must find a bigger home. There is not enough space here for the beautifully dressed Parvi Pennati." A jeweled button fell off his coat.

"Why not?" Timmo asked.

"We are too crowded." Wring, wring, wring. "We had a big, big fight last night and most of the Circulus left in anger, which they have done before but now they have not returned and our lovelinesses are fading." Two more buttons fell off. His black velvet hair-tie disintegrated— powdered hair flopped all over his shoulders.

Sure enough, where the Circulus had been, six or seven sorry-looking Parvi circled grimly as bits of their attire disintegrated.

"Where did they go?" I asked Rinaldo.

"We do not know. And these sad remaining few cannot do what must be done for the health and beauty of the Parvi Pennati. The Turpini must find a bigger home so we are not fighting."

"Forget that," I said. "It's time to ditch the Circulus and take back the Gemmaluna."

Rinaldo ceased the wringing activity and bobbed up and down in front of my nose. If he'd been bigger he would have been staring into my eyes, but since he could only handle one at a time he took turns, peering first into one, then the other. "You are meaning this? The Turpini will return our Gemma?" The plume on his hat curled up into a brown lump.

My stomach clenched. This was coming out much sooner than I wanted.

"A-i-i-i yi!" Lady Noctua whirred up to Rinaldo and slapped him so hard he flipped over backward, losing his hat. "You will end the Circulus? And what of me, your consort, who is so supremely skilled in the Magica Artificia? What of me, with no Circulus to be heeding my will?"

"*Ma chère*," Rinaldo said, "the time of beauty has passed. We must face this together, you and I and our Parvi Pennati. Perhaps we may find other beauties, through hard work and our original Magica Vera."

"*Tiens*! You betray me, Rinaldo!" Noctua lunged at him, missed, and flipped over herself, white-stockinged legs kicking in a swirl of petticoats. She righted herself and, weeping, zoomed out through the mail slot.

Rinaldo followed her. "Noctua! *Reveni!*" I think that means "come back," but she didn't. After a minute or two he returned, shaking his head. "My poor Lady Noctua."

"Tonight is the full moon," I said. "We can give you back the Gemmaluna this very night." At least Noctua wasn't around to hear the specifics.

Fidius appeared out of nowhere and hovered next to Rinaldo, waving his arms. "Turpini! Never do they listen to the Parvi Pennati!" His wings were turning brown. *Uh-oh.* "Melissa Angelica Turpin, you forget what I told you last night. We cannot take back the Gemma unless all the Parvi Pennati are present and answering 'yea.' And in case you haven't noticed, our Circulus is not here to say 'yea.'"

Circulus, Circulus, Who's Got the Circulus?

"Oh. Right. I'm sorry, Fidius." I reached for him with my gloved hand, but he folded his arms on his chest and turned his back, dark wings flapping.

"You must be finding our Circulus for us and be bringing them back," Rinaldo told me.

"That's ridiculous. I wouldn't even know where to start."

Durindana joined us, wings working hard to keep her aloft. "I know where to start."

"How are you possessed of such information?" Rinaldo asked contemptuously.

"I was outside last night, enjoying of the moon," Durindana said, hanging on to my sweatshirt sleeve to maintain altitude. Fidius's head turned slightly, but he kept his back to us. "Late in the night, I saw a great many Parvi Pennati entering a large black automobile. The driver was the giant walking *pupa* of which I told you before."

Rinaldo was so surprised that he plummeted a foot or two. He shook his finger at Durindana. "Why did you not tell us this?"

"Maybe it's because you all laughed at her the last time she tried to tell you about that big doll," I said. Durindana climbed my sleeve to settle on my shoulder in companionable fashion.

"What would this giant *pupa* want with our Circulus?" Fidius asked.

"Duh," Timmo said. "She doesn't want you to get the Gemmaluna back."

"Right," I said. "I bet she took your Circulus so we couldn't have the ceremony tonight."

"Then you, Melissa Angelica, must be finding her and bringing back our poor Parvi Pennati," Rinaldo said.

"No way. I'm not going near that plastic lady. Look what she did to me the last time!"

Durindana cooed soothingly in my ear.

"I'll go with you," Timmo offered.

"Yes, yes, you will have Timothy Oliver as your squire," Rinaldo said. "And Fidius reports that you have learned to fight her Magica. You may resist her now."

"No," Fidius said. "The Turpina is only a child and as usual you are an imbecile, Rinaldo. I know what she did yesterday to resist illusions. *I* will find the Circulus and rescue them from this walking *pupa*." He raised his hand to me in farewell, and flitted out the mail slot.

"Fidius!" I yelled. "Wait! We don't even know where she is!" I ran outside, Durindana clinging desperately to my shoulder, but he had disappeared. I went back in, feeling terrible. *Sheesh. He scolds me and then he sacrifices himself.*

"Has he learned to see through the Magica Artificia?" I asked Durindana.

"I do not know."

I turned to Rinaldo. "You can't let him do this alone. I can teach you how to see through the Magica Artificia, even the Magica Mala. I can teach all of you."

"There is not enough time." Rinaldo was flatly final.

Circulus, Circulus, Who's Got the Circulus?

"As you say, Fidius cannot succeed alone. You and Timothy Oliver must go now so we have our Circulus back by the twenty-third hour." He made a dismissive gesture and fluttered away to the bar.

"I'm not doing this!" I yelled after him. "I won't go!"

"Sure you will," Timmo said. "We'll be fine."

I rounded on him. "Shut up. Just shut up. You're nuts. This could be awful and it's not your fight. I'm the Turpina here, not you."

"Geez, I was only offering to help."

"Well, stop butting in, okay?"

He was boiling red. "Okay. Know what? You can have all this. It's cool and all, but I don't need any more meanness in my life, you know? There's plenty enough of it at my house. And I'm going back there now. Have a nice life."

Great. Now *he learns to stand up for himself.*

Timmo slapped the moonstone ring into my hand and stalked out, slamming the door. At which point I was even more alone than I had been five minutes before. *Nice one, Mellie.*

Alone, that is, except for Timmo's voice, floating in through the mail slot. "My sister told me all about you, by the way.

"Fairy Fat."

Chapter Eighteen

Monster Masks

TWO DAYS BEFORE, I WOULD HAVE BEEN HORRIFIED that Fairy Fat and the Tampon Incident had followed me from Boston. Now it almost didn't matter.

This isn't fair. I'm thirteen years old. I'm not supposed to be the one saving everybody. I should be the one with my head under a pillow, not Mom and Dad.

Tough. It's up to you.

I went upstairs to figure out how to (a) find Gigi Kramer before she hurt Fidius, (b) help Fidius rescue the Circulus, (c) organize returning the moonstone without Gigi hurting us worse than she already had, and (d) regain my former youth and beauty, ha-ha-ha.

I peeked in on my parents. They were snoring. I went into my room, took off my gloves, put on the ring, and opened the closet door so I could stare at Normal Mellie in the mirror. Maybe it would make me braver. On the other hand, I hadn't seen Mellie the Frog since that first rush of horror down in the pub. *How bad can it be, really?*

I took off the ring. There was the frog face, waxy, green, my brown eyes on either side of a pair of nose holes. As I watched, the mouth opened slightly and drooled.

My stomach clenched like a fist. I shut my eyes, fumbled for the ring.

No! Who's the boss here, anyway? I shut my eyes tighter and thought about Degas and *The Glass of Absinthe,* how I loved my parents and what dorks they could be, the times when I'd played "naked Venus" in front of the mirror back in Boston. How I won Best of Show at Science Fair.

My imagination tried to slink away from me, refusing to see anything except a green face with nose holes. But I wasn't having that. I was imaginative, yet firm. *I'm the boss.*

I opened my eyes and there was the real me: Melissa Angelica Toogh-peh, descendant of a paladin of Charlemagne. Time to stiffen the spine. Who was that female warrior Lady Noctua talked about? Bradamante. Time to be Bradamante.

I looked closer. I *did* have cheekbones.

Durindana wobbled in, her purple gown frayed around the hem. She tumbled onto my bed.

"Durindana, I'm going to help Fidius get the Circulus back. You have to keep an eye on my parents and make sure they don't jump off a bridge."

"That old man can watch the Turpini." One of her hairdo feathers disintegrated. "I am going with Melissa Angelica Turpin."

"No! Can't you do what I say this once? Somebody has to watch out for my parents."

She struggled into the air, bobbed in front of my nose. "Somebody must be watching out for Melissa Angelica Turpin. She and Fidius must not face danger without a friend." She patted the end of my nose, quick enough not to freeze me, and plummeted back onto the bed.

A friend.

My eyes fogged. Hey, I was tired. I blinked them clear. "I'll be fine. I'll have the Gemmaluna on. You would be in more danger than I will be."

"You are forgetting, Melissa Angelica Turpin. Sometimes I too see through the works of this *pupa magna*. Right now I am seeing you as Turpina, not as . . . how you say this . . . frog-face."

"That's great. But—"

"Fidius and Melissa Angelica Turpin will not battle this bad Parva all alone. If you do not take me with you, I will follow you. This is my final word."

I couldn't imagine how she'd help, but somehow I did feel braver. "*Merci*, Durindana." I wished I knew how to say it in Latin.

She curtsied. "*Ça ne fait rien*, Melissa Angelica Turpin. It is nothing." A cluster of silk flowers vanished from her gown.

"Now," I said. "Where do you suppose this Gigi Kramer creature is living?"

"I do not know."

"Is there some way you can tell where the Circulus is? Sense it, somehow?"

"I do not know."

"Could Rinaldo tell us?"

"I do not know."

I sighed and put on the moonstone ring. "Well, maybe Grand-père can help us out."

He'd made it upstairs to a guest bed, where he was flat on his back. I shook him.

"What now?" He didn't open his eyes.

"Get up. You have to watch Mom and Dad and make sure they don't jump off a bridge. Gigi Kramer's kidnapped the Circulus, so Durindana and I are going to get it back."

"Oh yeah? Where you going to find Gigi Kramer?"

My heart sank. "I was hoping you'd know."

"The youth of today, always expecting their elders to know things."

"You're the grown-up—why *don't* you know?"

"Top of Great Misery Hill, overlooking the ocean." Timmo walked in like a friend of the family. "Everybody's talking about it, Mom said. This nasty old mansion suddenly looks like Versailles. That was the palace of the French kings from 1682 to 1789."

"I knew that." I stood there, thinking I should say something else, but with no idea what that would be.

The silence got awkward.

"The youth of today," Grand-père said, "have no conversational skills."

"I came back," Timmo said.

"Yeah," I said.

"I'm coming with you. I don't care how rude you are."

"Durindana's coming too."

"Apology accepted."

I almost said "What apology?" but then I didn't. I wanted to ask something else, a yes or no question, but I couldn't make myself do it.

"I won't tell anybody," Timmo said. "About that stuff in Boston."

He was telling the truth. But . . . "Eileen will," I said.

"I'll shut her up." He frowned. "Somehow."

"What stuff in Boston?" Grand-père demanded.

I ignored him. "I guess you know where this place is," I said to Timmo.

"Yup. Used to be a really cool haunted house. When are we going?"

I was tempted to say, "Tomorrow, when I have parents." But we couldn't put it off—the full moon wouldn't wait. "Right now. Soon as this old man gets up and starts assuming some responsibility around here."

"Are you planning to walk through town like that?" Timmo asked.

"Like what?" I looked down at myself. Jeans. Sneakers. Sweatshirt. Moonstone ring on finger.

"I think the boy means, like a giant drooling amphibian," Grand-père said.

Oh. That.

"It'll be like the movies," Timmo said. "Panic in the streets. With drool."

I handed him the moonstone, took a whiff of Scotch. The three of us discussed putting me in a wheelbarrow with a tarp over me, so Timmo could wheel me through town. We thought about me wearing my Ugly Monster mask and fake hands. I have to admit, it was Grand-père who thought of the best plan: that *Timmo* would wear the mask and the gnarled monster hands that went with it.

We'd pretend we were a pair of goofy kids who couldn't wait for Halloween. Instead of a pair of goofy kids who had Halloween happening all the time.

We moved Grand-père downstairs to my mattress outside my parents' room. "Don't leave and don't fall asleep," I said.

"The youth of today—"

"Stuff it, old man."

The Halloween plan had its first test as we headed up Oak Street, Timmo under the monster mask, Durindana hiding in the pocket of his jean jacket with the moonstone ring. A lady came out of the community center and laughed at us. "What's the occasion, kids?"

"Only a hundred twenty-six shopping days until Halloween," Timmo said, muffled under his mask. I nodded vigorously. I had to avoid talking so no one would notice that my jaw really moved.

The lady looked at me and gave a big fake shudder. "Ew.

That's the ugliest face I've ever seen. Where on earth did you get that?"

I shrugged. "A friend gave it to her," Timmo said. "She doesn't know where it came from."

"And who's that under there?" The lady reached for Timmo's mask. "Is that Timmo?"

"Nope." Timmo backed away from her. "This is my real face."

The lady laughed like a grown-up. "Okay, okay. Have fun, kids." She headed for a red Saab parked at the curb.

As we scuttled up the street, Timmo started playing around, waving at cars and walking with an Igor limp. I tried to look like I was having a good time. "Lighten up," Timmo muttered. "Act like a kid for a change." So I waved at an electric company guy, and he waved back, grinning. I growled at a little kid until he squealed and ran away. I waddled like I had a wet diaper, and a car tooted its horn at us. I danced around like an ape for the next one, and it honked too.

I forgot that my parents were in bed with pillows over their faces. I ignored the fact that I was round with no friends. I pretended Timmo was my friend, to see what it felt like. *So sue me.*

"We're like the Ghost Head Nebula," Timmo said. "It looks like a ghost, with eyes and everything, but it's really gas and space-dust."

I told him about the Degas family wanting to be

called de Gas. He blew a fart noise under his mask and cracked up.

A parade of little kids started following us. "This could be a problem," I whispered. Timmo nodded. We started to run. The kids hooted and ran after us. A couple of bigger kids yelled, "Hey, who's that? Catch 'em!" We pelted around a corner and through a hedge and under somebody's porch, and they gave up. My heart was pounding. I loved it.

We followed Hale Street toward the sea. The neat houses with neat yards gave way to bigger houses with fields and woods around them. Tall fences and hedges and crumbly walls protected them from street noise, which right now consisted of running footsteps and a Parvavoice griping about what Timmo's pocket was doing to her hairdo.

Finally we came to a potholed dirt driveway flanked by chipped concrete lions. "Here we are," Timmo said.

I thought the lions' eyes followed us as we passed. "Get hold of yourself," I muttered.

We followed the driveway steeply uphill into the woods. It twisted a lot but tended toward the ocean, which we could hear pounding against a cliff as we neared the top.

"What's this place like?" I asked Timmo.

"Big. Rotting."

We came out of the woods onto a cliff top with a 180-degree view of the water. Timmo led me around one more sharp curve and went *unh*, as if he'd been punched in the stomach.

"Oooo." Durindana peeked out of his pocket under a mass of disheveled hair. "Pretty, pretty *domus*."

This was anything but a haunted house. It did, in fact, look like a mini-Versailles, all granite and marble and tall windows and ornate columns. It was a false front, though—a few yards down the side, the house turned back into a grungy old mansion.

"Guess she's only got enough power to change the front," I said. That was encouraging.

A path of polished pink granite led to a pair of double doors three times my height. We stood in front of them getting our courage up.

"Maybe they're locked." Timmo shucked his monster duds. I could tell he was hoping the doors wouldn't open. So was I.

"Warm dolts," Durindana observed. "Standing here will not make a rescue."

The doors weren't locked. They opened smoothly but with a rusty creak. "Guess she hasn't fixed the sound effects," Timmo said.

"Fidius?" I called softly, poking my head through the door. The front hall had new brocaded wallpaper, but the ceiling was a mass of chipped plaster. It was Parvi-frigid, and yet I could swear I heard a furnace humming—very faintly, very far away.

It wasn't a furnace. "The Circulus!" Durindana cried.

She wriggled out of Timmo's pocket and torpedoed straight ahead, down a hallway, through a door at the end . . . gone.

"Durindana! You can't barge in there!" I hustled after her, Timmo at my heels.

To my relief, she was waiting for us down a half-fancified hallway, bobbing up and down with impatient wing beats. "You must tear down this wall, Turpina."

"Sure. I'll get the sledgehammer out of my pocket."

"Hold on." Timmo put on the moonstone ring. "There's a door here. There's a keyhole but no doorknob or anything."

I peered at the foofed-up version. A neat crack ran from the floor through the molding and wallpaper to a point about a foot above my head, where it took a sharp left. "Can you pick the lock?"

"No. But maybe the key's around someplace," Timmo said. "You won't be able to see it, but maybe I can, with the ring on and all." He turned around in a slow circle, eyes darting.

"That's ridiculous," I said. "You don't lock a door and leave the key hanging around next to it. You put it in your pocket or stick it in a drawer or something. It could be anywhere."

"So what's your suggestion?" Timmo said. "Got that sledgehammer?" He wandered off down the hallway, searching floor, windowsills, molding.

Durindana fluttered up to a chandelier over our heads

and settled on a gold-encrusted prong. "What would this key smell like?" she asked.

"I dunno—metal. Keys don't really smell like much." I looked up at her. Her eyes were closed. "Hey, don't fall asleep up there. You'll fall off."

"I am concentrating, Turpina."

"Well, I guess I'm wrong," Timmo said, coming back. "I've looked everywhere."

Durindana gave a little cry. "Here! It is here!" She pointed at a hanging crystal, high in the chandelier. Timmo whooped. "She's right! There's a key hanging up there."

Durindana floated down to us with the crystal. Timmo grabbed it, stuck it into the wall, turned it, and—*snick*—a brocaded door popped open.

"Awesome, Durindana," I said.

"Hurry, Turpina," she said.

The door opened onto a narrow, cobwebby wooden staircase angling down and out of sight around a corner. The humming was louder. I eased onto the top step, which creaked like a gunshot. But it held, so I kept going and Timmo joined me, Durindana hovering fretfully over our heads.

At the bottom of the stairs, we peeked through a doorway into a large stone room. A cistern in the center had rotting wooden chutes feeding into it, probably for rainwater. At the far end of the room, a freight doorway opened onto the ocean. *We're inside the cliff*. Gigi Kramer hadn't bothered to foof this place up—it looked the way it must have a hundred years ago.

Except for the colorful circle of Small Persons speeding around and around above the cistern wall.

"*Tiens*, every lady should have her own Circulus," Gigi Kramer said from behind us, five steps up. "It is so much more convenient."

Chapter Nineteen

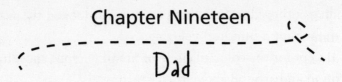

Dad

TIMMO WAS BREATHING FUNNY. I thought he was falling under Gigi Kramer's spell, but then I remembered he had on the moonstone. So he was seeing the mannequin, not Gigi the glam-queen.

"So agreeable of you to visit," Gigi Kramer said, sweeping us into the cistern room ahead of her. "Perhaps you will be staying for a while, yes?"

"No." I decided to memorize the room in case Gigi tried some kind of illusion on me. *Focus on one real thing.* The ocean sighed and slapped and splooshed outside the freight door, a constant noise, always there if you needed it—in case of trouble, I'd concentrate on that.

Durindana cried out and flung herself at a Circulus member who had dropped down to rest on the cistern. "This Small Person is not herself!" Durindana snapped her fingers in front of the lady's nose, shook her by the shoulders. "You have enchanted them with Magica Mala, you bad, bad Parva Pennata!"

Gigi smiled. "*Zut.* I shall release them when the Turpina is giving me the Gemmaluna."

"We don't have it," I said. Timmo put his hand in his pocket.

Dad

"I am surprised to hear that," Gigi said. "Because I am certain this horrified boy is seeing the doll, not the beautiful Gigantea. Therefore, he is wearing the Gemma."

"I don't have it," Timmo said. "I just think you're strange-looking."

The Circulus picked up speed, hummed louder. At my feet, a couple of stones flipped up and chains snaked out, wound around my ankles, held them fast. "Hey. Stop that."

"Stop what?" Timmo asked.

Sea noises, I told myself. *Listen to the ocean. Imagine what's real.* I closed my eyes and there it was behind the hum of the Circulus: *sigh-slap-sploosh, sigh-slap-sploosh.* I willed my foot to move, and it did. *Okay. So far so good. Remember, there aren't any chains, really.*

"You will be pleased to know that I am watching your *parentes* for you," Gigi said. "Why, observe! There is your father. What is in those little bottles?"

She got me—I opened my eyes. On the wall in front of me was a TV screen, and on the screen was my dad, sitting on the floor in the breakfast room beside the box of nip bottles. The box was open. I'd ripped the tape off the night before to get at the bottle I had in my back pocket right now.

Four or five of the little bottles were on the floor, tipped over and empty. As I watched, Dad unscrewed the one in his hand, downed it in one gulp.

"No," I whispered. "Dad, you said you wouldn't."

Ocean sounds. C'mon. Sea noises. The screen faded. I could see the stone wall through my dad's ghostly face.

But I could still see him. He opened another bottle, drained it. Then he buried his head in his hands and sobbed like a child. I'd never seen him cry. "Daddy," I said.

No! Concentrate! Ocean noises. Sigh . . . sploosh. But all I could hear was my dad, sobbing. I couldn't move my feet, couldn't take my eyes from the screen. Timmo spoke but I couldn't hear the words.

Dad wiped his eyes on his sleeve, raised his face to the ceiling, and howled like a dog. He stood up, swayed in place, then shuffled for the stairs, steadying himself with a hand on the wall. He trudged upstairs to the family quarters, then to the third floor. To the fourth floor.

He was heading for the roof.

"Dad!" I screamed. "No, no, no, no, no!"

I had to get out of there, run home before he jumped. But the chains held my feet immobile on the stone floor. I twisted myself around, writhed in place, my screams echoing in that stone-lined room. Timmo was yelling something, but I didn't care what it was. All I knew was that my dad was drunk and throwing himself off the roof, and all because I'd left that stupid box open.

I shouldn't have left them, shouldn't have left them, shouldn't have . . .

Gigi Kramer was beside me, laughing. She said something, but I couldn't hear that either. "Let me go," I begged her. "Please, please, let me go. I'll do anything. Please. Anything."

Timmo shoved past me, touched hands with Gigi Kramer. She waved and the television screen disappeared. So did the chains.

Sobbing, I stumbled for the door, but Timmo grabbed my arm. "Mellie, whatever you saw, it wasn't real. It wasn't real."

"My dad was drunk and going to the roof."

"Oh, yeah? How'd you see him? Somebody there with a camera?"

"Silly Turpina, your *père* is where you left him," Gigi said.

Which was when I noticed what she had in her hand. She held it up so the moonstone shimmered in the light streaming in from the ocean.

"The moonstone!" I made a swipe for the ring, but Gigi evaded me. "How'd she get that?"

"I gave it to her," Timmo said. "What did you expect, with you screaming like that? You said you'd do anything, so I did it for you."

I shoved him. "You had no right. That belonged to my family, not to . . . to . . ."

"Cattle?" Timmo was turning red.

I turned to Gigi Kramer. "So am I myself again now?"

She gave me a shark's stare. "I am finished with you, large child. You are what you are."

"I'm still a frog, aren't I?" I asked Timmo.

"Yeah. You are."

"So what was the point of giving her the ring, bird-brain?"

He got redder. "You were screaming, you freakin' dork. What was I supposed to do?"

I didn't get a chance to answer. Durindana, who had been following the action from Timmo's shoulder, took to the air. "Ai-yi-yi!" she shrieked, and dove into the Circulus.

It was like putting your finger in the water from a hose. Colorful figures ricocheted in fifty directions at high speed, some of them slamming into the walls, others hurtling through the doorway over the sea. Durindana fell out of the air and went *splat* on the cistern wall.

Magica Mala, it turned out, took a lot of power—especially when you'd been maintaining Versailles, entrancing fifty Circulus members, and balancing a mannequin on spike heels. And even the most skillful *maga* needed a Circulus at her beck and call.

All of a sudden, this one had no Circulus at all, not here and not across town.

Gigi took her gloves off, attempted to slide the moonstone ring on her finger, but she missed. She tried again, missed again. She stumbled on her high heels, as if the Parva inside was losing her grip on the mannequin.

Her blond hair started to look . . . I don't know . . . plastic.

Dad

And then it occurred to me: The moonstone wouldn't work for Gigi, and all I had to do was take it back. She could use it "only if given directly by us, its true owners," that's what Grand-père had said. Timmo had given the ring to her, sure . . . but he wasn't an owner, was he?

I didn't, didn't, didn't want to touch Gigi. But I hurled myself at the fist that held the moonstone, grabbed it in my two hands, tried to open the frigid fingers. *Cold, cold, cold, freezing cold, it burns! It burns!* One finger opened, then two. She staggered backward until I was close enough to ram her hand into the wall. She shrieked and the fingers opened, the ring bouncing across the floor.

I let go of Gigi and stuck my hands in my armpits— a handy frostbite-prevention tip courtesy of the Girl Scouts. Timmo retrieved the ring and presented it to me with a bow that might have been a tad sarcastic. I stuck it in my pocket and resumed the armpit maneuver.

Gigi lurched at me, but she'd lost control of her feet. Her hair was entirely plastic now, her skin shining weirdly, with faint neck cracks. She pitched past us and careened across the room, now regaining her footing, now losing it. She headed for the doorway over the ocean, but it didn't look like she wanted to. She got control and struggled backward, then lost it and stumbled forward again.

"Whoa," Timmo said, "she's going to fall through."

"Stop her," I said, but it was too late. After one final struggle to stay on her feet, Gigi gave a tinny wail and toppled out of sight, leaving behind one sequined shoe.

Timmo and I rushed to the doorway. The mannequin floated thirty feet below, a tiny figure scrambling around on her torso, too far away to identify.

"That'll keep her for a while," Timmo said.

The Circulus members were scattered around the floor, grooming their wings. They were supposedly the best of the Parvi, and yet they looked totally wiped out by their recent experiences. "Durindana," I called. "Is Fidius here?"

"I do not see him." Durindana gabbled in Latin to a little guy, who shook his head.

Durindana wobbled into the air, leaving a section of skirt to disintegrate on the stones. She too needed a Circulus. "These Parvi must leave quickly, while they can still fly," she shrilled, and aimed a stream of Latin at the wing-groomers. To my surprise, most of them obeyed orders and took to the air, streaming out the door to the stairs. Not one of them called her "Inepta."

A few, however, rose weakly into the air only to fall *splat*. "Too late for these guys," Timmo said.

"You must carry us." Durindana made a drunken beeline for Timmo's jacket pocket.

At least a dozen Parvi needed a lift. By the time we headed for the stairs, Timmo had three in each jacket pocket and two in each of the side pockets of his jeans.

Dad

The rest jostled for comfortable spots in my sweatshirt pouch.

"You look like you're pregnant with eels," Timmo said.

"Do you have to waddle like that?"

"Yeah," he said. "I do."

Upstairs, Gigi's handiwork was undoing itself fast, patches of mold staining the damask wallpaper. I looked at my hands—was it my imagination, or was the green fading?

Timmo peered into my face. "You have a nose. And you're definitely less green. If we time it right, maybe we can make it back to the pub before the Circulus starts up again. You'll look more normal and I won't have to wear that stupid mask."

"We can't leave until we look for Fidius," I said. "Who knows what she's done to him."

Timmo made a face and did a quick hula to adjust cargo. His pants pockets emitted a chorus of gripes and moans. "Do we have to? I'm not all that comfortable right now."

Durindana poked her head out of his pocket. "The Parvi Pennati will disembark while Melissa Angelica Turpin and Timothy Oliver Wright search for Monsieur Fidius."

We left the Parvi sitting on the stairs chatting morosely in French. Timmo set off to roam around the first floor. I headed upstairs, Durindana perched on my shoulder.

It was a mess up there. The last residents had left rugs and furniture behind, and in some rooms the ceilings had fallen right on top of it all. The air was sickly sweet with wet wool and rotten wood.

I creaked around calling for Fidius, feeling stupid and hopeless. Durindana kept saying, "Hist! Do you hear?" But the sound always turned out to be something or other decaying.

We were searching our third room when Durindana gave a start. "The Circulus! I feel the power of it!" Which meant the Circulus had made it back to the pub and started up again. I looked at my hands. Yup. Greener.

Durindana fluttered off my shoulder, wavered, and sank down again. But Fidius was better at tapping strength from a distant Circulus—maybe this was helping him, wherever he was.

"Fidius!" I yelled. No answer.

Another room, another and another. Finally, we reached the end of the upstairs hallway and one last door, which opened onto a narrow chamber lined with shelves and musty drawers. I opened the drawers and poked around in the corners. Durindana, a little stronger, wobbled off my shoulder to search the upper shelves.

Nothing. "This sucks," I said. "We'll never find him."

"This metal door is cold like a Parvus," Durindana commented from across the room. It was a square door of mottled gray metal, about three feet off the floor,

Dad

hinged at the bottom, with a horizontal bar for a handle.

When I got closer, I saw that the mottling wasn't from rust or age or moisture.

It was frost.

"Fidius!" I flung myself at the door, pulled it open. It was some sort of chute—for laundry, maybe. It went all the way down to the cistern room—I could hear the sea sploshing and splooshing.

And there, clinging to a rivet . . . was Fidius.

"Turpina," he whispered. "Turpina."

I plucked him out of there by his raggedy tunic and sank to the floor with him on my knee. Durindana fluttered around us like a maddened moth.

"Fidius, what did she do to you?"

He closed his eyes, and his nasty tunic turned into a velvet coat. But still he lay there, seemingly exhausted. "Magica Mala, Turpina," he said. "She entranced me, and when I awoke I had no powers, could only climb, climb, climb up that"—he wafted a hand at the laundry chute—"that chimney, or whatever it is." He sat up to groom his wings. "But I begin to feel better now."

"The Circulus stopped for a while, but now it's started up again back in the pub. You probably can fly."

To be companionable, the two Parvi rode my shoulders back downstairs. Durindana told Fidius what had happened in the cistern room.

"My little Turpina," he said in my ear, chilling it. "You succeeded where I failed."

"I had help. You were all alone."

"Still. My little Turpina is very brave."

Timmo was waiting at the foot of the stairs. "The Parvi took off," he said, obviously relieved not to be waddling home. Fidius flitted off toward the pub. Timmo and I trudged down the driveway, Durindana nestled in Timmo's pocket.

"You're a frog again," he said, "but you're not drooling yet." He got out his bleach-dripped paper towel and sniffed it. "Better take precautions, though. Watching you makes me retch."

"Thanks." I handed him the moonstone ring.

"Hey, you try looking at a steady stream of saliva—"

"No, I mean it. Thanks. For being here and all."

He was so surprised he shut up all the way back to Oak Street. When we got to the pub, Rinaldo announced me as "the Turpina who is giving back the Gemmaluna." A knot of ladies and gentlemen started shouting and shaking their fists when he said that, but most of the Parvi cheered. Ladies threw roses at me—actually swizzle sticks from the bar, Timmo said.

An admiring crowd clustered around Fidius and, I was pleased to see, Durindana. Not Rinaldo, though, because he had more hand-wringing to do. "My Lady Noctua has not returned," he quavered, bobbing up and down in front of the mail slot.

"Hmm," I said. "So, Rinaldo . . ."

He stopped wringing. "Turpina?"

Dad

"Um. So. Lady Noctua. She's not too happy about us giving back the Gemmaluna, is she?"

He returned his attention to the mail slot. "My Lady Noctua will accustom herself."

"But . . . with no Circulus for her to run . . ."

Rinaldo bobbed closer, spoke softly. "The Lady Noctua and myself, we shall live in a mossy place with a view of the sea. In a cave we shall build with the magic of our ancestors."

Lady Noctua and mossy caves didn't exactly go together. I was pretty sure Rinaldo had a shock coming. Part of me wanted to warn him . . . but what did I really know? Gigi sounded like Noctua . . . but so did a lot of Parvi, and how much effort would it take to throw in a *"tiens"* here and there? Both Gigi and Noctua were very clear about not wanting the Parvi to take back the Gemmaluna, but that wasn't unique either.

On the other hand, I couldn't remember a time when Gigi and Noctua had been in the same place at once. And who better than Noctua to lure a Circulus away and set it up someplace else?

I pictured myself saying to Rinaldo, "Pardon me for butting in, but I think your wife is the evil Gigi Kramer, Circulus kidnapper and user of Magica Mala." (a) He wouldn't believe me. (b) He'd give me acne on top of my frog face.

Rinaldo murmured on, more to himself than to me. "My Lady Noctua loves the sea above all things. And in this mossy place we shall eat food we create with our hands, wear real clothes." He sighed. "Noctua and myself."

Love is blind, that's for sure.

Timmo and I went upstairs, where the grandfather clock was sitting at the kitchen table. "I told you not to move," I snapped, and pelted up the stairs. Mom and Dad were sound asleep in their bed. When I returned downstairs, all nip bottles of liquor were full and accounted for.

I'd known everything Gigi showed me was a fake. Still. It was a relief to be sure.

Bong, the grandfather clock said. I fumbled for my nip bottle, gave it a sniff. Grand-père reappeared, glowering. "It's several hours past lunchtime."

"I told you to stay with them."

"They were asleep. I'd hear them from the kitchen if they started walking around. I came down to see if you'd left me a sandwich. You hadn't."

"I thought you couldn't eat."

"I grew legs, and I got hungry."

"The Circulus stopped for a bit. Then it started up again, and right now you're definitely a clock. Are you still hungry?"

"I *remember* being hungry. Maybe I could try eating something."

"*I'm* hungry," Timmo said.

I got out baloney and bread while Timmo told Grand-père how it had gone with Gigi Kramer. He glossed over the Dad Is Drunk illusion, which was good. I didn't want Grand-père to tell Dad I was afraid he'd start drinking again. I'd been surprised by that myself.

When nobody was looking, I snagged myself three flies. Tasty, but they didn't do much for my human-sized stomach, which was hollow. I made myself a baloney sandwich, although I wasn't looking forward to the effort involved in eating it.

"Hey," Timmo said when I handed him his sandwich, "did you notice Gigi tried to put the moonstone on her finger? How would the ring affect some fiberglass walking dummy, even if the right person gave it to her?" I'd explained about the "true owner" issue.

Grand-père sniffed his sandwich. "Blast. I'm not hungry anymore." He put the sandwich down without taking a bite. "The boy raises an interesting point. If Gigi is as good at the Magica Mala as she seems, she may be so connected to that mannequin that she thinks the moonstone would work for her as a ring. If that's so, she can wear the ring while the other two magics are still in force. She'll have access to the Three Magics, and heaven help us all."

I pondered this. "She'd need the Circulus for two of the magics though, right? How would she convince the Parvi to keep it going for her?" I gagged on a bit of baloney.

Grand-père shrugged, watching Timmo wolf down his sandwich. "No one knows how the Three Magics work.

Maybe once she united them she'd be a sorceress for good, wouldn't need a Circulus anymore. She'd have absolute power—you'd be a real frog, I'd be a clock."

"I think she likes being human," Timmo said.

I saw again the way Gigi admired herself in the pub mirror. "You're right," I said.

"Interesting," Grand-père said. "Perhaps she thinks the Three Magics will make her a human body."

"Do you think they can?" For some reason, I found that thought revolting.

"How should I know?" Grand-père said. "Do I look like a *magus*?"

"Well," Timmo said. "We've got the Gemmaluna, so that's one magic she doesn't have. We'll never know what she could have done."

"Never say never." Grand-père sniffed his sandwich again, a look of longing on his face. "I never thought I'd crave baloney."

Chapter Twenty

The Blanket in the Air

GRAND-PÈRE WENT BACK TO HIS GUEST BED around four. I wanted to take a nap before moonrise, so I tried to relax. I reassured myself that we'd left the mannequin floating in the ocean, and even Gigi would have trouble pulling herself together after that.

But the better part of my brain knew perfectly well that whoever was in that mannequin wasn't going to give up.

"The mannequin may be waterlogged, but whoever's running it was moving around fine," Timmo said. "I bet she shows up again."

"I don't know what to do about it," I said. "Except try to keep a clear head."

"Lock the doors and take a nap," he said. "I'm going home. I'll try to sleep too, if I can do it without my mother deciding I'm sick or something. What time should I come back?"

"You don't have to if you don't want to," I said. "My parents will be back to normal at nine twenty-six."

"Don't be nuts. I want to see the ceremony."

"Okay, so come back around eleven, I guess. What'll you tell your parents?"

"Nothing. I can climb out my window onto the shed roof."

He handed me the moonstone ring. "Oh geez," he said, eyes wide, "I forgot what you look like as a frog." He took a whiff of bleach, and I got a full frontal assault with the galaxy grays. "Phew. That's better." He got up to leave.

I put the ring on. "Timmo," I said, and then I couldn't go on.

He paused in the doorway. "Yeah?"

"Do you . . . do you think . . ."

"Geez. Spit it out."

I swallowed hard. "Do you think we could ever be friends? After this is all over, I mean. When the Parvi aren't around anymore." I wished he was seeing me as a frog, because then I wouldn't be blushing.

"You're wacked," he said. "We're already friends."

Warmth flooded over me. That was the absolute truth.

To celebrate, I took off the ring and snagged myself a fly going up the stairs for my nap. Might as well enjoy them while I could.

I checked on my parents. They were restless—no surprise, considering they'd been sleeping for twenty-four hours straight. Mom was sitting on the edge of the bed when I went in.

"You look pale, sweetie," she said.

"I'm okay. How are you feeling?"

"Sad."

"Sad ain't the half of it," my dad muttered into his pillow.

Fidius settled on my shoulder, chilling my ear. "May I be of help to the Turpini?"

Mom scowled at him. "What could you do for us?" She fingered her frostbitten ear.

"He's been very helpful, Mom."

"To tell the truth, Turpina, I tried and failed. Veronica Turpin is right—I am no hero."

"Well, it's not heroic but I need to sleep. Can you watch my parents for me?"

"'Watch my parents,'" Dad grumbled. "Like we're three-year-olds. Which we might as well be, for all the good we are to anyone."

"I'm not sure I can live with you anymore," Mom told him. "You're so depressing."

"Go back to bed, Mom. I'll get you up at moonrise. You'll feel better in no time."

"I will stay here," Fidius said. "Rest, Turpina."

I left him there, sitting straight-backed at the end of the bed, beady gaze shifting from one blanketed lump of parent to the other. His wings were brown around the edges, not surprising after the day we'd all had.

I hauled my mattress back into my room, leaving my door open a crack so I could hear if something happened. I put a wastebasket of books against it so I'd wake up if somebody tried to sneak in and steal the moonstone. As an added precaution, I kept the moonstone on my finger with my hand clenched. With all that on my mind, you'd think I'd never fall asleep. But as I snuggled into my pillow, my brain played back Timmo's voice: *You're wacked. We're already friends.* I don't remember a thing after that.

It was dark when I woke up, starving and with an ice cube on my shoulder. Icy hands tugged at my earlobe. "Turpina! Wake up, Turpina!"

It was Durindana. Her tone of voice woke me as if she'd fired off a cannon.

"What's the matter?" I sat up and she took to the air, bobbing distractedly up and down. She was wringing her hands, Rinaldo-fashion.

"I do not understand what Fidius is saying to them. Why is he saying such things to the parents of Melissa Angelica Turpin?"

I fumbled for my sneakers. "What? What is he saying?"

"He has told them that you, their daughter, Melissa Angelica Turpin, face danger alone while they are in their beds." *Wring-wring-wring.* "He is talking and talking, never allowing them to sleep, saying this bad thing and that. And now . . ." She buried her face in her hands, bobbing up and down.

"What? What now?"

"Now the Turpini are on the roof!" she wailed.

I didn't tie my shoelaces, just booked it up the stairs. A clock on the fourth floor said quarter past nine—eleven minutes before moonrise.

The roof was cool and breezy, the sky dark overhead, a line of gold to the west where the sun had set, a wash of silver where the moon would rise in the east. Facing the moonrise, my parents stood hand in hand. My dad had one foot up on the parapet around the edge of the roof.

"No!" I ran to them, covered their clasped hands with both of mine. "It's not true, it's not true. Whatever Fidius said to you, he was wrong, wrong, wrong."

"He was telling the truth, Mellie." *Dad's so calm, how can he be so calm?* "Let us go."

"I won't," I said like an angry four-year-old. "If you jump I'm not letting go. We'll all go down together."

"Oh, sweetie." Mom slid her hand from Dad's grasp and mine. I got hold of their T-shirts, pulled as hard as I could. They stumbled backward. Dad's foot came off the parapet. Progress.

I flung myself between them and the edge, arms out wide like a crossing guard. "You're not doing this." *Come on, moon. Rise. What must it be now, five minutes? Four?*

I heard a car turn the corner from Oak Street. "Help!" I shrieked. "Somebody, help me!"

The stairwell door slammed open and Grand-père staggered out, wild-eyed. "No," he panted. "No. Stop." He stumbled to us, clasped Dad's arm, bent over, catching his breath.

Dad shook him off, no longer calm, his face contorted like some Halloween mask. "Get away from me, old man. What do you care, anyway?"

"Is this to punish me? Idiot boy, as if I am not already punished."

Dad wheeled to face him. "IT'S. NOT. ABOUT. YOU." I didn't recognize him, this bellowing, spitting person. "It isn't always about you! Can't you see anything through that haze of selfishness you live in? This is about me, about us—other people. NOT. YOU."

"Roland, I cannot argue with you. I know what I am. But you must not do this. Please. . . ." Dad turned back to the parapet, grim-faced. Grand-père took my mother's hand. "Veronique. You have some sense. You cannot leave your child."

Mom let him hold her hand, but otherwise she ignored him. "Mellie, it's cruel to prevent us. You'll be better off without us. Fidius says you've been doing all sorts of dangerous things while we've been lying there. You don't need us anymore."

"But I do need you, I really do. Not that much happened to me, and I had Timmo and Durindana with me. They did a lot of it. And everything is much, much better, much, much safer with you here. Who will I live with? Who will take care of me?"

"You can live here with the old man," Dad said. "The Parvi will take care of you."

"Are you *nuts*?" Okay, maybe that wasn't the smartest thing to say.

"Roland," Grand-père began. Dad faked to my right, I matched him, he veered back to the left and seized Mom's hand from Grand-père. The two of them stepped up on the parapet.

The Blanket in the Air

They leaped out into nothing but air.

"Roland, nooooo!" Grand-père grabbed at Dad but he missed.

"NO!" How could I live after this? I lunged for the parapet, because I had to jump too. Grand-père wrapped his arms around me, held on, tight. I clawed at him. "Let me go, let me go!"

"No," he gasped. I knew he was too weak to hold on to me for long. *I'll wait for him to let go, that's all.* But he was stronger than he looked.

Which was a good thing. Because if they'd had to catch me too, the Parvi couldn't have saved my parents.

Which is exactly what they did.

It was the weirdest sight I'd ever seen—and you'll admit, that's saying something. It must have been every single one of the Small Persons, their wings beating like mad, clutching a pink blanket with my parents writhing around in the middle of it. Slowly, painfully, the Parvi hauled their burden up to the roof. They lowered my parents to the asphalt and collapsed around them with a tinny group moan.

Grand-père slumped onto the parapet, wheezing. I wasn't in much better shape, standing there hiccupping because I'd forgotten how to sob. I wanted to fling myself on my parents but (a) I couldn't move and (b) I didn't want to step on any Parvi. I can't remember what (c) was.

Durindana wobbled over to me and sank onto my shoulder. Fidius hovered nearby, keeping his distance.

"We have saved the Turpini," Durindana panted. "Ogier told us what to do."

"Thank you," I whispered. But I was looking at Fidius.

His wings were beautiful, glimmering. "I am sorry, Turpina. This is not what I intended."

"Intended?" I said. "*Intended?*" There was so much to say, but I couldn't sort it out.

He didn't wait for me to sort out anything. He swept me a bow, flitted over the parapet and away.

"The moon is rising," Durindana said. I turned to look and there it was—a sliver of salvation, just showing over the horizon.

My parents hadn't moved. But then Dad reached over and took Mom's hand. She covered her eyes with her other hand and said something I couldn't hear. Dad stroked her cheek.

One by unsteady one, the Parvi were rising into the air. Durindana got airborne too. "We must prepare for the Gemma's return." She bobbed in front of me, eyeing my clothes with disapproval. "The Turpini also must dress for the occasion."

"Sure." My voice barely worked. "Panoply, coming up."

She flitted away with the other Parvi. My parents, Grand-père, and I were alone on the roof.

"I'm going downstairs," Grand-père said. "Give me the Gemma. I want to say good-bye."

I pulled the ring off, watched him turn into a clock. Before I could get my nip bottle out of my pocket a strong, physical memory stabbed itself into my mind: Grand-père's scrawny old arms clinging to me, keeping me from jumping after my parents.

The clock faded and the old man appeared, studying the moonstone ring on his pinky.

Mom sat up, held out her arms to me, frog face and all. I hustled over to her. She took me in her arms and held me. It was awesome.

"Sheesh." Dad was still lying there. "That was the pits."

"Still is, in a way," Mom said.

I sat up. "What do you mean, still is? You're supposed to be back to normal."

Mom gave me a squeeze. "I feel much better, lovey. I'm sure Dad does too. But I don't have amnesia—I do remember how I felt an hour ago. It's hard to explain. I know what I thought about my paintings and about you and how you didn't respect me. To some extent, it's all still true. It just doesn't stab me to the heart the way it did before."

"I respect you. And your paintings are amazing."

"They're as good as they could be when I've spent most of my time doing other things. And you respect me as much as you could, considering what I'm like and what you're like." She stroked my froggy face. "And the fact that you're growing cheekbones."

"You're a great kid, Mellie," Dad said, his eyes shut. "I'm very proud of you."

The door to the stairs creaked open. Grand-père was

leaving. Dad sat bolt upright, seeing Grand-père for the first time without the elixir. "Huh. A floating clock."

"Welcome to my world," I said.

"*Mon père*," Dad called to Grand-père, "I am deeply in your debt."

Grand-père halted in the doorway. "I will not lose my father *and* my son to this blasted elixir." He gave me a lizard's thin smile. "Thinking only of myself, as usual." He left.

"What did he say?" Dad asked. "All I heard was bonging."

I told him.

"Ogier," Mom said. "Sheesh."

Dad shook his head, pondering the moon. "Hey. Aren't we returning the moonstone tonight? What time is it?"

"It must be ten o'clock," Mom said.

"We have to put on the panoply of our state," I said. "Find a pillow for the moonstone."

"Most of the panoply in my wardrobe has paint on it," Dad said. "But it'll have to do."

We got up, folded the blanket, and clattered down the stairs to the fourth floor. We didn't notice that anything was wrong until we opened the door at the foot of the stairs.

And saw the flames.

Chapter Twenty-one

Burgess Persuaded

LIKE IDIOTS, WE STOOD THERE in the stairwell door, gaping at the inferno that used to be the fourth-floor corridor. It was a tunnel of swirling flames, the roar deafening. Where was Grand-père?

Dad shoved Mom and me back into the stairwell and slammed the door shut. "Back up to the roof," he shouted over the tumult.

We were halfway up to the roof door when the molding around it burst into flame.

"We may have to get through that door," Dad yelled. "Let me think."

"Think about what?" Mom glared at him. "We don't have time—we'll lose the air. We have to get out on the roof and yell like crazy!"

I was shaking so hard I couldn't talk. The human body is weird, you know? There I was, crammed into a stairwell with my parents, fire everywhere. You wouldn't think I'd be freezing cold, but I was.

The roar filled my brain, leaving no room for rational thought.

"Roly," Mom shouted. "Move. Now."

"Okay, okay," Dad said. "Let's get out there."

The entire door to the roof exploded in flame. The downstairs door too was a sheet of fire. We were stuck on the stairs.

My mom lost it. "Oh my god we'll never get out now! OhgodMellie'sonlythirteen, ohgodohgodohgod."

Something didn't make sense. I tried to block out the noise, tried to think. The door to the roof crackled like a log on a fire.

Wait a minute.

I shouted in Dad's ear. "Isn't that door made of metal?"

He frowned, nodded.

"Does metal burn like that?" I shouted.

He shook his head.

"This is no time for materials analysis!" my mom shrieked. "What are we—" She shut up, stared at us. "No. It doesn't, does it?"

Huh.

I closed my eyes, took a deep breath of the chilly air, looked for that one thing I needed, that one clue. "Anybody smell anything?" I yelled, opening my eyes.

"*Smell* anything?" Mom shouted. "Mellie, we don't have time for guessing games."

"Mom, tell me what you smell. Dad, you too."

We all sniffed the air. I smelled mildew, as usual. But not a whiff of smoke.

"I don't think we'll ever get rid of this mildew," my mom shouted.

I concentrated on mildew, thought about the nasty

fourth-floor carpet, how it looked when it wasn't on fire.

Mildew. I sneezed. The thunder of the fire receded, almost died completely.

For me, anyway. My parents were hollering as if they could barely hear their own voices.

"How come we're not hot?" That was Dad. "We should be hot, with fire everywhere."

"I'm freezing," Mom shouted.

"That's because there's no fire," I yelled, sounding ridiculous to myself in the now-quiet stairwell. "It's an illusion."

Dad squeezed past me, heading down. "Nick, wrap yourself and Mellie in that blanket. I'm going to see what's really happening."

"Oh, Roly." Mom gripped his arm. "I don't know."

"It's fine, Mom," I said. "Really."

Mom wrapped us both in the blanket. Dad stopped at the bottom of the stairs and blew her a kiss. He hesitated, getting his courage up, and I knew that for him the fire still roared. But he straightened his shoulders and opened the downstairs door.

My daddy, protecting me.

Reality hadn't returned to me completely—I didn't hear the fire anymore, but I saw it. It was scary watching Dad walk out into this madly flickering hallway, closing the door behind him.

Mom and I huddled on the stairs, shaking with cold and nerves.

After a long, long minute, my dad opened the door.

"You can walk right through these flames. It's pretty weird, but you don't feel a thing."

It *was* weird. We walked across the hallway to the stairs with flames towering over us and licking up from the carpet. They acted like real fire—when you stomped on them they sparked and went out, then came back when you moved on. But they didn't even tickle, let alone burn us.

The stairs to the third floor were a dragon's throat, flames swirling around and around and around, crackling and roaring. I had to shut my eyes to force myself into the stairwell, even though it was freezing cold. When we got to the bottom the third floor was normal. We looked where we'd been and that was normal too.

"Who on earth would do that to us?" Mom said.

"Gigi Kramer," I said. "She wanted to keep us up there until it was too late to give back the moonstone. She must be close by."

"Who's Gigi Kramer?" Dad asked.

Durindana catapulted up the stairs from the second floor, wearing white satin with diamonds and gold lace, her hair pouffed, powdered, and ostrich-plumed. "What are you doing, Turpini? It is thirty-seven minutes past ten of the clock and you are not at all foofed in the panoply of your state. Hurry! Hurry!"

"We had to walk through flames to get here," I said.

"Turpini. Always they make excuses. Hurry! Hurry!"

I was starving. Mom and Dad must have been too. But we dutifully went to our rooms.

My little china guy was grinning like a jerk on my bureau. I sank down on my bed. *What had Fidius intended?* Why had he said all that to my parents about me being in danger, about not needing them? Part of me wanted to believe that he'd just been in a brown-winged mood, and regretted the results. But then why wasn't he the one who warned me when my parents were on the roof?

I caught a glimpse of my frog face in the mirror and gave myself a shake. One more hour and all this would be over. My parents were laughing next door. *I wonder what they're wearing.*

I wonder what I'm wearing.

Because we would be in the pub with a bunch of chill-inducing Parvi, I unpacked my best winter outfit, a red wool jumper with a turtleneck and tights. In the mirror it didn't look much like panoply. I blamed the frog's head and the drool.

I rummaged further and came up with a gold cape that had been the basis of several Halloween costumes, the most recent and lamest being the Princess Superhero from Hell. I didn't bother looking for the werewolf teeth that went with that one, but I did find the tiara and stuck it on my bald, green head. The tiara had fake blood all over it, but it would have to do.

When we gathered at the top of the stairs, Dad was wearing a white bedspread as a cape over his gray suit with the cadmium yellow paint on the knee. Mom had a silvery silk bathrobe, given to her by her mother, over an ancient turquoise pantsuit with a split seam in the butt.

Snappy dressers, the Turpini.

"Hey, Mellie," Timmo yelled from downstairs. "Are you up there?"

He put us all to shame in a Dracula costume complete with black tie and red-lined cape. It was too small for him—it looked like the Lord of the Undead was wearing capri pants—but he got an A for effort.

The clock was sitting at the kitchen table. I didn't have my bottle of whiskey, so I shut my eyes and tried to feel Grand-père's scrawny old arms, pulling me back from the parapet. The memory already was fading. *Imagine what's real. Concentrate.*

And there he was, holding the moonstone ring, gazing around at the rosy silk hangings, brocade wallpaper, gold filigreed this and that. "*Mon Dieux, c'est beau.* Beautiful."

He put the ring on his pinky. "Lie to me."

I didn't hesitate. "You're not my grandpère, and I don't like you very much."

"Mellie!" my mom said.

Grand-père put his head back and hooted. "Not bad for an amphibian."

"Mellie," Dad said. "Can you understand him? What's he bonging about now?"

"Tell him it's time to go downstairs." Grand-père stood up. "Time to end all this and see what it's like to be cattle. Get me a purple velvet cushion."

I translated. Mom rummaged under the sink and came

up with . . . a purple velvet cushion. "This may be a floor sponge," she said.

"Give it to Grand-père. He's supposed to carry it."

I learned what "looked askance" means—bug-eyed with a hint of "dang it"—although all Mom said was, "Does he have hands?"

"You were seeing him as an old man before the elixir wore off," I pointed out.

"A lot can happen in two hours." She held the pillow out to Grand-père. "I can't tell if he's got it. Does he have it?"

"He's got it," I said.

Grand-père processed out the door to the reception lounge. He looked fine to me, but of course everybody else saw him as a floating clock with a pillow wafting along in front.

"Cool," Timmo whispered.

Grand-père led us in a ceremonial procession down the stairs and into the night, where he pounded three times on the pub door. That wasn't specified in the instructions, but it felt right.

Rinaldo hurled himself out of the mail slot. "Noctua, my Lady Noctua! We have searched and we cannot find her. If she does not return, the ceremony will fail! The others, they will expel her from the Parvi Pennati!"

"It's after eleven," I told him. "You don't have much time."

Rinaldo bobbed up and down, wringing, wringing, wringing his hands.

"Time to be a leader," Dad said.

Rinaldo gave him a beady-eyed look, stopped wringing, straightened his shoulders. "I know this, Roland Turpin. We must begin without *ma chère*. And hope that she returns in time."

The Parvi were milling about on the floor in a mass of silks and diamonds. When we walked in, Rinaldo yelled something tinny in Latin. Almost all of his people rose into the air, hovered below the spinning Circulus. A small cluster of Parvi huddled on the bar, backs to the rest of us. *Noctua's supporters*, I thought.

Durindana flitted over to hover near me. I couldn't see Fidius right off. Just as well. Part of me still loved him, the friend of my childhood, but a much larger part wanted to stomp on him.

Rinaldo faced his people, wings flapping. They stared back at him, waiting. "*Circulo desistite!*" he shouted. "Stop the Circulus," Mom whispered.

The crowd moaned. The Circulus slowed, colors unblurred, individuals became distinct. Slow . . . slower . . . then it stopped, the members fluttering down to join their friends. Durindana's ostrich plumes dried up and fell out of her hair, disappearing before they hit the floor.

Rinaldo beckoned to us, and Grand-père led us across the now-empty floor. I was losing my grip on my imagination, and now saw him as a floating clock.

"Turpini," Rinaldo said, "will you part with the gem

of insight, legacy of the Archbishop thy progenitor, dispelling the Obligatio Turpinorum for all time?"

The moonstone ring glistened on its purple velvet pillow that was really a sponge. It had been mine for three days or all my life, depending on how you looked at it. Archbishop Turpin had worn it in 775, then his children, then their children, down the generations for twelve hundred years. It gave us a special relationship with magical winged creatures no one else knew existed.

If I wore it, I could find out who liked me. I shot a glance at Timmo, who winked. *Maybe I can find another way. Imagine what's real.*

"Too bad," Dad muttered. "I was looking forward to buying a good used car."

"May I remind you," Mom said, "that our daughter is a frog?"

Dad took both our hands in his, her normal one, my green one. "Good point," he said. "Yea, Rinaldo. We'll part with it."

"Yea," Mom said.

"Yea," I said.

Bong.

"We'll take that as a 'yea,'" Dad said.

And, simple as that, the Gemmaluna wasn't ours anymore.

Someone shoved me, hard. Sprawled on the marble floor, I looked up to see a pair of hot pink ballet flats sashay by. Sashaying fast.

She pushed Grand-père over, pillow and moonstone flying through the air. The Parvi let out a piercing group scream. Dad snatched at the ring but not fast enough—it arched right into Gigi Kramer's pink-gloved hand.

Gigi Kramer had the Gemma. And she hadn't stolen it, because it didn't belong to anyone until the Parvi voted to accept it.

A white-and-gold blur zipped past me. "Durindana, no!" I yelled, scrambling to my feet. "She'll hurt you!"

Durindana rapped Gigi on the nose. "Who is inside there? The Gemma is not yours, you bad Parva. No one shall own the Gemmaluna except the Turpini and the Parvi Pennati!"

"The Gemmaluna is for the making of elixir." Rinaldo joined Durindana in front of Gigi's nose. "It is for all of us, not one alone."

"Zut," Gigi said, and cackled. "Zut, zut, zut, zut, zut." She held the ring out to Rinaldo, who dove for it and flipped over in midair when she pulled it away. "How blind can you be, my dear Parvi? It doesn't matter who owns the Gemma. All you need is the hand and mind to wield its power. Fifteen years have I hidden my work from the magi, and now I understand our magics as no one has before, even Imprexa herself. Behold!"

She slipped the ring on her finger and flung her arms wide, palms up, cupped hands wafting back and forth as if scooping the air. Durindana retreated to my shoulder. "She tries to use the Magica Mala," she said in my ear.

"It requires gesture when other magics do not. But this cannot work. She has no Circulus to give her power."

Gigi grinned. "Mademoiselle Durindana thinks all Parvi Pennati are as inept as she is. Some of us can store the power of the Circulus, remember?"

She doesn't have Versailles to keep up. And she's wearing flats. Gigi learned from experience.

Muttering in Latin, eyes closed, Gigi raised her arms slow, slow, deathly slow until her cupped palms met over her head. "*Donum potestatis peto*," she intoned—"I seek the Gift of Power," Durindana translated in a whisper. Gigi went rigid, arms straight in the air, fingers splayed like sunbursts. The lights flickered. The hovering Parvi moaned like February.

We waited for . . . something. "Did anything happen?" Timmo whispered.

"I don't know," I whispered back.

Gigi's eyes flipped open. "Hmm. Not enough power for the Three Magics, apparently. No matter. The Circulus must begin again."

"Never," Rinaldo said.

Gigi smiled. "Size is power, Rinaldo. For example . . ." Quick as a snake, she nabbed Rinaldo in her fist. He struggled to free himself but he was helpless, his wings crushed in her fingers. A picture flashed into my mind from long ago, from kindergarten—Fidius trapped in a glass jar with no room to unfurl his wings, his panic and anger.

Gigi pressed Rinaldo to her cheek, his face a fraction of an inch from her shark-like eye.

Noctua, I thought. *How could she?*

"Open your eyes, Rinaldo," Gigi said gently, squeezing him in her fist, muttering more Latin. He stopped struggling, went limp in her hand. "*Circulum incipe.*"

"She says, start the Circulus," Durindana whispered.

"*Circulum,*" Rinaldo muttered. "*Incipe.*" My heart sank. He was a zombie.

"Tell your people now, Rinaldo. Tell your Parvi Pennati." Gigi opened her hand. Rinaldo collapsed on her palm, but his wings unfurled and shook themselves out. He jerked into the air and faced the fluttering horde.

"*Circulum incipite!*" he cried, waving his arms. "*Circulum incipite, Parvi Pennati.*" ("Start the Circulus, Parvi Pennati," Durindana whispered.)

A cheer went up from the Small Persons on the bar. A handful of Circulus members lined up under the chandelier, ready to begin again. But the rest of the crowd hovered in place, not sure what to do.

I remembered the Circulus in the cistern room. "She enchanted almost the whole Circulus last time," I whispered.

"Too many of us now," Durindana said. "And her power will not last without a Circulus." She left my shoulder for Rinaldo's side. "Rinaldo, no, do not start the Circulus. *Noli Circulum incipere.*"

Gigi grabbed for her, but Durindana darted away.

"*Nolite circulum incipere*," she called to the Parvi. They gave one another the fish eye, but they obeyed her: Nobody moved, nobody else joined the circle under the chandelier.

"You wish to fight me, Inepta." Gigi smiled. "Very well." She recaptured Rinaldo, whispered to him, flung him away from her as if releasing a bird. He landed on the bar and stood there, uncertain. Gigi drew a complicated shape in the air and said, "*Incipe*, Rinaldo."

Tears ran down Rinaldo's expressionless face. On their own, seemingly against his will, his hands crept over his shoulder, grasped the top of his right wing.

He gave a mighty shriek and ripped the top of his wing right off.

Every Small Person in the room shrieked with him. Rinaldo sank to his knees, the dead iridescent fragment pressed to his cheek.

"Dang it!" Mom yelled (more or less). Dad held her back, I guess so she wouldn't get turned into a frog.

Rinaldo had a hand on his left wing now. My eyesight blurred with tears. Timmo was breathing so hard I could hear him.

Bong! Bong! Bong!

"*Circulum incipe*, Rinaldo," Gigi said. Rinaldo mouthed the words, kneeling there with a healthy wing in one hand, a ruin in the other. But he made no sound.

A fast-moving smudge of rose-colored silk whirred in through the mail slot, landed on the bar next to Rinaldo.

I blinked my tears away so I could see. She helped him to his feet, murmuring to him, soothing him.

It was Lady Noctua.

She's not Gigi.

My brain went numb.

Gigi gestured. Rinaldo twisted free of his wife, pulled his hands from her grasp. He reached back and ripped the top off of his left wing.

The Parvi screamed, and Noctua buried her face in her hands, sobbing. Rinaldo didn't make a sound, just swayed in place, eyes closed.

Who is inside that big doll? Who could do this?

But I knew who it was, and Timmo did too. "Mellie," he said. I didn't reply, because talking about it would make it real.

I stepped toward Gigi. "Stop this. Please."

She raised her hand. "Mind your own business, Fairy Fat."

But her hand was shiny. My own hand was a fainter shade of green. I squinted at Gigi. Was that a neck crack?

Durindana, Timmo, and I must have had the same thought at the same time. Without exchanging even a glance, the three of us charged, Durindana tumbling into Gigi's forehead while Timmo and I hurled ourselves at her torso, shoving her hard.

"No!" Gigi shrieked. She fell, her head hitting the bar with a sickening crack. She sat up immediately, but her head hung off her shoulders like a hood.

I managed not to puke by reminding myself that this was a mannequin, not an actual person.

The outside door banged open: Timmo's dad and his sister, Eileen. "What the frig is going on in here?" Chief Wright shouted. He did not actually say "frig."

They saw me, a human-sized frog who might or might not be growing a nose. They saw Timmo—out of bed at midnight, dressed like Dracula, surrounded by five hundred Small Persons with Wings and Grand-père, who had grown human legs but still had a clock face.

Chief Wright sagged onto Eileen, whose face twisted with annoyance. Then Eileen noticed Gigi Kramer sitting on the floor with her head hanging backward, and that was too much even for a blonde with perfect makeup. Eileen's eyes slid back into her head.

"They're fainting!" Dad and Mom got there just in time—he caught Chief Wright while Mom got Eileen. They managed to lower father and daughter to the floor.

Timmo was rooted in place. The expression on his face reminded me of *The Scream*, painted in 1893 by Edvard Munch, who . . . Yeah, never mind. Anyway. Timmo looked horrified. "What'll we do?" he moaned. "They saw everything."

Dad was chewing his lip, sometimes a sign of brain activity. "Magica Mala," he said. "It's the only way."

"No. No," Rinaldo said weakly, struggling to sit up on the bar. Noctua supported him, cooing. The Parvi launched into an agitated murmur. Gigi Kramer fell over sideways and lay on the floor, inert and increasingly plastic.

Mom slipped the moonstone ring off the mannequin's finger and held it clenched in her fist.

"I know it's forbidden, Rinaldo," Dad said. "But these Gigantes can't know about you—they'll put you in a zoo or something."

"A glass jar," I said. "Like Fidius." All around me, Parvi sucked in their breath.

Durindana joined Rinaldo and Noctua on the bar for a spirited Latin debate. At last, Noctua rose majestically into the air. "I will do this thing. My morals may withstand such an onslaught."

I wasn't standing all that close, but I was pretty sure Durindana rolled her eyes.

"Uh," Timmo said. "I'm sorry, but won't the Magica Mala wear off without a Circulus? Like, by tomorrow?"

Lady Noctua looked down her nose at him. "*Tiens*. It is simple, Timothy Oliver. The Circulus shall begin again, long enough to enchant the minds of the Gigantes and send them to their beds. When they wake tomorrow they will believe they dreamed us." She gestured, and a handful of Circulus members began whirring around for one last power-surge.

Timmo didn't look convinced. "It'll be fine," I whispered. "You said your dad only believes what he already thinks. He'll *want* to believe he dreamed us."

And then I was struck by a blisteringly brilliant idea. *It might even work.* I whispered it to Durindana, who consulted Lady Noctua and gave me an encouraging nod.

We Gigantes scuttled the Wrights into their moonlit backyard, draped them in deck chairs by the pool. Noctua hovered at Eileen's nose, snapped her fingers. "*Vigila!*" Eileen's eyes opened, unfocused. Noctua hovered close, staring into her right eye. She murmured in Latin. I heard "*oblivium,*" which sounded like it had to do with forgetting.

"How about making Eileen forget the whole Fairy Fat thing?" Timmo whispered.

Wow. Great idea. I opened my mouth to ask, but then I remembered that I was a Stoic descended from a warrior archbishop. "Nah," I whispered back. "I'll deal with it."

Eileen got up and walked like a zombie toward the sliding glass door. Noctua moved on to Chief Wright, again muttering in Latin I couldn't catch. Except toward the end, when the stream of words slowed down, I thought I heard "*filius*" and "*nauta ad stellas.*"

"Son," I found out later. And "sailor to the stars." *Cool. My idea turned into Latin.*

Chief Wright followed his daughter into the house. When he woke up, he'd think he dreamed about fairies. And about the heroic astronaut who was his son.

Chapter Twenty-two
Elixir in the Moonlight

GIGI KRAMER WAS RIGHT WHERE WE LEFT HER. I couldn't stop myself—I prodded her head with my toe. "Mellie," Mom said warningly.

The head twitched. A bump appeared under the nylon wig, traveling south. And then he crawled out from behind Gigi's ear, his velvet coat already burlap, his black hair ribbon gone, his hair in disarray. He sat down on Gigi's nose, exhausted, rubbing his head where he'd banged it in the mannequin's fall.

Fidius, my imaginary friend.

Bad enough that he had turned me into a frog. Sick, sick, sick that he had made Rinaldo destroy his own wings. And he'd tried to kill my parents. Kill them! My parents!

But what really, really hurt me, made my eyes sting just thinking about it, was Fidius calling me "Fairy Fat."

"*Mendax!*" Durindana shrieked at him, Lady Noctua holding her back by the skirt. "*Proditor!*"

"Liar. Traitor," Mom translated.

Durindana burst into tears and dove back to my shoulder, where she huddled against my turtleneck. I couldn't offer comfort without freezing me or squishing her. Plus, if I moved at all I'd find myself picking Fidius up and drop-kicking him like a football.

I must have looked upset, because Timmo put an arm around me and gave me a quick squeeze, careful not to crush Durindana. Unlike Benny in Boston, he meant it. I didn't need the moonstone to tell me that.

The Parvi were so quiet you could hear their wings beating. A thousand beady little eyes homed in on Fidius— some of the faces frowned slightly, already recovering from the Magica Artificia.

Rinaldo struggled to his feet and broke the silence, speaking in Latin. Durindana pulled herself together and translated into my ear: "Gubernator Rinaldo says, because the Parvi Pennati must not harm others, and must not use the Magica Mala for unnatural control of persons and objects, Fidius is no longer one of the Parvi Pennati. He must leave this place. We will never see him again."

Fidius's pretty mouth took on the hint of a sneer. "I survived exile before, I will again," he said in English. "I need no one."

Rinaldo switched to English too. "Yes, Fidius? Do you not require magic to fly? Where is this magic to come from, if there is no Circulus and you do not drink the elixir with us?"

"Pah! You forget, you *magi*, how long I have pursued the Magica Mala. For years I sought power to protect us all, small against large, Parvi against Gigantes. But then you drove me away, and I studied merely to protect myself from all of you. Melissa Angelica Turpin will tell you of my experiments, miles away from the Circulus." *A galloping My Little Pony. Swaying palm trees on my wall.* "I will find a way. Always."

"You deceive yourself," Rinaldo said. "As we have seen this very night, the Magica Mala fades without the power of the Circulus."

Fidius shrugged and said nothing.

Rinaldo reverted to Latin, and Durindana took up the translation again. "Gubernator Rinaldo says we are not murderers. He says we will make the elixir at midnight of each full moon, and when we have drunk of it ourselves we will leave it under the sky to become one with the air as ritual requires. If Fidius wishes to drink of it then, no one will stop him. Thus may he fly and care for himself in the world."

Wings fluttering, Lady Noctua allowed herself to drift toward Fidius. She stretched out a hand to him, spoke in Latin. "Twice in recent days, Fidius has befuddled her with Magica Mala, keeping her from her place among the Parvi," Durindana said, "but still the Lady Noctua is very sad. Fidius showed promise, and his parents were beloved members of the Parvi Pennati."

Fidius unfurled his beautiful wings, flapped up to confront Noctua. "*Tiens,*" he said—and he did sound exactly like her. "*Zut, zut, zut.* If that was love, I prefer hate."

He pivoted toward my parents and me, raised his hand in farewell. "Turpini." He flew through the mail slot, but then poked his head back in. "I give you the Gemma, by the way. You did not think of that, Rinaldo, did you?" And he was gone.

"Sheesh," Dad said. "He's right. He was still the owner."

Durindana stroked my hair. I felt numb.

A clump of flowers dropped from a nearby lady's gown, fizzled into nothing. My hands were normal color. Soon, it would be as if Fidius never existed.

"I . . . *bong, bong* . . . hate to intrude," Ogier said, his mouth visible under the big hand. "But anybody got a . . . *bong* . . . watch?"

"Eleven forty-seven," Timmo said. "I set my watch by the U.S. Navy online."

I had a watch too, but it was upstairs in the top drawer of my bureau. I wasn't sure it was set right. *We need a computer. I don't care what Dad thinks.*

"We better get this show on the road," Dad said.

Mom put the moonstone ring on the bar next to Rinaldo. The gubernator flapped his poor, ruined half-wings and rose four inches from the bar, but crashed down again. Noctua fluttered over to support him. "Rest your poor wings, consort."

Rinaldo straightened his shoulders, stepped away from her. Standing on the bar, he lifted the moonstone ring high, showed it to the Parvi. "*Magi. Venite*," he said.

"He asks the *magi* to join him," Durindana translated.

Ten or so ladies and gentlemen fluttered out of the crowd, a couple of them from Noctua's crew, still huddled at the far end of the bar. They weren't dressed in any special way, but they all had one thing in common—while buttons and plumes disappeared from the other Parvi, the *magi's* clothing was unchanged. They were the best of the lot when it came to the Magica Artificia.

Which meant they had the most to lose.

"Will Lady Noctua agree to take back the moonstone?" I whispered to Durindana.

"No one knows what she and her followers will do. If they say no, the ceremony fails."

Rinaldo raised the moonstone, spoke in Latin. "You, Parvi Pennati," Durindana whispered, "descendants of the Larger Gods, will you take back the gem of insight, recapturing the powers of old?"

Silence. All over the room, Small Persons with Wings fluffed the lace at their wrists and rearranged their skirts, even as flounces fell off, jewels disintegrated, silks faded back into rags.

Lady Noctua unfurled her wings in all their glory. Tears ran down her cheeks, but she stood straight and tall. "I have been by the sea this day, as yesterday, watching the Gigantes. They fling their arms up, face to the sun, and say, 'Smell that air!' I wish to smell the air. I will live alone with my Rinaldo by the sea, even without my silks and jewels."

She turned to her people at the end of the bar. "Therefore, although I wished to prevent this day from coming, I say before you all . . . Yea!"

"Yea!" Rinaldo and the other *magi* shouted.

"Yea!" Durindana called from my shoulder, waving her arms. "Yea!"

The crowd was silent.

"Freedom, my Parvi Pennati," Rinaldo said softly. "The taste of food, the scent of the earth. No longer the elbows bumping, the Circulus humming in the night. Silence and stars, solitude, the Magica Vera shaping the real."

Rinaldo raised his arm like a band leader. "Now, my Parvi Pennati. We shall work magic together, one more time."

Here and there, a little lady straightened her shoulders, a little gentleman set his jaw. They stopped fawning over their clothes. Everyone, in the air and on the bar, watched Rinaldo's hand, raised above his head.

He swept it down.

"Yea!" they cried, in one tinny voice.

Everyone looked at everyone else, but nothing changed except the gentle fraying of lace.

"What time is it?" Grand-père's face was almost back to normal except for a **12** on his forehead and the stubborn pair of clock hands at the end of his nose. They said four twenty-eight.

"Three minutes to twelve," Timmo said.

"*Aqua!*" Noctua squealed. Water.

"*Vide*, see!" Durindana called, pointing to a large porcelain bowl. "Quickly! Quickly!"

Durindana took one of Rinaldo's arms, Noctua the other. They hauled him into the air, moonstone ring in his hands. His people stayed where they were, eyes fixed on that moonstone.

"Give us a countdown, Timmo," Dad said.

"Two minutes, five seconds," Timmo said, intent on his watch. "One minute, fifty-nine seconds. Fifty-four. Forty-nine. Forty—"

"Spare us," Grand-père said.

"Maybe you could wait until ten seconds before," Mom said.

We all fell silent as Timmo hunched over his wrist, shoulders tense. He was taking his responsibility seriously. *Four days ago I didn't even know this kid*, I thought. *Now our whole future depends on whether he set his watch right.* I couldn't believe I hadn't remembered to bring my own watch.

The Parvi began to murmur, worried. At my feet, a little lady burst into tears from the tension. "Isn't it time yet?" I asked.

"Twenty-five," Timmo said. "Twenty-three. Twenty."

Rinaldo shifted his grip on the moonstone ring. "*Miseria!*" a tinny voice cried. Misery.

"Ten," Timmo said. "Nine. Eight. Seven. Six. Five. Four. Three. Two . . ."

One. Right on time, Rinaldo dropped the moonstone ring into the water without even a splash. "*Cupimus videre,*" he said. We want to see.

A vapor rose from the water, as it had when Mom made the elixir. Once again, it clarified all it touched. The pub returned to the way it was when I first saw it—greasy, moldy, and cobwebby—and yet for a moment it seemed like a beautiful truth, the essence of Pub.

With a wail, the hovering Parvi fell to the floor, wings flapping but not holding them up. Rinaldo, Noctua, and Durindana plummeted into the water bowl, now a red plastic dog dish.

The floor was a mass of struggling little creatures, each dirtier and raggedier than the one before.

Considering that they hadn't had a bath or any new clothes for thirteen hundred years, I guess they looked pretty good. The thought crossed my mind—thanks to the vapor—that this was the way they were supposed to look. Essence of Parvi Pennati.

Rinaldo hauled himself out of the water bowl and stood on the greasy bar, dripping and wiping his mouth on the tattered rag he wore as a toga. "Parvi Pennati!" he shouted. "Magica Vera is in the elixir—drink, drink, and you will fly! See! See!" He waved his hands at Noctua and Durindana, who fluttered into the air.

Noctua gathered cobwebs, and then landed at the end of the bar. "Durindana," she called sharply. "*Veni.*" That's "come here" in Latin. It didn't sound all that polite.

She draped the cobwebs over Durindana and stood back, cocking her head like an artist assessing a painting. She scraped the cobwebs off, laid them on the bar, and plunged her hands into them. It was hard to see, because she was so small and the light so bad, but she seemed to be working at the cobwebs with her fingers. She was humming, a one-woman Circulus.

Everybody—warm and cold alike—watched in fascination. It was clear Noctua didn't know what she was doing: The cobwebs kept sticking to her hands so she'd have to scrape them off and start over. But before long the gummy stuff began to form itself into something like a dress.

A very ugly dress—colorless and shapeless, and gooey to boot. Noctua held it out to Durindana. "*Vestem sume.*" Clothe yourself.

Durindana hesitated, took the dress. She didn't put it on, though. Instead, she laid it down on the bar and began moving her own hands over it, sculpting it almost. It smoothed out, acquired a waist, lost its stickiness. You wouldn't have caught the old Durindana wearing it, but at least it looked like clothing.

She ducked behind a dusty napkin dispenser and came out wearing the dress. She looked cute, like a fairy in a kids' book, tendrils of cobweb wafting around her bare arms and ankles.

When Durindana had started working on the dress, Noctua had stiffened as if insulted. She was accustomed to being the best. But she got interested in the process, and before long she was leaning in to see how Durindana moved her hands. When Durindana came out in the dress, Noctua swept her a haughty curtsy, which Durindana returned with equal haughtiness.

I was feeling pretty good about Durindana's future.

The other Parvi were climbing the bar. Mom and Dad and Timmo and I used our hands as elevators for some of them—I could fit four or five at a time, with my sleeve pulled over my hand to ward off frostbite.

I caught a glimpse of myself in the mirror behind the bar. There I was—round, pink, and curly-haired, not a speck of drool. I squinted. Hey! Cheekbones!

"Welcome back, sweetie." Mom shook the chill off her hand before picking up some more Small Persons with Wings.

I looked for Grand-père, and there he was too, slumped on the grungy bench. When I waved at him, he nodded back as if he were Charlemagne instead of a scrawny old man in a moldy pub.

"Our thanks to you, Turpini." Rinaldo was standing on the bar, supporting himself on a swizzle stick. His mangled wings dangled limply from his shoulders.

"Your poor wings," I said. "Can you fix them?"

"They will grow. But they will never more be beauties."

"That's terrible," Mom said.

He drew himself up straight. "One pays the price for one's people."

"You are a good leader, Rinaldo," Dad said.

"Yes, yes. And now the Parvi Pennati will be fixing this inn for you, the Turpini."

"Are you sure you know how?" Dad asked. I could see his point. Lady Noctua flew by, wobbly and weeping, her second attempt at a cobweb dress having turned into a sticky blob. She looked like one of those chewed-up balls you find in a dog exercise park.

"We are learning," Rinaldo said. Nearby on the floor, Durindana bustled among Small Persons with Cobwebs—the stuff was plastered all over their hands, hair, and feet. Durindana smoothed and sculpted, smoothed and sculpted, increasingly harried.

"Durindana is very good at all this," I said.

Rinaldo shrugged. "She is among those whose bodies resisted the Magica Artificia. This naturally will mean she regains her native skills before the rest of us."

"I know." I couldn't help myself. "Now aren't you sorry you called her Inepta?"

Rinaldo gave me a disdainful look and stalked off to the other end of the bar, where a cluster of Parvi was contemplating a couple of dead slugs and a pile of crickets. One little guy was trying to start a fire.

"Hey!" Dad said. "Not right on the bar! Sheesh!" He grabbed a metal ashtray from a nearby table and hustled over to avert disaster.

The last gentleman thrust his face into the elixir and emerged snorting and choking and flexing his wings. Timmo gave a jaw-cracker of a yawn.

Mom grabbed his wrist and looked at his watch. "It's almost one in the morning, and we never ate. Let's go upstairs, think about how to get Timmo home without waking up his mother."

"I could stay here and go home early," Timmo said. "I get up before they do anyways."

"Wearing your Dracula outfit?" I said.

"It's happened."

We'd settled down around the kitchen table when Durindana flew in and landed gracefully on the toaster. She *was* a lot more together now that the Magica Artificia was gone. "I shall rest with the Turpini. The Parvi Pennati are *inepti*." She smirked. I didn't blame her a bit.

Mom gave Durindana a Proud Mother smile, but then her face collapsed. She dropped her cheese and cracker on the table, plunged her face into her hands. "Fidius! He tried to kill us!"

"He stayed with me for a while," Grand-père said. "I never liked him. Something false about him—I could tell if I put on the moonstone ring—so I sent him to you."

"Gee, thanks," Dad said. "Your own granddaughter."

"He never did anything bad to me," I said.

"He frostbit your nose," Mom said from behind her hands.

"He was scared. He thought I was going to take him to school and they'd put him in a jar. That happened to him once. I think it's what made him go bad."

"I can't believe you're defending him," Timmo said. "He called you . . . you know."

"Fairy Fat," Grand-père said. "Not inaccurate, if I may say so."

"You can keep a civil tongue in your head when you

refer to my daughter," Dad said, jutting out his chin. I actually thought Dad was being a bit harsh. Grand-père's a nasty old coot, but he did save our lives. I felt sorry for him. I handed him a cracker and cheese.

"I don't need your sympathy," Grand-père said. But he ate the cracker. When Dad handed him another, he ate that one too.

Mom decreed that Timmo had to go home rather than spend the night. I walked him down the back stairs and through the yard to the fence.

It was like daytime, the moon was so bright. The whole world was silver and black-green, except for one spot of red: the plastic dog dish with the last of the elixir in it.

"Evaporating," I said. "Which means—"

"Becoming one with the air," Timmo said in a dreamy voice.

We leaned against the fence, contemplating stuff.

"I have to admit," Timmo said, "you're pretty brave."

"Thanks."

"Smarter than most of the girls I know."

"You're the only smart boy I know."

"You're sort of obnoxious sometimes."

I started to say "You too," but I had to acknowledge he really wasn't. "Yeah."

I could feel his breath on my cheek. I turned my head to see what the heck he thought he was doing, and was surprised to find that his face was inches from mine, his eyes closed. His breath smelled like cheese.

I panicked and backed up. He got interested in his shoes.

"Uh," I said. "It's just that—"

"Experiment," he muttered.

Something splashed, over by the dog dish. A tinny voice said something in French.

"Fidius," I whispered.

His moonlit shape rose from the dog dish, wings glowing silver. He wiped his mouth and shook himself, drops of elixir shimmering as they fell. Then, faster than a thought, he was hovering before me, hand outstretched as if he was going to frostbite my nose again. "Turpina."

"You tried to kill my parents. You turned me into a frog."

"I did not wish the Turpini to die. I wished them out of the way, so there would be no ceremony."

"They would've died."

"I would have been sad then. And I would have turned you back into yourself once I had the Gemma."

"You had the Gemma yesterday," Timmo said. "And you didn't fix her then."

"Stay out of this, boy. I saw you try to kiss my Turpina."

You can't tell if someone's blushing by moonlight. "I'm not your Turpina," I said.

"No? Good-bye then." With a mighty flap of his gorgeous wings, Fidius rocketed out of sight over the inn roof.

I wasn't sad to see him go. Not. At. All.

Chapter Twenty-three
Buttoning Up

WE ARE TRESPASSING, BUT TIMMO SAYS the landowners will never know.

It's a Saturday in October, almost four months after I first met Durindana—one of those fall days that make you think summer is overrated. The sky is so blue you wouldn't believe it if you saw it in a painting. The air is warm and sweet, smelling like dead leaves and the good kind of mold, the kind that stays outdoors.

Timmo and I are walking a path along the edge of a low cliff, woods on one side, rocks and ocean on the other. Moss is everywhere, deadening our footfalls, the only sound the slapping of the tide against the rocks below.

Except, when we round the bend by the fallen oak, for a tinny voice raised in song. Humming, with no words I can distinguish.

Durindana and the other Parvi still have work to do at the inn, but the major renovation is done. They have to work at night now, so the guests won't see them. Today, though, they are working on their own houses, Durindana having stressed to everyone the need to get ready for winter. "We must button up our *domicilia*," she said. *Domicilia* means "houses."

Buttoning Up

And there she is, buttoning up. Or, more precisely, driving her herd of slugs underground through a hole she's made in the moss. She hovers over them, humming, wings flapping, while she prods them with a stick.

When she sees us she flutters to a deck paved in sea glass by her front door, halfway up a five-foot-tall bank of moss on the landward side of the path. She flops into an easy chair of sticks and moss, keeping half an eye on the slugs. They continue to ooze into the hole she made for them. We sit down on a couple of boulders she's set up for visiting Gigantes.

Durindana thinks of everything.

I'd give a lot to see her *domicilium* on the inside, because the outside is gorgeous. Her bank of moss faces south, taking advantage of the sun peeking through the trees. She either made holes in it or took advantage of existing ones, framing them with scraps of wood and closing them in with five-inch-tall driftwood doors that open without a creak.

From the deck in front of the main door, mussel-shell steps lead to another small porch, this one with a roof on it in case of inclement weather. (The steps are for show—why do you need steps when you can fly?) Other doors below the main entrance lead to storage rooms and workrooms of various types. Durindana has plaited sticks and seaweed into windscreens, which she's set up on the ocean side of every door.

She is looking very nice today, in a dress woven from

various colors and textures of moss, silky yet nubbly. The hem's raggedy, but that's deliberate. Her brown hair is loose and flowing down her shoulders. Lounging there on her sea glass deck, she looks like a pre-Raphaelite heroine. (The pre-Raphaelites were nineteenth-century painters who liked fairy tales and King Arthur and women with a lot of hair. I can tell you more if you . . . Okay, no.)

"So," I say as Timmo and I settle down, "how are Rinaldo and Noctua doing?"

"Come see." Durindana darts down to give the rearmost slug one last prod, then flits off down the path.

It's hard to follow a flitting Parva through shadowy woods. If you try to keep up with her, you'll trip over a root and fall head over Nikes into the ocean. You just have to take your time, mind your step, and put up with this little winged lady zigzagging back to you crying, "Keep up, keep up, warm dolts!"

Rinaldo and Noctua's *domicilium* is about a hundred yards away, right beside the path.

It's lame.

They made—or, more likely, found—a hole at the base of a rotting tree stump. A sad excuse for a door hangs there, lopsided. When we arrive, Rinaldo is trying to tighten it with blue twine that floated ashore from a lobster boat. Noctua is seated daintily uphill on a tuft of moss, making herself a necklace out of straw and shards of sea glass. Her cobweb dress has some shape but is littered with pine needles and twigs—she hasn't solved the stickiness problem.

Durindana hovers, watching, then shakes her head and lands next to Rinaldo. "*Desiste. Ego id faciam.*" That means, "Stop. I will do it."

He stands back and watches her while she fiddles with the door. Sometimes she seems to be doing what anyone would do, shoving the doorjamb upright and weaving the twine through it. But she's humming the whole time and sometimes she's just laying hands on the wood.

Whatever. By the time she's through, Rinaldo and Noctua have a door that will withstand a gale. As it will have to at some point.

Noctua makes her way down the hill, wearing her new necklace. Durindana, hands on hips, says in English, "Winter is coming, my lady. This is no time to make a necklace. You must be herding your slugs."

Noctua's chin trembles, and Rinaldo intervenes. "My Lady Noctua tended the crickets all day yesterday. She deserves a day of beauty."

Durindana shrugs. "This is your choice. But the snow will not wait for you." She rises into the air and leads us back to her house.

Durindana is happy.

In spite of their door problems, Rinaldo and Noctua seem happy.

Even I am a little bit happy, despite the fact that Eileen did tell everyone about Fairy Fat and the Tampon Incident.

Timmo told me as soon as it happened. I told Mom. Mom did not tell Dad or Grand-père. Instead, she sat me down and gave me a grandeur lesson.

As a result, the first day Timmo and I joined his friends at the beach, I had a tampon pinned to my T-shirt like a brooch. I thought I'd die walking through town like that, and an old lady called me a "little tart." But the other kids thought it was hysterical.

Timmo called me Fairy Fat in front of everyone. I called him Fairly Flat. Everybody thought that was funny too. Then he called me "Smellie," which I thought was too much.

Anyway. Grandeur rocks.

I'm still round. I don't wear eye makeup. I like words with lots of syllables. So sue me.

Timmo's happiness is a work in progress.

As Noctua predicted, Eileen and Chief Wright didn't say one word about seeing the Parvi the night of the full moon. Eileen said only that she'd had a "wacked-out dream." When Timmo experimented, describing the antics of the parakeets I was raising in the pub, they pretended they hadn't heard him.

Encouraged, Timmo wrote away for a space camp brochure and handed it to his father at supper one night in early July when I was there for moral support.

Chief Wright turned the brochure over and over in his hands. "What's this?" he asked.

Timmo looked him right in the eye. "It's for space

camp. I'd do it instead of basketball camp. It's more expen-
sive, but I'll mow the lawn for free this summer and—"

Chief Wright gave his brains a shake. "Have I seen this
before? Seems like I've seen it before."

"Uh. I don't know. Maybe."

"Somebody said something." Chief Wright furrowed
his brow. "Can't remember . . . something about sailing
to the stars." Apparently, Magica Mala had a universal
translator.

Timmo was barely breathing. "So . . . what do you
think?"

"Heroes." Chief Wright set the brochure down beside
his napkin, lined it up with the table edge. "This person
said astronauts are heroes."

"Sounds like a yes," Eileen said. "But don't anybody
think *I'm* going to police academy."

The next day, Timmo and his dad went fishing. His dad
called him Spaceshot all day and said basketball's a real
game whereas baseball's for sissies. He sent the check in
for space camp, though.

My parents don't own the inn anymore, but we decided to stick around and run it for Grand-père as long
as the Parvi could fix it up without us having to borrow a
lot of money. Dad managed to swing a part-time teaching
job that will keep us in spaghetti and Roland's Big-Time
Teriyaki Chicken until the inn makes a profit.

Everyone agrees that my college fund is out of
bounds.

Everyone agrees that my parents will be allowed time to paint.

Nobody listens when Grand-père says the inn should have a Versailles theme.

We don't keep whiskey in the house anymore. Grand-père goes to Alcoholics Anonymous meetings as a condition of us sticking around, but sometimes he comes home drunk. The dang-it factor is pretty high on those occasions. But I think we're staying anyway.

The inn renovation began in August, once Durindana felt that the Parvi were good enough at Magica Vera. This was a legitimate concern. In early July, her first attempt at slugs in truffle sauce turned into an oozy mess so disgusting I had to take it outside and dump it for her. The practice house she built out of tree bark and moss (collected by Timmo) caved in on itself after a couple of days. Everybody's cobweb clothing fell apart in the rain.

The Parvi's sense of taste came back in the middle of July, and they discovered that slugs in truffle sauce tasted like . . . well, slugs in truffle sauce. Durindana and a couple of others figured out how to make it taste more like chicken.

On August third, Dad suggested that the Parvi test their renovation skills by repairing the pub's oaken floor, which was all cracked and splintery with board ends poking up everywhere. When I walked in the next morning, the place looked like one of those pictures you see of monarch butterflies swarming in South America. The floor was a mass of fluttering wings and little prostrate, cobweb-clad bodies, Durindana flitting overhead giving instructions. The Parvi seemed to be stroking the floor with their hands, kicking at it with their bare feet.

I wanted to look closer, but I was afraid of stepping on somebody. So I left.

The morning after that, the floor looked new. Also turquoise, which is a funny color for oak, but Mom thought it was cheery-looking, so we didn't complain.

Mom and Dad had their own aesthetic problems to worry about.

As soon as we'd decided to stick around, they each claimed one of the guest rooms for a studio. It took a full month to set up the studios to their liking. The first day of actual painting, Mom worked for two hours, burst into tears, and shut herself in her bedroom for the rest of the day. Dad went out for a long walk.

"If it's that painful, why do they bother?" Timmo asked, smearing organic peanut butter on a slice of whole wheat bread, slapping it together with a jelly-smeared slice, and handing the sandwich to Grand-père.

"Idiot boy." At first I thought Grand-père was objecting to the PB&J, but then he said, "Painting is one of the grand arts. Once it is begun, one does not simply drop it."

"You did," I said.

"Not without considerable effort," he said haughtily. I handed him a glass of milk, which he shut up and drank.

I was worried that my parents would turn into Grand-père—unhappy and unsettled and hard to live with— because of having drunk the elixir and found out terrible things about themselves. But they didn't. On their second painting day, Mom got up and went into her studio and shut the door. Dad did the same. They came out for meals and to check on the Parvi's progress and to impress the building inspector. (He has his brains back now, so we have to pretend we're the ones doing the renovation work.)

After three weeks, Mom had finished a painting and Dad was close. Mom didn't like hers, but she said she could see what was wrong and what to do next time. She almost looked happy.

"That's my idea of courage," Mr. Watkins said the next day in art class. He likes to use my parents as an example of real, live artists who aren't too weird. Unlike Paul Cézanne (1839–1906), who wrote a poem about a family eating a human head for dinner.

Mr. Watkins lets me share interesting facts about artists as long as I don't monopolize the whole class. On the other end of the spectrum is Ms. Tally, the science teacher, who likes me best with zipped lips.

I'd been looking forward to science class. I wanted to learn about light waves and how the brain interprets information it receives from the eye, such as a gold filigree refrigerator door handle. But October in the eighth grade is when the Baker's Village school learns about phyla, subphyla, and other biological classifications, and Ms.

Tally couldn't care less if you already memorized half of them by fourth grade.

"Fairy Fat must've memorized the whole encyclopedia by now," Janine said. "That's what you do when you don't have any friends."

Yup. You read that right—Janine.

Turns out she's the friend's cousin who told Eileen about Fairy Fat and the Tampon Incident. And her parents moved out from Boston the end of August so they could be near family and away from bullies in the schools.

"You're lucky you even memorized your own name," Timmo said. "Teen Queen Janine." The rest of the class hooted, and a new nickname was born.

"Spaceshot," Janine said, but everyone had been hearing that one for years. "Snooze alarm," somebody said.

"Settle down," Ms. Tally said. "Who remembers the Latin classification for the green frog?"

Timmo squinched up his face. "Amphibia Anura—"

"Drool-idae," I said.

He and I cracked up. Everybody looked at us like we were nuts.

"How come Janine hates you?" Akira Manning asked me at recess. Akira is a Shakespeare fanatic who eats two desserts every day, trying to expand into her excessive height and stick legs.

"Janine had a bad birthday in kindergarten," I said. "She blames me."

"Geez," said Annie De Luca, who makes jewelry out of sea glass. "She should get over herself."

They might be my friends. I'm not counting on anything, though.

That afternoon was one of the bad ones, when the heat's on too much and the sun's streaming in the windows and the teacher's droning on and on and all you want to do is put your head down on your desk. I was staring dully out at the golden trees when Durindana rose into the air—right outside the window!—wings beating furiously, clutching a sheaf of the fancy tall grass that grows next to the building. She likes it for weaving.

Durindana peered in the window and waved at me, then flitted away. Somebody behind me made a choking sound.

Janine, white as new slush.

"Is something wrong, Janine?" I asked, in the most syrupy, sympathetic voice you ever heard.

Her glassy eyes met mine. She knew that a real, live fairy had waved at me, and we both knew she'd look like an absolute dork if she said anything.

Grandeur.

*

*

*

Acknowledgments

DURINDANA FIRST TOPPLED FROM her chandelier online, in the madcap company of the Leaky Marauders. Contributing to her character development were: Sue Barnowski, Connie Paragas Bolinsky, Georgiana Daniel, Anne Ehrenberger, Meg Ford, Craig Graham, Andrew Grimwade, Verena Grützun, Dorothy Hiser, Belinda Hobbs, Laura Holland, Donna Hosie, Connie House, Monica Hultin, Ruth Meyer, Liesl Muller, Michele Myers, Sarah Parsons, Katy Powers, Marie-Lyne Pratt, Lily Prudhomme, Matthew Roberts, Martje Ross, John Sanchez, Dianne Suzuki, Christine Bosworth Watkins, Christopher Watkins, Mike Weinstein, and Sandi Young.

Nobody would have toppled from anything anywhere if not for Kathy Dawson, genius editor, whose diagnostic skills and sense of character are astounding. Kate Schafer Testerman truly is a super-agent, and Shelly Perron is a goddess of language and logic. Sosha Sullivan was an early and astute reader. Mellie benefited from the insight and support of Lisa Heldke and Peg O'Connor. Lauren Curtis gave expert advice on Latin and French, and understood why I had to ignore it in places. (Any mistakes are mine, of course.)

Deepest thanks, admiration, and affection to my writers' group: Deborah Brewster, Maggie Davis, Ann Logan, Becky McCall, Gail Page, Kim Ridley, and Susa Wuorinen.

And nothing good ever happens without Rob Shillady, who could be an editor if he ever gets tired of painting.